The Guardian

Georgia Le Carre

Prologue
ZOLA

"I still can't believe you're actually here," I exclaimed with a small laugh of happiness.

My father chuckled and it made me realize again how much I loved hearing him laugh in that low comforting way that he only did when he was with me. Whenever we were together hearing him laugh wasn't rare, but the problem was we were rarely ever together.

"How long are you going to torture me about not being around enough?" he asked softly.

"Forever," I replied as I stirred the cake batter.

"Trust me, it *will* get better. I *will* reduce my workload," he promised.

"But by then I probably won't be here anymore." I lifted my eyes and watched the smile slowly disappear from his face.

Silently, he slid the lined baking pan over to me.

I bit my bottom lip and set the spatula down. "I don't want to make you feel bad, Papa. I just want us to take advantage of the precious time we have together now. Don't forget, soon I'll be graduating from high school and off to college. And after that, I'll probably be too occupied finding a job and life in general. Or am I wrong?"

"I'll do better, Zola," he said gravely, but his eyes were twinkling with amusement. "But please don't do that passive-aggressive thing with me. It intimidates the hell out of me."

That amused, guilty look tugged at my heart but I couldn't show him that. I folded my arms, one eyebrow raised. "That's all you have to worry about? Me being passive-aggressive."

That smile stayed, curving the corners of his lips. "I suppose it could be worse. You could be doing drugs or ... getting pregnant."

My eyes widened and suddenly I was so embarrassed I couldn't meet his gaze.

"Your cheeks have gone red. Is it too hot in here?" he asked innocently.

I pretended to laugh airily. "Why do you have to be so awkward all the time, Papa?"

"What is awkward?" he asked. "Because I mentioned you getting pregnant? You surely can't possibly know how that works at your age."

Now I was horrified. "Oh, for heaven's sake!"

But he was on a roll and refused to stop. "Oh wait! You know how that works?"

"Papa," I warned. "I swear, I will walk out of here this instant if you don't stop."

"Why are you so shy?" he asked, staring directly into my eyes.

I squirmed internally.

The Guardian

"Oh, my God. I really have been absent, haven't I? You seem to know more than you should."

I set the bowl I'd been about to empty into the pan down on the counter and turned to walk away, but he caught me by my wrist and drew me toward him for a hug. I relished every single moment of this closeness. Though, of course, the last thing I was going to do was let him know.

I pretended to groan. "Let me go."

But he only squeezed me tighter and playfully growled, "Never."

"Ugh yuck," I complained, but I couldn't help giggling.

"I better hold on tight before I'm not able to anymore," he said and planted a sloppy, noisy kiss on my cheek as if I was still a child. "You're already sounding way too mature for me. I can't even make up my mind if it's a good thing, or if it's my fault you had to grow up so fast."

I didn't bother sparing his feelings. "It's a hundred percent your fault. The cake's gonna burn," I said, pulling away.

"Impossible," he refuted. "We haven't put it into the oven yet."

"Well, we should. It's almost midnight and if we don't do it now, it's not going to be ready for my birthday at midnight."

"Calm down and enjoy being a teenager, Zola," he murmured gently. "You're not an adult. Stop being so fixated on time and results."

"Look who's talking," I teased.

I hurried over to the marble counter, transferred the batter into the round baking pan, banged the pan on the hard surface a few times to let the air bubbles out and slid it into the oven.

"Done," I said, shooting him a smile, but I was disappointed to see his cell phone had once again made its appearance.

I was determined not to say a word in protest as he scrolled through his messages. Instead, I focused my attention on making sure the oven temperature was right. But when I turned around and saw him texting rapidly into his device, a huge frown across his forehead, I knew I had to say something or he would be lost to me again.

"Papa," I called just as his phone began to ring. He lifted a finger in my direction and, taking the call, began to bark out orders in rapid Italian, probably to one of his staff.

My heart fell as I tried to convince myself there was no need to worry. He'd promised that he had cleared the entire night for me. And so far, whenever he had said that, especially on my birthdays, he always came through.

I returned to the counter and grabbed a napkin to wipe my hands before turning on the iPad so I could review the instructions on how to make the cream frosting.

Fabiola, the housekeeper, had stocked up on all the ingredients I needed so I headed over to the refrigerator to retrieve them. As I was grabbing a pack of strawberries to add to the pile I'd already gathered in my arms, my father came over to help me.

"Here, let me," he said, but his voice was different. It was no longer playful but full of tension.

I let him, but I didn't have the courage to look at him. I already knew what was coming. He helped me set the ingredients down on the counter, but his mind was elsewhere. I could feel my throat begin to clog up. Eventually, I couldn't stand it anymore. I knew I had to let him go.

"When will you be back?" I asked.

"One hour, tops," he said, and the relief in his voice was palpable.

"One hour?"

"Yes," he replied with a grateful smile. "This is an emergency. You know I won't leave on your birthday. I just need to go pick a kid up and bring him here."

"You're bringing someone *here*?" I asked, surprised.

"Yeah," he replied. "He's just a kid who needs a helping hand. He will stay with us for a short time while I handle his case."

I didn't know how to respond. It made no sense as to why my father was suddenly bringing a stranger to our home, and the absence of any details left me feeling muddled.

"Don't start icing the cake without me," he said, his eyes on the oven. "It should be perfectly cooled and ready by the time I return."

"The cake and I will be waiting right here for you," I assured.

"Good, because I always keep my promises," he said and hurried out of the room.

I stood in the middle of the kitchen and listened to his footsteps echoing in the foyer. I heard the sound of his keys, and then the front door shut.

Once he was gone, I was surrounded by a persistent, pervasive, dense silence. It was nothing new though. It had come to live in this house since Mama died four years ago. She left me with a father who distracted himself from dealing with her loss by filling his time with endless work and pursuing noble causes.

As he was doing tonight.

No matter how hard I tried, I couldn't stop him or make him understand how much I longed for him to spend a bit more time with me. I didn't know how to intrude in his intentionally busy life so I chose to trust instead that someday, hopefully soon, he would reduce his workload, and I would have him home again the way he was when we were a happy family of three.

With a sigh, I headed over to the living room.

I lay on the couch and tried to keep myself entertained by scrolling through Instagram. Eventually, the oven's timer pinged. I switched it off and took the cake out. It smelled good. I left it to cool and went back to my phone. Three hundred and thirty-three images of gorgeous birthday cakes later I slipped into sleep. I awakened to the sound of the door lock clicking open. I could hear masculine voices, but I couldn't quite make out the words.

My father called out to me, but I was still somewhat half-asleep and a bit grumpy so I didn't respond to the first call. Still, I could never stay angry with my father for any length of time, so by the third time he called I felt remorseful enough to lift my hand and wave it.

"Here," I called drowsily.

He came over to the living room and cocked his head at the sight of me sprawled on the couch.

"You became tired?" he asked, and I spied a bit of guilt in his voice.

"I lost interest," I replied.

"Go easy on me," he murmured and turned to the

unwanted guest he'd brought with him. "Come over, Dante, and meet my daughter."

I immediately shot up, horrified that he would think to introduce me in such a state.

"Papa!" I muttered, shaking my head and straightening the oversized T-shirt I was wearing.

"Dante, this is Zola," he introduced.

I lifted my gaze. I didn't know what I'd been expecting, but the vision in front of me was not it. My father had called him a 'kid', but the young man standing before me was surely no one's idea of a kid.

He looked more like an avenging angel.

Tall and broad with jet-black hair that curled around his collar. His features were so perfect he looked as if he'd been chiseled from stone. He was ... indisputably, and undeniably beautiful. He stood there like a living, breathing work of art.

A fiercely beautiful, staggeringly beautiful masterpiece of creation.

The most astonishing thing about his tanned face was his eyes. They were the most piercing, brilliant blue I'd ever seen. They burned like twin blue fires and I had to tear my gaze away from their awesome beauty.

He had jammed both his hands into his trouser pockets, which to my inexperienced eyes, just made him look both rebellious and so impossibly cool that none of the boys in my high school could ever compare. Saying nothing, those electric blue orbs stared at me with neither shyness nor awkwardness while I could feel my face begin to heat up and flush like crazy.

Confused and disconcerted, I turned towards my dad

and tried to look normal, but it was hard to overcome my body's reaction to how obviously attractive the young man was.

My father smiled benignly. "He'll be staying with us temporarily until a few issues with his case are sorted. So don't be startled if you see him lurking around."

He was going to be staying with us!

I became even more curious about him. Even if he looked darkly dangerous, he must be the victim and not the accused. I knew my father would never bring someone even slightly risky into our house to stay with us, kid or no kid.

"I'll just show him to the guest room, then we'll ice the cake together, okay?" my father said.

But I had completely lost interest in the idea of icing the cake with him. Nothing we did could live up to those hundreds of amazing creations I'd seen on my phone. I took a deep breath to control my racing heart and shook my head. "No, don't worry about it, Papa. It's already way past midnight. I'm going to bed."

"Zola," my father called plaintively.

I felt guilty at the unhappiness in his tone as I was aware he had been looking forward to icing my cake together, but the presence of the beautiful but broodingly silent young man had totally thrown me. The longer I stood here the more I felt those eyes burning into me.

"It's okay, Papa. It's just a cake. Not the end of the world if I don't have one," I said with a forced smile.

Then I fled from the room like the devil himself was at my heels.

I locked my bedroom door, got into my bed, and pulled the covers up to my chin. My wish was to sleep, not to entertain any useless thoughts about the young man or how I had just utterly and completely humiliated myself, but an hour and a half later I found myself still wide awake. I kicked the covers away and thought of what I could do instead of restlessly tossing and turning in bed.

Since it was already technically my birthday, I didn't want to entertain sulking of any type. I looked toward the shelf that was stacked with books, but I couldn't bear to read anything new due to the potential for disappointment, which I didn't want to deal with on my birthday. I got out of bed and headed over to grab my favorite story, *As You Wish*.

But my hand stilled as it reached for the spine of the book.

No. Not that now.

The truth was I felt agitated and no longer wanted to stay in my room. It was a hot, sultry night and my air-conditioner was playing up. I opened a window and leaned out. The night sky was filled with stars.

Without my consent, my lips whispered his name. "Dante."

It was the name worthy of such a ferocious avenging angel. It suited him perfectly. A thrill ran through me. I remembered the way his remarkable eyes had moved over my body ... making my body flush with heat ...

Oh, God.

I stopped myself cold, right there, and quickly I thought about my mom instead. I imagined her wishing me a 'Happy Birthday'. I could almost smell her soft sweet fragrance. Tears filled my eyes, but I didn't let them fall. I didn't want to cry on my birthday.

A swim. A swim was what I needed.

I changed into my swimsuit, grabbed a towel and headed out to the kitchen. Underneath the starlit sky, the pool glistened invitingly.

I dived into the cool depths.

Oooo ... bliss.

DANTE

https://www.youtube.com/watch?v=KT44aQ_1oXM

Marco Leone's daughter was way too hot.

And I wanted to fuck her.

I was lying on the bed thinking how inconvenient that was when I heard the splash. I sat bolt upright, immediately on alert. Acting purely on instinct, I switched off the bedside lamp, sprinted over to the window, and parting the blinds with my fingers, peered out.

I could see a pool illuminated by the light from the pavilion.

Zola was in the water, doing laps. I stared at her body moving through the water for a few seconds. She was a very beautiful girl with a very, very sexy mouth, but she was forbidden to me. But even more importantly, I was in too much trouble to be thinking about girls, no matter how delectable. I told myself to turn away, but at that very moment, she began to lift herself out of the pool. Water ran down her delicious body in rivulets and dripped onto the tiles.

I couldn't look away from the sight.

I was frozen with an irresistible desire to have her. Her white swimsuit glimmered in the dark as she walked toward the cabana. Then suddenly, and without warning, I felt a rush of sensation in my gut, the old instinct that had always served me well.

Something bad was about to happen.

Even as the thought became a shape in my head, her foot slipped on the wet tiles and she lost her balance. It happened so fast. One moment I was lusting for her, the next moment, her arms were flailing as she landed on her back. I saw her hand flutter towards her head and realized she must have hit it. Grabbing the edge of the pool with her other hand, she twisted her body and tried to get up, but her body suddenly became limp, as if had lost consciousness.

And she slipped into the water noiselessly.

Fuck! I turned from the window and ran from my room through the unfamiliar house. Most of the lights were off and navigating through the dark was a nightmare. It felt like a lifetime passed before I finally burst through the back door.

The water's surface showed no ripples. It was eerily still, but a dark shadow was slowly sinking. I dived into the cool water, grabbed her descending body, and pulled her towards the surface. The moment I emerged out of the water I began to yell out to her father.

"Mr. Leone!"

"Mr. Leone!"

I laid her on the tiles and looked down at her pale,

motionless face. Up until that moment in my life, I'd been attacked with every sort of weapon imaginable, but I couldn't recall ever feeling as afraid as I did then.

"Don't die, *bella* Zola. Please don't die," I urged urgently.

Then I opened her blue lips and, taking a deep breath, put my mouth over hers.

Ten Years Later

Chapter 1
Zola

"Well, what happened next?" Nina asked.

I reached for my wine glass. A small smile played on my lips as I sipped the exquisite *Garblèt Suè Barolo*. The fruity notes of raspberry and the smoky aroma of the dark wooden barrels that the wine had lain in for years flowed down my throat.

I had to admit my colleagues were right. This wine was the perfect splurge for celebrating my promotion to a fully-fledged agent at the Gray Swan Literary Agency ... but two glasses on an empty stomach had loosened my tongue and led me down the unfamiliar path of sharing my old stories with them.

"She's enjoying this," Stella, one of the editors, accused.

"Actually, there's nothing more to say," I replied with a smile. "The story ends there."

"What do you mean, it ends there? You lost consciousness and fell into the pool in the middle of the night. You obviously didn't drown so who saved you? Was it the beautiful man-boy? It was, wasn't it?" Steven, a flamboyantly gay intern demanded dramatically.

I set my glass down. "Yes, it was him. He ... resuscitated me. My father called for an ambulance and I was rushed to hospital. I was concussed and a bit ill for a little while, but I was fine in the end."

"I knew it. What happened then?" Steven asked in a hushed, excited voice.

I shrugged. "I never saw him again."

A murmur of dissatisfaction swept around the table. I glanced at their faces. They were expecting some sort of grand resolution, but to hear that the end of my first crush had been so abrupt seemed to disappoint them all.

"Wait, you guys never spoke or kept in touch?" Steven asked in disbelief.

I shook my head.

"So ... you've always been useless around men then," Steven concluded, shaking his head. "I'd have got his number the moment I set eyes on him."

The table erupted into tipsy laughter.

"Wow, that's a shame," Nina commented softly.

I agreed silently.

"Still, better first crush story than all the nonsense I've had to sift through today in my emails," Linda, one of the three literary assistants muttered with a shudder.

"What kind of nonsense?" Janice, her immediate boss asked.

"Like the way, the query letters and samples are just getting worse and worse. I had a woman today, who sent me three photos of herself in different poses and the assurance that she had a whole lot more if those were not suitable for the book jacket cover. I mean, come on. Your story has not even been selected and you're obsessing over the cover photo."

"That sounds like something I would do. Was her book any good though?" Steven enquired.

"No. It was some sort of a weird mermaid tale. Mermaid sex in the second chapter." She shuddered. "I was a bit creeped out, to be honest. Too fishy for me."

Steven shrieked with laughter. "I'm sure I could have been tempted by a slippery male mermaid. Imagine, no lube needed."

Janice groaned. "Oh please, Steven! We all know you'll fuck anything that moves. Now behave yourself. This is a work-related event." She turned to me. "You used to read too, didn't you, Zola? How long were you an assistant for?"

"Two years under Jodie, and one and a half under John."

She nodded in acknowledgment. "You've paid your dues then and now it's time for the fun to begin ... building your own client list."

"I guess so." A big happy smile spread across my face because I was just so super excited about my new job. "Excuse me, but a trip to the Ladies seems to be in order," I murmured and rose to my feet.

In truth, I didn't need to use the bathroom. I just wanted a bit of a break to hide my great excitement. The bathroom was blessedly empty. I took a couple of deep breaths to dispel some of the hundreds of butterflies fluttering away inside me since my promotion was confirmed and looked at my reflection in the mirror. I looked pretty sober until I allowed myself a grin. Then I looked like an insanely happy Cheshire cat.

"You did it," I crowed to myself. "You are now a full-fledged agent two years earlier than anyone had expected."

An image of my father flashed into my head. He had been so excited about the prospect of my promotion, but it was almost eight o'clock and he hadn't even sent me a little congratulatory text.

I wanted to give him the benefit of the doubt, but I had to consider the possibility he had simply forgotten. I pulled my phone out of my purse and hit my father's number, but to my immense disappointment, he didn't pick up.

I guess you'll be too busy to walk me down the aisle on my wedding day too, won't you?

My stomach churned as it tried to talk myself out of being hostile, but I couldn't stop my fingers as they carried on flying across the screen.

You know what? I won't even bother inviting you. The last thing I want that day is more disappointment, so it will be best to celebrate it with strangers. Thank you for helping me make such an informed decision ahead of time.

And before I could change my mind, I hit send.

There. It was done.

I waited a few minutes, but still, there was no reply. I took another deep breath. Where was I going with this? This was my very special day. I had worked my ass off to get here and nothing was going to ruin it. Not even Papa. What did it matter if he didn't call right now? He loved me. I knew that. With great determination, I put him completely out of my mind. After reapplying my lipstick, I walked to the bar and ordered myself a Cosmopolitan.

My grip was tight around my phone as some part of me still hoped and waited for a response from my father. However, nothing came, and I became upset again. *Calm down, Zola. When he has untangled himself from whatever urgent work he is currently immersed in, he will call you.*

"Here you go, Miss," the bartender said.

I grabbed the glass and downed more than half of it. I was still too upset to return to my colleagues so I looked around and allowed myself to appreciate the gorgeous tropical-themed space.

The walls had murals of palm trees to complement the actual palm trees dotted around the restaurant. Together with the rattan lamps, island scents, and candlelight it made for a lovely and warm ambiance. It was a wonderful place and I promised myself I would come back to it when I was less irritable so I could properly enjoy it.

I drained the last of my drink, and as I stood, I noticed a man in a corner. He was nearly shielded from view by one of the palm trees. He sat alone right next to the window with what seemed to be an untouched glass of Scotch before him and his gaze was fixated on the entrance door, but what drew me to him was his cartoonish blue and yellow Donald Duck tie. It was as familiar to me as my own name.

For a couple of seconds, I was so shocked I couldn't move. My throat choked up with emotion and all I could do was stare at him, but he must have felt the intensity of my stare for he frowned and turned in my direction.

His eyes widened in alarm as our gazes connected.

To my astonishment, he quickly turned away as if he didn't recognize me. Picking up his phone he began to type furiously into it. I continued to stare at him. For one crazy moment, I actually wondered if that man was my father's doppelganger, but that was impossible. That tie, those mannerisms, that hairstyle ...

When he stopped typing, a message arrived on my phone, and I understood what was happening. For whatever reason, probably because he didn't want to be distracted by me, he had decided to act as though he didn't know me. I wasn't having that. Not today. Without even bothering to check his message I began to walk toward him, but the moment he saw me approaching, he sprang to his feet and literally scurried away.

I stopped in my tracks in amazement.

'Dad!' I wanted to shout, but I didn't want to bring the attention of the whole restaurant to me. Seconds later he was at the entrance door and before I could do anything else, he slipped out without looking back. My father's behavior was so strange I couldn't help but feel slightly alarmed. I regretted not calling out to him.

He'd told me he wouldn't be able to make dinner with me because he would be working late, but here he was, waiting to dine with someone else. Perhaps it was a client but, even so.

At that moment, I heard Samantha call out to me. When I turned around, I found all my colleagues watching me curiously, probably wondering why I was just standing in the middle of the restaurant staring stupidly at the door.

I returned to the table slowly and sat down.

"Zola, we were just wondering why the gorgeous man-boy was brought to your house in the first place," Steven cried.

I looked around the table. "What?"

"The man-boy?" Steven repeated impatiently. "Who was he?

I pushed my worry about my father aside. Today was my special day. No doubt I would get an explanation from him later. "Maybe ..." I began with a mysterious smile. "Dante was in my house because he was part of the mafia, but afterward he was killed in a terrible gang war. Maybe that's why I've never seen or heard from him ever since."

The table went quiet.

Then Stella spoke up. "You're weird, Zola."

"Maybe not," Steven said softly. "Maybe she's just creative. Her style has always been interesting after all. So ... does this human god even exist?"

"He does." I nodded.

"Really?" Samantha asked doubtfully.

"Really," I confirmed.

"And the bit about the mafia?"

I smiled at her. "My dad is a criminal defense attorney, you know?"

Her mouth fell open. "Wait, oh my God. She's of Italian descent y'all. She might not be kidding."

"I'm not," I said.

"Did he really die?"

"No idea."

"Oh! Okay, let's move on. I think Zola is having way too much fun at all of our expense."

The conversation moved to something else and I took the opportunity to pull my phone out of my pocket and look for the message I was certain my father had sent to me before he hurried out. The moment I saw the words that he had written fear gripped me.

Don't approach me, he'd written. **Don't act like you know me.**

My eyebrows furrowed with confusion. What? *Don't approach me. Don't act like you know me.* What the hell was going on?

I put the phone away and thought back to our conversations recently which had been about how a new criminal defense case had taken all of his time. He didn't seem eager to tell me much about it so I hadn't pressed him for details. All of my annoyance from earlier disappeared. I quickly excused myself from the table and I called him as I walked away.

His phone began to ring but the call was then abruptly disconnected. My heart fluttered with fear. What kind of mess had my father got into? Willing myself not to panic I rushed outside and got into the first taxi in the queue.

The driver met my gaze through the rearview mirror and I gave him my father's home address. He nodded and pulled away. I couldn't just sit back and wait as we headed toward my father's house. Instead, I tried calling him again. Over and over until eventually, he picked up.

I was so relieved I nearly collapsed ... and then I was furious.

"What the hell is going on? "I yelled. "I've been worried sick."

"Where are you? You're not back at the restaurant, are you?" he asked urgently.

"No, I just left."

The Guardian

"Good," he said. "Come home. I need to talk to you."

Consoled that he was alright or at least he sounded so, I took a deep breath and released it. "Yeah, I'm on my way."

I slumped back into the seat and watched the passing streetlights as we rode through the city. It had been more than three months since I'd last visited him, precisely on his birthday. Even then, I'd had to drag him out of the office for a night out. I loved what I did too, but his obsession with work was unfathomable. Until now I still hadn't found the courage to suggest to him that perhaps his obsessiveness had something to do with my mother and could be resolved with some therapy.

We arrived at the house and I paid the driver and got out of the cab.

His housekeeper, Catalina, had gone home for the night and as was always the case, he was home on his own. This had concerned me when the time for me to move out had come, but he'd managed to convince me I couldn't stay with him forever. If anything, he was the one who was worried sick about me being on my own.

Thus far things had gone well, but more and more I was beginning to get the uncomfortable feeling that perhaps my father was somehow vulnerable. Why I felt that way I couldn't say, but his behavior today was strange to say the least.

He didn't seem happy to see me when he opened his front door. In fact, he wasn't even looking at me. Instead, he was apprehensively looking behind me and glancing out toward the gate and the neighboring houses.

"What's going on, Papa?" I asked, confused.

He caught my hand in a strong grip and quickly pulled

me in. I knew how he got when he was worried about something, but when he shut the door behind us and locked it nervously, I understood that things were really not well at all.

In the bright light of the hallway, I saw dark circles under his eyes, the strange pallor of his skin, and a terrible fear in his eyes.

"What the hell is going on?" I urged anxiously.

He didn't respond. Instead, his gaze perused me, and this gaze I was familiar with, he was checking to see if I was alright.

"For God's sake, Papa. What's happening? Why did you have to pretend you didn't know me at the restaurant?" I cried.

"Come with me," he said, then turning, headed toward his home office.

He pushed the door open and I followed him in. He went behind the desk and settled into his old leather armchair. He was watching me intently, but for once I couldn't gauge his mood as he deliberately kept his face expressionless. It reminded me of that night my mother had passed away and how he'd been trying to hide the grief he was feeling so I'd be convinced everything would be fine in the end. He regarded me silently as if he was deciding what he could reveal to me, and the quieter he became the more afraid I became.

"Dad, you're scaring me."

"Sit down. I want to talk to you." With a defeated sigh he got out of his chair and went over to the cabinet next to him. On top of it was a single bottle of Scotch whisky. I watched my father, who was not much of a drinker, half-fill a thick, crystal tumbler and down it in one go. My eyes widened when he began to pour another. I walked over to the chair in front of his desk and sat down.

"How bad is this case?" I asked quietly.

He brought the half-filled glass over to his desk and sank down heavily into his chair. For a few seconds, he seemed lost in thought. Then he said something astounding.

"Do you remember Dante?" he asked.

I stared at him in shock.

A sliver of a smile curved the corners of his lips. "Maybe you don't."

I shook my head. "Of course, I do. You brought him here when I was sixteen. You were working on his case ... and he saved my life."

"Yes, he saved your life," he murmured. "I don't think I ever told you what his case was about."

"No, you never did," I replied with a frown. "But why does it matter now?"

"Well, it matters now because the case I'm currently working on is for him."

"For him?" I was surprised. "Are you trying to acquit him of murder? Again?"

"That's not exactly how it was," he replied slowly. "But let's just say back then he helped me put a few nasty individuals away and now they're coming for him."

"What?" I exclaimed.

He nodded.

"And he came to you? Why you?"

"Who else can he trust? And who else is better?"

I frowned at his words and wished he wasn't good at all.

This thing he was involved in sounded downright dangerous.

"Anyway," he said. "The reason I couldn't acknowledge you at that restaurant was because it wasn't a simple meeting. I was supposed to meet an informant who had incredibly sensitive information. We chose that location because of how busy and anonymous it was. And that was why I was so shocked to see you there."

"We went there because it's a block away from my office," I murmured.

He nodded absently. "Yes, of course. I had forgotten."

"If you were waiting for your informant, why did you leave?"

"I think we might have been compromised or my informant got spooked because he didn't turn up. I would have waited a bit longer, but when you started to come up to me." He stared at me reproachfully. "You should have known better. I've told you time and time again you should be careful about associating with me in public, especially when I'm in the middle of a case or I'm acting strangely. For this reason, I didn't even allow you to take my last name. How could you be so careless?"

I understood his words and scolding, after all, I had heard them a thousand times from when I was younger, but on this particular day, I couldn't bear to hear him.

"I got promoted today," I reminded him.

His expression immediately softened. "Of course. I'm an old fool. Please forgive me, *amore mio*. I'm so sorry."

"I was hoping to celebrate it with you but instead I was congratulated by strangers. I'm sorry, but when I suddenly saw you waiting for a guest when you told me you couldn't spare any time to even have dinner with me, I was shocked and wanted to approach you immediately."

"Are you happy?"

"I was ... until I saw you." I rose to my feet. "I'm going home."

He too rose to his feet. "Wait ... Zola."

I stopped and waited.

"You're here now. We could have dinner."

"I've already had dinner," I told him, and continued on my way, but just as my hand closed around the door handle there was the faint but unmistakable sound of glass shattering. I whirled around to face my father.

We didn't say a word, but our eyes held the same urgent question.

"What was that?" I whispered.

My father immediately placed a finger over his lips, warning me not to speak, and returned his attention to his computer. In no time, he had the surveillance cameras for the house pulled up on his screen. As he peered at the screen, his gaze moving from one monitor to the other, I could tell he wasn't able to detect anything.

"Maybe it's a squirrel or something," I said in as low a tone as I could manage, but he gave me a harsh warning look. Chills ran down my spine. I began to think of what he had said about his suspicion of being compromised earlier and went closer to him.

"Dad, call the cops," I urged.

He immediately picked up his phone, but it was not the cops he was calling.

"Dante?" he whispered.

My eyes widened. Jesus! He had called the avenging

angel himself. He continued in low conversation telling him about the sound we'd just heard. I stared at the door and then back at him.

Suddenly, he pulled out his desk drawer and retrieved a gun that I'd never been aware he had.

I nearly gasped out loud but managed to slap a hand across my mouth in time.

"I'm calling the cops," I whispered fiercely, and he didn't stop me.

"I've checked the cameras but nothing is out of place," he said into the phone.

"The meeting was at eight-fifteen. I waited for about twenty minutes, but I had to leave immediately because I ran into Zola."

"Yeah, my daughter."

There was a brief silence as he listened, his eyes darting toward the windows, and then he headed over to the door to make sure it was locked.

"Alright," he said as his gaze connected to mine, and then his call came to an end.

He watched me silently for a few moments and I saw something in his eyes I had seen only once before. When my mother died, it was a mixture of inconsolable sadness and pity. The pity was for me.

"Papa," I called worriedly.

"I should never, never have let you come here tonight. Yes, call the cops," he said, his voice bitter with regret. "It's better to be safe than sorry."

My fingers shook as I fumbled with my phone, but somehow, I managed to keep calm as I dialed nine-one-one.

I got connected almost immediately and was able to give

my report. I returned my attention to my father and saw him still watching me.

"They're on their way. They'll be pissed if it's a false alarm," I said praying that was all I would have to deal with.

He lifted the pistol. "You know how to use this right?"

"Yes, but can you please stop scaring the hell out of me," I muttered.

He smiled sadly. "I should have insisted that you take your lessons more seriously back then. Anyway, you'll be fine. Dante is on his way."

"What do you mean by Dante is on his way?" I asked. "The cops are on their way too."

"They'll be too slow," he said, and right then panic shot through my system.

"So, there's really ... someone out there. An intruder?"

"You grew up here," he told me. "Have you ever seen a squirrel?"

I looked at him.

"For once could you just clearly explain to me what is going on?"

He stepped forward and tried to pull me into his arms. I was so frightened I didn't resist. "Congratulations on your promotion," he said softly. "I've been in a great mood for the last few days because of it."

I thought of his words and then mumbled into his shoulder. "You didn't call me."

"I was going to. I was going to stop by your apartment later on tonight. The day just turned out a bit different from what I'd been expecting."

"It's okay, Papa. I know you love me even if you don't know how to show it."

He opened his mouth to speak, but before he could there was the undeniable sound of a man's voice coming from behind the door. As though he were speaking on a phone. I immediately jumped backward, a scream in my throat, but before I could make any sound my father's large warm hand was over my mouth. I stared in shock at him. His eyes had changed. They were unrecognizable.

I had never seen such an alert and almost lethal look in his gaze before. For a moment I couldn't register anything else that was going on around us. Suddenly, I found myself being pulled around his desk.

"Shhh," he warned sternly.

I couldn't stop myself from trembling.

Then he mouthed to me. "Everything is going to be fine."

As I stared at him in shock and fear, he set his gun on the table and pulled away the rug underneath him. To my surprise, it exposed a latch which he pulled open, revealing steps leading down into a secret underground space.

I was shocked because I had lived in that house for so long and never knew that something like that existed.

My eyes widened as I stared at him, and then he started to guide me towards the hole in the ground. Before I could say a single word, I was hurrying down the narrow stairs. At the bottom, I turned around to wait for him but he was not coming down. He smiled at me. It was devoid of the warmth I had long come to appreciate and anticipate whenever he looked at me. Instead, his face was sad and cold, and it broke my heart. I couldn't understand why he was looking at me that way, but then I began to hear the lock to his office being fumbled with and I almost passed out.

The Guardian

"Quickly, Papa, come down," I urged desperately, but he didn't come down to join me.

Instead, he squatted and said softly to me, "You'll get an email from me."

I was confused as to what he was talking about. "What?"

"I love you," he said, and before I could respond the door was shut and locked. I was encompassed in complete and total darkness.

Chapter 2
Dante

I heard the gunshots over the phone.

And everything inside of me went cold.

The intruders would be professional killers with silencers. That must be Marco Leone, either he was just shooting warning shots, or wildly shooting at the intruders. Either scenario meant bad news for him. Instinct told me he was probably already dead, but he would have hidden his daughter though. A few seconds passed, but it felt like an eternity.

"Boss? Boss?" Luca called.

I gripped the phone hard. "Are you inside?" I barked.

"Yes, Boss. We're navigating our way through the living room."

"Head straight to his study," I instructed. "That's where they are."

"Yes, Boss," he said.

"Take a left when you get out of the dining room," I told Luca.

"We just did," he replied, his tone low and cautious.

The Guardian

"Go into the living room on the right ... you'll see a door at the end of the hall. That's where they are."

"Yep, I see it."

"Be careful and precise in your movements in case the intruders are still there. And you must protect the man ... if he is still alive, and his daughter at all costs. Do you hear me?"

"Yes, Boss," he replied.

I sat back to wait and hear every word they said, how they interacted, and how all of their actions were purposeful.

The worst feeling of dread imaginable was already affecting every single cell in my body. I was worried, furious, and frustrated all at once but I had to remain calm.

"We see his office-"

"Any signs of a struggle?" I interrupted impatiently.

"Yes," Luca replied softly. "Someone is crying?"

I tried my best to remain calm, but my blood was boiling. "Get ready to kill on sight. No hesitations. If it's not Leone himself or his daughter, take them out. Don't waste a fraction of a second."

"Yes, Boss," he said, and I listened as they continued in.

I heard the first shot fired, deafening as it rang from the receiver and echoed through the confines of the private airplane. Then the sound of the door being broken down. A few shouts. Another gunshot ... and then another. A window shattering ... shouting ... and what seemed to be a pursuit. Instructions were shouted, most of which were too urgent to decipher.

The moment things seemed to quieten down a little, I

called out to Luca. In the background was the unmistakable whimpering of someone who was absolutely terrified.

"Is she okay?" I asked. "What of her dad? Where is he?"

There was a moment of silence and then I heard her heartbreaking scream.

Luca exited the room then and everything was even quieter. In the distance, I could still hear her scream or perhaps it was now just etched into my mind.

Either way, I waited until he was ready to speak.

"She seems to be alright, Boss. A bit bruised because the attacker was trying to pull her out of an escape hole under her father's desk. We walked in just in the nick of time. He had his gun facing her head, but we startled him and he turned the gun on us. We took him out."

"Her father?" I asked. "Where is her father?"

And he spoke a single sentence that would hurt me like nothing else ever could in my lifetime.

"He's dead, Boss. We saw him lying in a pool of his blood before we entered."

I felt cold inside, icy cold with fury. Revenge was like a poison inside me.

"And his killer?"

"We couldn't get a good look at him," he said. "He fired at us and escaped through the window. His bullet hit Aldo in the shoulder."

"Where are the others right now?" I asked quietly.

"In pursuit, Boss," he responded. "I'll update you if they catch him when they return."

"And the girl?"

Before he could respond, however, I heard sirens in the distance.

"The cops are there?" I asked.

"Yup. We'll have to leave now, but what about the girl? Do we take her with us?"

"No, leave her with her father and get out of there quickly," I instructed. There was nothing further that they could do except protect themselves.

As I cut the connection, regret came over me. I shouldn't have listened to him. I should have followed my own instinct. In my mind, Marco Leone's voice echoed convincing me that he didn't need protection.

"Look, Dante, why have you got your men watching and protecting me around the clock? They're not interested in me per se. I'm just a lawyer with inflexible morals. Less valuable than a used condom to them. You should be diverting all your resources to protecting the whistleblower. We really need him. Without him, we're cooked. I don't know how else I can tell you, but he is absolutely pivotal to us winning your case."

He had sounded so confident, so utterly sure in his conviction, I'd taken him at his word. I'd decided to listen to him this one time and now I was too late. My men were too fucking late. Inside, I was raging, but there was nothing I could do. I was still forty-two thousand feet in the air. Impotently, I slammed the phone to the floor and watched it smash into pieces.

No one said a word or even attempted to come around me. I couldn't lose control. Not yet and not now. I needed to be clear-headed so I could stay on top of things and make decisions as needed.

"How much longer till we get to New York?" I growled.

One of the air hostesses who was standing in the corner

with her head slightly lowered responded. "Forty-five minutes, Sir," she said.

I unclenched my fist, took a deep breath and leaned back against the seat. There was pain in my chest. With my eyes shut I thought of the man who, from the time I was a kid, had treated me with concern and dignity. He had believed in me and helped me when no one else would, and I had failed to protect him.

"How much longer until we land?" I asked and the response soon came.

"Forty minutes, Sir."

Only five minutes had passed, but it seemed like forever.

Chapter 3
Zola

I wondered if the nightmare would ever end.

Sooner or later, I would wake up and find none of it had been real. But the sun rose, chased the darkness away, and confirmed, all of it had been real. My father had died in my arms the previous night.

I could barely speak.

The shock was still too palpable.

In many ways, I imagined I was dead as well because apart from the fact I was still somehow breathing, no other part of me felt real. I felt completely numb.

The moment I'd heard the gunshot my first instinct had been to scream and run up those narrow steps, but something else even more powerful inside me couldn't allow whoever the bastard was to find me, so I covered my mouth and crouched down to hide my face between my knees.

But the nightmare had only just begun because a mere second later I heard him begin to stomp his foot on the floorboards around the table. I'd known then he was aware of the latch and of the crawlspace I was in and I wondered why.

And how? I'd lived here practically all my life and had been denied access to this room, but I'd never discovered it. It was obvious to me this attack had been meticulously planned and orchestrated by people knowing more than they should have about my father.

And that was further confirmed when he flipped open the door, saw me, and pulled me up the steps by my hair. My scalp burned like it had been torched, but as soon as I saw my father I didn't care if I was dead. All I knew was I wanted to hurt that murderer more than anything I'd ever wanted in my life. I saw my father's gun on the opposite side of the room. It must have been flung out of his hand.

I started to crawl to it but before I could, my attacker kicked me so viciously on my side that I went flying in the other direction.

As I sat in the back of the police car I thought he must have broken a couple of ribs but I could barely feel it. I looked out of the window and watched as we drove past the familiar residential buildings that would take me to my apartment.

It all still seemed the same, and yet everything had changed.

I couldn't shake off the image of my father lying on the floor. His blood had seeped out and pooled around him in a deep red puddle. It seemed unreal. Like watching a movie.

But the shocking thing was how peaceful his face looked, almost as if he was sleeping. I shuddered. It was madness. He was such a kind and caring person that they couldn't take the beauty out of him even by killing him in such a gruesome way.

My lips parted to speak. I wanted to tell the cops to take

me back to the house because I suddenly felt he wasn't dead. I'd made a mistake ... he was fine. Either that or this was a dream. I pinched myself and felt the sting. But I couldn't get myself to speak.

My inability to speak continued at the station. A lot of the details escaped me as I made my report as I was unable to speak more than a few disjointed sentences at the time.

I hadn't even been able to give a coherent response to the cops as to how I'd been able to briefly get the gunman off me. I had bitten the back of his ankle. I bit down so hard that he cried out and nearly crushed my head under the force of his boot in anger. I didn't blame him. I had put all my horror and terror into it so it was sure to have hurt. I could still taste his blood in my mouth. My only lifelong regret was that I had not reached the gun and killed him myself.

And then there were the men that had come much too late. At that time I did not feel grateful to them, only panic. My perception of their sudden appearance was of more attackers arriving to make sure I definitely didn't make it either. But then they shot my attacker who quickly catapulted through the window and escaped. They went in pursuit of him and I rushed to my father.

Everything else ceased to exist.

On my way back to my apartment I leaned my head against the window of the car and shut my eyes, but snapped them open again immediately. It would be impossible, I felt, for me to ever shut my eyes again because when I did, all I could see was my father lying in the red pool of his own blood.

The cops led me into the elevator and all the way up to

my floor. At my door I became suddenly aware of the fact my purse with my keys was at my father's house and my roommate, Antoine, would not be home. Even if he was, he would definitely be asleep, and no one would be able to wake him up.

I turned around, ready to leave and refusing to say another word to the cops. All the strength had left me making it a miracle I was even standing. One of them stopped me gently with a slight touch on my shoulder. My gaze went to it and then to his kind eyes that eerily reminded me of my father's. I pushed his hand away and frowned. I wanted to howl at him not to touch me. I wanted it to sting because they had come too late. Much too late. They should have been faster and I hated them for it.

Which made me wonder about the men that had come to my rescue earlier. They'd been Dante's men and had arrived in minutes. But why had they been so close to our home? Had they been watching us? My dad's nervousness from earlier was beginning to make perfect sense to me.

There seemed to be too many moving pieces. Too many parts I had no clue about and had no idea how I could even begin to decipher them. Perhaps my father had been aware of them and perhaps this was why he hadn't seemed very concerned from the start. I wished I could ask him. I couldn't. I wouldn't ever be able to.

Suddenly I heard my name. I stopped in my tracks. The voice was familiar ... extremely familiar and in a way, it felt almost warm. It was the first human response my heart had since the beginning of this nightmare and I couldn't help but respond to it.

I turned around and saw my roommate standing at the open door.

"Zola?" he said, confused. He was in his robe and looking at the uniformed police officers and detectives like he was seeing ghosts.

I heard a male voice call to him from behind. "Antoine? Is everything okay?"

He turned around. "Yes, yes, wait for me in my room." He turned back to me. "Zola, come in. What are you doing? What's happening?"

I walked into my apartment. Whoever he had been talking to had disappeared back into the room. "Sorry for interrupting," I said.

"What are you talking about?" he said. "I just came out for some water."

My facial muscles moved and words came out of my mouth. "Always after thirsty work."

He started to smile at our old joke, and then he stopped. "Zola?" he called anxiously.

I seemed to be on the verge of collapse. I gazed at him as though I had seen a ghost and he watched me in alarm. Tears began to gather in my eyes and spilled down my face.

"Zola," he cried as he hurried over to me and took me in his arms.

Antoine bore the brunt of my crushing embrace and to my surprise, he didn't say a word. Even though I knew him well enough to be aware he wasn't the biggest fan of these kinds of affectionate gestures.

When I stepped away, he looked around at the cops who had brought me.

"She needs to rest," the detective whose name I couldn't remember said.

They were speaking to him when I turned around and walked to my room. I just didn't care about anything beyond the comfort that was awaiting me in my room. I closed the door and sat on the bed until Antoine knocked softly and stood at the open door.

He came over and crouched down before me. "Sweetheart," he called softly.

But I wasn't able to look at him. I turned my face away.

"I don't know what's wrong, but I'm here for you. Tell me whatever you need, okay."

I nodded.

"I'm going to leave now okay," he said gently. "So that you can rest. If you need me just call me."

I looked at him and nodded again, grateful for his care and concern.

I wasn't ready to talk ... at least not yet.

I lay down and pulled the covers over my head. When I closed my eyes, I saw my father. Millions of images of him that I'd accumulated through the years.

Chapter 4
Dante

The media fanfare surrounding the murder of Marco Leone was incredible.

Obviously, it was not what I wanted, but there was a silver lining to the entire farce. The breathless nightly coverage of the murder meant the authorities had to take Zola's protection more seriously or risk a hit on their reputation should she be harmed on their watch.

My name was still out of the news as the unnamed businessman her father had been working on defending, but I knew it was only a matter of time before this would no longer be the case.

I also knew it was only a matter of time before they tried to hurt her again.

It was inevitable because of the rumors that she might be able to identify her attackers and that her father had shared valuable information to her about the case. This made her the ultimate loose end and it completely robbed me of sleep.

I also needed to talk to her but that didn't seem to be a

possibility. I ground out the cigar I'd been smoking and looked out at the picturesque nightlife skyline and considered my next steps.

The door behind me slid open but I didn't bother turning around.

"Boss?" Luca called. "Detective Hudgens is on the line for you?"

He came into my line of vision, a cell phone in his outstretched hand. I took the phone.

"Moretti," he said in his nasal New York accent. "Long time no speak."

I frowned at the grating voice of the meddlesome detective. "Well, we had a chat last month at my office so I don't think it's been that long."

"Oh, it has been," he said. "After all, Leone was alive last month, wasn't he? In fact, he was alive and well barely a week ago."

I ignored the jibe. "How many people do you have at her apartment?"

"One or two?" he replied.

I was even more annoyed by his careless tone. "One or two?" You're not sure?"

"Moretti, you have no right to interrogate me. She's safe. This case is only as big as it is right now because they know someone very high profile is behind it. But I guarantee you that in a few days, it'll blow over. The media will move on to something more interesting."

I could feel myself grow even colder at his words.

"I want to supply extra security for her, how can we make this happen?"

"You can't," he said and there was great satisfaction in

his voice. "And neither can we. At this point, we're doing all we can."

I didn't believe him.

"The media are reporting that she might be able to identify her attacker. You don't know how serious that is? There is no way they are going to let her live."

"When did you become so concerned about our witnesses? You've never been this way before."

"Marco Leone died to protect his daughter. I owe him to see that she is safe."

"At the moment she has chosen to stay at her apartment and we've got men outside guarding it, but we're going to put her into the program after her father's funeral in a few days. Security will be amped up during the funeral, and afterward, once things settle down a little, we can assess the situation more clearly."

I was shocked. "You're going to put her in the program?"

"Of course."

I had no desire to continue the conversation with him, but I had to. "Has she actually agreed to be in the program?"

He paused. "Uh ... I have to check up on that, but why wouldn't she?"

I couldn't believe the level of stupidity I was dealing with. "I want to see her. How can it happen?"

"It can't," he replied. "Perhaps at the funeral. People will be free to go up and speak to her then."

I acknowledged the truth in his words as I ended the call.

Chapter 5
Zola

The sound of the hairdryer was strangely soothing, and for a few minutes, I was almost able to believe I could completely focus on it and not remember my beloved Papa was gone. Gone forever. He was never coming back.

When Antoine cut off the dryer, I was once again greeted with silence and my loss seemed even greater.

"There. I bet you're glad you have one of the best stylists in the city as your roommate."

I curved my lips at Antoine's words and hoped it passed for a smile. "Yeah."

"So ... do you like it?" he asked, pumping hair serum into his hands and rubbing it through the ends of my hair.

"Yeah," I nodded, staring at my lifeless face in the mirror.

"You should put some makeup on, darlin'."

Our eyes met in the mirror. "I don't want to."

He nodded and didn't ask me any questions or push me to talk, even though I was certain he wanted me to share my burdens with him. I just couldn't, so this was where our little bathroom session came to an end. I thanked him, got to my feet and went to my room. I slipped quickly into my black dress, grabbed my purse, and was on my way out when I caught my reflection. For a second an old memory of my father resurfaced.

When I was a child, my father always loved my hair down, but whenever it would get in my eyes, which was all the time since I could never quite sit still, he would call me over and help me tie it up.

He always seemed to have a hair tie on him. I had always wondered how this was so. I had asked him once and he gave me some funny fantastical answer of how he was secretly a hair tie genie and it made me laugh until my sides hurt.

Antoine had done a wonderful job, but the perfection of my hair suddenly annoyed me. I grabbed a hair tie and turned it into a messy knot that I was certain would break Antoine's heart.

Then I grabbed my phone off my dresser and headed into the kitchen to find breakfast for one waiting.

"Eat up, darlin'. You need your strength today."

"Aren't you going to have any?" I asked.

He shook his head. "Nah, I'll just have a Kiwi smoothie later."

"Thank you," I said and looked down at the omelet, sausage, and toast breakfast he had obviously put so much care into making for me.

I really appreciated the effort so I ate as much as I could, but my appetite was gone and it was hard going.

We went down to meet the police officers waiting and

followed them to the unmarked police car. They never spoke and neither did we. I was grateful for the silence all the way to the cemetery.

I had been made aware of the potential danger that now surrounded me, and even though I believed I was in danger, I still couldn't find it in me to be worried or even scared. I would never say it out loud, but sometimes I felt so sad I hoped they would come so that I could escape this cold, numb, hollow emptiness. For three whole days, I couldn't find a lick of sleep. I had literally become the walking dead.

I stared out of the window at the vibrant city and wondered when or if I would ever feel like these people again. Living their lives with a frown or even a smile on their faces. Feeling anything beyond this soul-crushing grief that seemed to want to completely suck my life away at every moment.

I shut my eyes, no longer willing to think.

Finally, we arrived at the cemetery.

Papa's funeral, as I had expected, was packed full. The media kept a reasonable distance and I was sure this was due to the police's insistence that they stayed away. However, more people than I cared to know were present.

In fact, I had invited no one, hoping I would be able to do this as intimately as possible and without any observers, but this courtesy, I realized, would not be given to me. From the moment I entered the cemetery, I ignored any person that came up to me with their empty platitudes, making the message clear, I didn't want to talk to anyone.

My gaze never left my father's casket while the prayers were recited and he was lowered to the ground.

It would be the last time I ever came close to experiencing his existence physically. Even though I tried to control myself as he disappeared into the ground, I couldn't help the tears that filled my eyes and flowed down my face.

Antoine didn't hold me. He knew I would have hated that. Instead, he edged closer, encouraging me to lean against him. I readily accepted the offer of support as my legs were close to giving out.

Soon enough it was over, and people began to go their separate ways.

My father's secretary, Rosa, came up to me and this was one face at least I recognized. She gave me a warm, sweet hug, which I had no choice but to accept. Afterward, I knew she wanted to say more but after observing my frozen expression, she hesitated and then thankfully, went on her way after telling me she would be contacting me later on in the week with some information for me.

Papa's business associates began to come up to me ... and although I wanted to escape from them, I couldn't help feeling as if that would be disrespectful to my father. I kept myself together until I couldn't any longer. At that point, I looked to Antoine and he led me to the car while ensuring I wasn't stopped on the way. Eventually, we were seated in the dark-tinted vehicle. The cop turned to face me.

"Ready to leave?"

I shook my head. I couldn't stop staring at my father's grave in the fields. "I want to wait here for a bit. I want to spend a little more time with him. Maybe you can take Antoine home and come pick me up later."

"Sorry. Can't leave you here," he answered flatly.

"I'll find my way back. You stay," Antoine said and got out of the car.

It took about half an hour for the crowd to clear out. I was then able to return to the grave site in peace.

I sat on the grass and began to whisper to him. I found that although there were a thousand things I wanted to share with him, the only ones that bubbled up clearly and irrevocably were four words.

"I miss you, Papa."

The dam broke with those four words. I poured out everything I felt in my heart until I realized I was no longer alone. Something about the way this person moved made me freeze. The hairs at the back of my neck stood and I stopped breathing. The steps behind me were incredibly quiet and controlled. I waited, hoping I was just imagining things. It was just someone passing by.

I wasn't.

I heard the crackle of dry leaves behind me ... much too close. Instinctively, I jumped up and whirled around, but my fear-fueled reaction was so sudden I couldn't maintain my balance and I felt myself begin to fall backwards. Before I could land on my ass on the grass, a solid grip caught my hand and pulled me upright.

For a second, I thought I was losing my mind as I looked up and saw the face before me. The sun in the sky slightly hindered my vision for a moment, but soon it cleared and my vision was perfect.

He towered over me and I recognized him instantly. I stared at him in shock. God, he looked even more like a beautiful avenging angel than I remembered. All I could do was stare stupidly up at him until he broke the spell by speaking.

"Are you alright?"

The Guardian

"No," I said and rudely pulled my hand away.

I saw him stiffen and instantly hatred filled me. "I guess you had to come, right? To see the results of your handiwork?"

I was so sarcastic that for a moment even I was shocked. I hadn't meant to say that to him because even in my grieving state, I knew it was not his fault, but I still couldn't help the resentment I felt when I saw him look so strong, vibrant and alive just after I'd buried Papa. The air between us crackled with tension, resentment, and ... something else. I felt my heart beating erratically in my chest.

Suddenly he glanced away from me towards my father's grave and I could see for a moment the sadness on his face. Then it was gone, and he continued speaking as if I'd never uttered my ugly comment.

"I don't think the safety measures around you are appropriate," he said evenly. "For one, too many people were able to come up to you. That's unacceptable given the danger you're currently in."

"Rather than kill my father, why didn't they kill you?" I asked. "Whoever the madman behind all of this is, he only had to get rid of you, right? Why take my father out instead?"

He looked at me in surprise. "I'm not that easy to kill, Zola."

"Ah," I spat furiously. "So you enlisted the help of a man who was?"

He sighed. "I'll say this because I want to try to get you to listen to me. I tried my best to ensure your father was protected. However, that evening and after he had lost the informant at the restaurant ..." he paused, and I could tell he was wondering whether I knew any of this or not.

I scowled at him. "Tell me the truth for the love of God."

"That evening he wanted me to divert his security detail to finding and protecting the whistleblower because he believed their canceled meeting meant his identity had been compromised and he was in danger.

"I sent additional security to replace the ones I had sent to follow your father's request, but they arrived too late."

"So, what do you want from me?" I asked with a lethal glare. "Understanding? Forgiveness? I'm fresh out of both, I'll let you know when I restock."

Without waiting for him to respond I stepped to the side away from him and started to walk away, but his words stopped me in my tracks.

"You're in danger. I'm sure you know this."

I stopped and turned around to face him. "So? What's it to you?"

"I'm told you're considering getting into the witness protection program," he said.

"Again, what's it to you?" I asked.

His eyes narrowed. "Don't. I can tell from personal experience they're incapable of giving you the protection you need. The man who murdered your father will run rings around them. I want to help. I have to help. I can't let anything happen to you."

"You want to help?" I scoffed. "The same way you helped my father?"

It must have stung because I saw his expression go cold.

"Yeah, I thought so. Thanks, but no thanks," I spat

bitterly. "I think my family has been associated with you for long enough. Do me a big favor and stay away from me."

Then I turned around and stormed away. I was still fuming when I returned to the car which felt weird because it was the first time since this nightmare had begun that I'd felt anything beyond the crippling, heart-wrenching sense of emptiness and loss. But the rush of fury and adrenaline faded as I got in and closed the door. As I was driven away from the cemetery Antoine called.

"You okay darlin'?" he asked.

"Yeah, I'm fine."

We both knew it was a lie.

Chapter 6
Dante

I sat in a meeting listening to the briefings from the newly appointed lawyer.

"The trial will proceed, but now that Attorney Leone's daughter has been caught in the middle of it, we're hoping a testimony from her can reveal something that'll give us the upper hand. Or perhaps maybe some extra information her father might have left her in his final minutes? There is no doubt sooner or later she will be subpoenaed as a witness but as to what she will say or not say, no one knows."

He paused then.

"What is it?" I asked.

"Are you in any way close to her? I heard you had a somewhat personal relationship with Marco Leone so perhaps this could be enough to talk his daughter into revealing any inside information to us?"

My heart sank.

"My relationship was with her father. As you can imagine, due to what has happened since, she wants nothing to do with me."

"Mmm," he said. "Is there any way we can convince her? Right now, we're on somewhat solid ground, but it still doesn't guarantee a win. We need irrefutable evidence. What about the informant that he'd been waiting for at the restaurant? Any news on that?"

"My men are working on tracing him."

"Alright. We'll get to work building our defense for the next hearing so please keep us updated in the meantime."

"Of course." We parted company then, but I didn't feel any hope at all in the wake of his departure. And that, I realized, had to be one of the great things I would miss about Marco Leone. He was rare. Not only was he a wonderfully talented attorney, but someone I completely trusted. He represented me with all of his heart. As if he was my protector. Almost a father, I dare say.

If only I had listened to him. That tiny lapse without security was all they needed to take him out.

My chest felt heavy with sorrow at his sudden passing. I hadn't shed a tear for the man that meant so much to me. It would be a weakness that could be exploited. I felt alone. More alone than I had since I met the man more than a decade earlier.

I could still recall how we first met. It was after my indictment and the court's subsequent assignment of a lawyer who didn't give a damn whatsoever about me. I had already accepted that the justice system was going to crush me in its jaws and my life of freedom was practically over, but then Marco Leone came out of nowhere and gave me new hope.

I came from a brutal world where everyone was out to get you and I had been distrustful of him, but his kind eyes and pure smile made me question my initial distrust of him. Then he bailed me out and brought me to his home. No one had been able to do that given the evidence that had been stacked against me. But he had, and from then on, I was fully converted. He was the real deal.

His daughter on the other hand ...

From the start, it was hate at first sight for her. She eyed me haughtily and probably regarded me as a lowly criminal, but I was fine with that because it made it easier to curb my strong desire for her. I was indebted to her father, and the last thing I wanted to do was betray him by hooking up with his daughter.

I thought back to that night when I had covered her mouth with mine. I believed it would be the end of my interaction with her, but life sure had a way of bringing back loose ends you hoped would stay that way forever. And in the most gruesome way.

I recalled my conversation with her at the cemetery and the terrible pain in her eyes. She blamed me. I knew it would be nearly impossible to reach her. But whether she could help me or not, my number one priority from now on was to ensure she was safe and taken care of in every imaginable way. Marco had given up his life for her so I would not let the sacrifice be for nothing.

Zola didn't know it, but I was now her guardian.

Chapter 7
Zola

Antoine got smoothly to his feet from sitting cross-legged on the floor. "I have to return to work at the restaurant tomorrow," he told me. "It's been a few days now. Any more and I think I'll get canned."

"Of course," I said, and he came over to squat in front of me.

"What?" I asked.

He softly brushed my hair out of my face. "I don't know if I can leave you alone yet?"

I smiled. "What do you think I'm going to do? Slit my wrist?"

The smile was immediately gone from his face. "And that," he said firmly, "is the reason why I'm not comfortable leaving you on your own."

I reached out and tousled his messy hair. "I was kidding. I will be fine. I wouldn't dare hurt myself. Wherever my dad is right now, he would look down and be so disappointed. Plus, I don't exactly like the idea of doing that before I find the bastard who caused this and make him pay.

After that, you can be worried about me. But for now, I'll stay grounded."

He narrowed his eyes. "I hear the determination in your voice, so I'll agree for now. But I'll keep listening for desolation or anything else alarming and then I'll act."

Tears filled my eyes as I wondered about how I would have been able to survive if I had been all on my own. Before he could see them, I turned my face away towards the television. It had been stuck on the news channel ever since that devastating night, but it suddenly changed to a different channel. Startled, I looked up and saw Antoine with the remote.

"You should watch something else," he said.

"No," I said as I tried to snatch the device away from him.

He evaded me and instead put on a cooking show of some sort.

"I won't know what's going on," I complained under my breath.

"Everything there is old news. Any important development will be communicated directly to you by the police standing guard outside, so rest your poor mind and heart, please."

He blew me a kiss before he left, and I settled down to watch the show. I allowed myself to be distracted by the visual stimulation until I fell asleep.

I woke up suddenly. The apartment was in darkness. The only light was from the television and for a second I was terrified. I sat up but was too scared to move any further.

"Antoine?" I called, but I didn't get a response.

The Guardian

He was probably still out. I forced myself to get up and turn on the light. The moment the warm golden ambiance filled the room I was able to relax somewhat. I looked out of the window and wondered just how long I would be forced to remain cooped up in here. I didn't necessarily want to leave the apartment right away, but I wondered if I ever would without looking over my shoulder.

Just then my phone began to ring. It was the detective in charge of my father's investigation. I was glad to hear from someone who seemed to be in some sort of control because I most definitely was not.

"Miss Leone?"

"Yeah." I was gripping the phone too hard.

"I'm just calling to let you know that you will be subpoenaed as a witness. You may want to hire your own legal counsel to guide you through the process. Also, if there's anything incriminating to either party that is different, or in addition to what you've told us so far, then please let us know immediately. Perhaps since the incident, you have remembered some details that might have slipped your mind initially. Any possible identification marks on the assailant ...?"

He remained silent, waiting for me until I responded.

"I haven't thought much about it," I replied.

"Alright. You've asked for some time to consider being in the witness protection program, but always remember you can willingly refuse based on your own personal preference perspective of risk." He paused for a few seconds, then continued. "If you have any further issues or feel unsafe, please don't hesitate to contact us. Stay alert and be guarded at all times. Contact us if anything seems amiss."

"Sure," I replied, but as I stared out of the window, I realized I had one more question for him.

"Can I go back to work?" I asked.

"You can," he replied. "But we strongly advise against this for the time being."

"Until when?"

"My personal suggestion will be after this trial has been concluded."

"And when will that be?" I asked.

"I don't have the answer to that yet," he said.

Chapter 8
Dante

"She what?"

"She returned to work this morning, Boss. She's heading there right now."

I couldn't believe it.

I was on my way to the office, but I knew if I wasn't able to talk some sense into her the rest of my day would be rendered useless.

I ended the call and instructed my driver to change my route immediately. In less than half an hour I'd arrived at her literary agency. As I stepped out of the car, I noted there was no reasonable police security in place. Thank God, my men had their eyes on the building and on her. I'd also planted one of my men as a security guard for the building through their supplier company, but having only one man to guard her did not put me at ease at all.

He gave me a discreet nod as I entered the building.

I took the elevator and got off at Zola's floor. I was the last person any of her colleagues could have been expected to recognize, but given that my photos had been broadcasted over all the TV channels yesterday, I was immediately identified.

"Mr. Moretti?" one of the ladies blurted out with widened eyes. "Um, this is such a surprise. How can we help you?"

"I'm here to see Zola Leone," I said and her eyes seemed to widen even further.

"Um sure, certainly, I'll get her for you."

The only issue ahead of me was getting Zola to listen to me. It wasn't going to be a small feat but I had to try until I got through to her. In memory of her father.

While I waited I called my secretary and asked her to shift all my meetings for the next couple of hours. Fifteen minutes passed but Zola didn't show up. I wasn't ready to spend any more time waiting. There were other ways to reach her. I got to my feet and was about to leave when the CEO of the agency appeared out of nowhere and hurried over.

I recognized her from the brief search I had ordered of the company.

"Mr. Moretti." She approached with a smile, her curly dark hair bouncing all around her.

I accepted her handshake, then she ushered me into her office.

"What an honor it is to have you here," she gushed, leading me to the seat in front of her desk.

I remained patient and politely listened to what she had to say.

Her cheeks were flushed and she was wringing her hands nervously. "I just wanted to extend my sincerest apologies for what is happening to you. The media sure has a way of painting everything and everyone in a negative light. I didn't know you were personally connected to Miss Leone, although um as we have learned her father was your lawyer."

"I don't have a personal connection to her," I replied. "I only had one with her father. I came here today to speak to her about some urgent issues, but since I haven't been able to see her, I'll find another way to contact her."

She studied me, the smile on her face faltering slightly before she leaned forward and I knew there was an uncomfortable question she wanted to ask.

"I have several appointments today so if you have nothing further to say I'll take my leave."

"Oh no," she immediately jumped up. I looked at the near panic in her eyes with interest.

"Um, I guess there's no delicate way to put this. I just ... Miss Leone has been with us for a couple of years now and while we do immensely appreciate her talent ... due to the recent developments we also can't help but be um ... be concerned for the safety of our office. Especially now she has returned to work. We offered to put her on paid leave for a little while so she could recover and get her family affairs in order, but she insisted that she needed to work to keep her mind off things so we had no choice but to accept. Um ... I'm ready to put my foot down and insist that she leave if there is a solid reason to believe her presence here might put the rest of the office in danger since the trial her father was handling ... yours, is still un——"

I cut her off, unable to deal with her rambling any further.

"Are you asking me if you should fire her?"

She attempted to smile. "Well ..."

My answer was simple. "If you're asking if her presence here poses a risk to the safety of your office then my answer is yes. As to whether you have to fire her or not that is up to you. That is your company's decision and not mine."

She stared at me.

"Um ... but if you were to give a recommendation?"

"It's best that she not be here," I replied bluntly. "At least for the time being."

An awkward silence struck the room as I got to my feet. She did the same, but before I could leave, she had another request for me.

"This might be a bit forward, Mr. Moretti but this is my card," she murmured, coming around the desk. "After the trial concludes, I might come knocking at your door. I hope you'll be able to grant us an audience. We're just ... we're hoping to get your side of the story."

I raised an eyebrow. "My side of the story?"

"Yes," she replied. "In book form, of course. We want to represent you."

I watched her. "I'm sorry, but I don't think what's happening is entertaining enough to be told to anybody. Have a nice day."

Chapter 9
Zola

"What?"

I gazed at my boss, hoping the words she was saying to me were not true.

"Paid leave?"

She sighed. "You need some time to recuperate, Zola."

"And what I'm ... that's what I'm trying to do right now."

"Zola ... I'm already being quite generous. I truly don't know what else you want me to do. I'm so sorry, but this is the best for everyone. There is still so much attention on you and the case and ... I really have to think of the well-being of the other employees here."

I could now clearly understand what she meant and what she was trying to do.

I couldn't complain. I lowered my head and mumbled that I understood her situation.

A short silence passed between us before she added with forced brightness, "You can still handle your workload during your leave. You can work virtually, and we can hold meetings since most of your work, as you build your client list, now will be scouting out deserving writers. I think this time at home will allow you to carefully sort through your pile of submissions and find unique talents and stories. Either way, I see it as a win-win. Plus ..."

She leaned over, her eyes sparkling with excitement. "I didn't know you were very well acquainted with Mr. Moretti. So, if you're able to talk him into a book deal for us, we would immensely appreciate it and you will be celebrated here. Your first client possibly? That will be a massive win for you."

I was so struck by her words that for a few moments, all I could do was stare blankly at her. Unable to believe what she was telling me at first, but then it all made sense and my eyes widened with understanding.

"Ah, non-fiction."

"It would be riveting," she said to me, but must have realized she was speaking to one of the victims of her non-fiction story so she changed her opportunistic expression.

"I mean ... it would be incredibly moving. This whole case and events are almost unreal and there are so many sides to it we would never get to know all of them, but I do believe if we were able to, then it would really help a lot of people. You have experience with being an editor and agent plus due to your ... association with Dante Moretti. I have no doubt you will be the perfect person for this."

I managed to work up a smile. "You know what? You're right. What I need is rest so I will take that personal paid leave. I'll let you know when I've healed and recovered enough from my father's murder to work again. I truly appreciate all your advice and assistance so far. Thank you."

The Guardian

All the enthusiasm seemed to drain out of her face as she stared at me, but she didn't dare say anything else.

At first, I felt nothing as I cleared my things and emptied out the desk I'd only set out for the first time that morning. My very own office. Inside I was cold and numb, just like I had been over the last few days. I thought of how it had been coming in this morning and drinking coffee with my other coworkers. They had shown only sincere kindness for me and it had made me feel a little warm inside.

But then that bastard had to come in and ruin it all. I could feel the chill slowly seeping into my bones again.

Great anger swept over me. Had he not done enough damage to me? I wanted to hurt him.

When all my things were in my box, I marched out of my office building and tossed the box into the backseat of my car. I didn't even give a damn when all those things that I had lovingly collected fell and spilled out and rolled onto the floor. I got into my seat and pulled out my phone. I didn't know how to reach him, but a quick Google search for his investment company later, I was able to get to his office.

"Dante Moretti's office," a crisp voice answered.

"Tell him Zola Leone is on the phone," I growled.

She went silent for a few seconds.

"I'm afraid Mr. Moretti is occupied at the moment. Would you like to leave a message?"

"Tell him if he doesn't call me back in the next five minutes I'm coming to his office with a loaded gun and I'm going to kill him. I swear to God I will."

And with that, I ended the call and tried to calm down, but there was no possible hope of me calming down. I was so fired up it felt as if sparks of electricity were shooting out of my skin.

How dare he? How freaking dare he? The audacity!

I started the ignition and zoomed out of the parking lot.

I decided I really wanted to give Dante a piece of my mind, the angrier the better. I drove to his office building and parked in a reserved parking bay. Slamming the car door, I marched up to the entrance.

Chapter 10
Dante

I was catching up with one of the delayed meetings for the day with my financial director when Ellie pushed the intercom button. She knew better than to disturb me during a meeting so it had to be urgent.

"What is it?"

"Zola Leone called. She said that she'll be here with a loaded gun in five minutes if you don't call her back. Should I contact Security, Sir?"

For the first time in a really long while a smile came to my face. "No. Show her in when she arrives."

I set down the phone and returned to my meeting, but I couldn't concentrate. It dawned on me that I was really looking forward to seeing her again.

I ended my meeting and sat looking out of the window at the sea of skyscrapers. She would be annoyed at my interference at her workplace for sure, but I had no choice. She wasn't taking the very real dangers surrounding her as seriously as I wanted her to.

Half an hour later Ellie announced her arrival. To be honest I was surprised that she had even bothered to stop outside. I'd almost expected her to barge in and point a gun straight at my head.

I tapped my fingers on the table as Ellie showed her in.

"Miss Leone, Sir," Ellie said and directed her to one of the seats in front of my desk. Ignoring Ellie, she glared at me.

Ellie didn't linger. She shut the door behind her and I turned my full attention to the woman before me. Her face was pale, and she was dressed in a fitted skirt and linen shirt but all in black. She probably thought she looked as if she was in mourning, she had no idea that she looked like the sexiest woman alive. If the circumstances were different ...

"You're smiling. Is this all amusing to you?" she raged.

"I thought you were bringing a gun," I said and settled more comfortably into the chair.

"What did you think you were doing?" she asked, and tears of anger and frustration were welling up in her eyes. "Do you know what you took from me today? That job was my last lifeline. I wanted to hold on to it and find a way slowly to stay alive and you took that away. Why?"

Every trace of amusement immediately left me. She was in pain, immense and heartbreaking pain and I understood that. I knew what the pain of loss felt like.

I softened my tone, something I couldn't ever recall doing.

"Zola, I don't know how I can make you believe it, but you are in extreme danger and it was the only way I knew to protect you."

The Guardian

At my words, the pain in her eyes turned to a murderous fury. "All of a sudden I'm supposed to believe you care for me?"

I told her the truth because I didn't know how else to get to her.

"Not you, but your father. If anything happened to you, I'd never forgive myself."

"So, in order to protect your golden conscience you took my job away?"

The way she was putting it didn't make me feel good, but there was no way she could convince me that I had done the wrong thing.

"You might not believe this but I owe your father everything. I am here today ... because of him."

"And where is my father?" she asked. "Because of you, he is gone, and yet you're still not willing to leave me alone? How can I make myself clear? Oh yeah, stay the fuck away from me."

It was obvious to me that exchanging words in this way would not be productive so I got straight to the crux of my offer. "There are rumors going around that you might be able to identify the murderer which makes it certain there is a hit out for you right now."

She sank into the chair nearest to her and stared at me with a mixture of horror and disbelief at her situation.

"I can protect you, Zola, and it's very frustrating to sit here and not be given the chance, but it's either me or the witness protection program, and trust me they will not be able to protect you the way I can."

She shook her head as if in a daze. "Why does everyone

keep assuming I saw something? I haven't made any such claims to the police when they interviewed me so why is there even an offer that I should join the witness protection program?"

I studied her. "It doesn't matter whether you saw something or not ... you're not someone they want alive. You were with your father before he died so they must take into account that he could have given you some information that none of us are aware of. Actually, there could be a hundred different speculations, but what I'm trying to say is they don't need a hundred and they don't need one either. The moment they have a suspicion about a possible threat, they immediately eliminate it. Their motto has always been better safe than sorry."

She sighed, but I could tell that rather than agreeing with me she was simply trying to control her temper.

"I'm going to give you one last warning to stay away from me. If you don't, I'm going to give testimony alright and it's going to be against you."

She stood and started to walk out of the room.

"Your father wanted to defend me," I said.

At first, she kept going, but then her steps slowed until she came to a complete stop.

"What the hell does that mean?" she asked as she glowered at me. "Are you trying to shift blame from yourself?"

"No," I replied directly. "It is my burden to bear, but here is a little history for you. I was once falsely accused of murder. Like you, I was in the wrong place at the wrong time so I knew it was only a matter of time before they also tried to get rid of me. The dead don't talk.

"I knew how to take care of myself. That was no problem, but I didn't know how to stop them from throwing me in prison and letting me rot in there for the rest of my life ... until your father believed in my innocence and was genuine in his kindness, he footed the entire cost of defending me and worked tirelessly to ensure I came out a winner in the end.

"I owe him my life and I'll forever be grateful to him for that. So ... I also feel his loss deeply. His presence had been something I'd treasured for so long. The world was a better place because he was in it.

"I don't know what your father told you, but I did not hire him to work on my case. I would never put him in danger. For precisely that reason I gave the job to someone else, but he kept working on it on his own steam. It was he who uncovered the whistleblower. Then I had to listen to him. All I could do was try to protect him the best way I could, but because of a momentary lapse in judgement, I failed in that and it's a scar I will always hold."

"Instead of defending you, he should have been with me," Zola muttered inconsolably.

"I'm sorry for your loss, but you have to understand, your father held his work in high regard. He would always go to great lengths to defend those who had been accused but didn't have anyone to fight for them. Do you know why his dedication was so immense?"

She shook her head slowly, her eyes full of curiosity.

"He was so focused and driven because early on in his career, before he opened his own firm, he had been part of a defense team to represent a murderer, but they had not prepared well and they lost the case. The result was the mother of three was taken from her kids and sent to prison.

The woman died in prison and your father was devastated. It haunted him for years. And then ..."

I hesitated briefly but decided to continue.

"And then he lost your mother. In the depths of his broken heart, he considered it retribution for taking that mother from her three kids.

"I'm not trying to gain your understanding or compassion, but you shouldn't refuse my protection because you ultimately judge your father's murder to be my fault. Whether I liked it or not, the moment your father heard of my case he was going to take it because he saw me as his own. And now that he's no more I have to be a source of strength and protection for you, but I need your cooperation even in the smallest way to make that happen. You cannot be out and about right now because it's still too dangerous. Ugo, my boss before the time I met your father, is behind this, and believe me when I tell you, he is an evil psychopath. He could cut your throat with a song in his heart. And he could do it for no other reason than he felt like it."

I had said much more than I wanted to, but I was sure this could be the last chance I was going to get. I needed her to at least hear and consider my words.

For a second neither of us said anything, then she turned around and fled from my office. I picked up my phone and called Luca.

"She's leaving the building. Double your team and keep your eyes on her at all times. Ensure that nothing happens to her. And for fuck's sake, find me that informant."

"I believe we'll have word on him today, Boss," Luca said. "Rocco and his team found the motel he had booked into a few days ago. We suspect he's severely injured from trying to escape Ugo's men. We'll find him."

My fingers drummed the desk surface. "So, he truly is an informant and not part of Ugo's men?"

"Looks like it, Boss."

"Alright," I said. "Update me as soon as you have him."

Chapter 11
Zola

What I hadn't expected to be, after my meeting with him, was visibly shaken.

I leaned against the headrest of my car and thought of the way Dante had spoken of my father. About the motivations behind his work, the work I had despised so immensely, and suddenly, I was filled with a terrible regret. I couldn't control the tears that flowed out of my eyes.

If only I'd known this while he was alive.

Why couldn't he have told me about his earlier experience and the way my mother's death had haunted him? If only he had told me. All those years I spent bickering with him and holding a grudge for his absence wouldn't have happened.

It wasn't long before I realized I had never asked. I had whined and complained about him not spending time with me over and over again, but I had taken him for granted. He was always there. Papa. I thought he would always be there.

The Guardian

Dante showed me that my father had not wasted his life. Instead, he'd poured himself into something that soothed and fulfilled him and changed other people's lives for the better.

"I'm sorry, Papa," I whispered.

Lowering my head I tried to picture him the way he was before that night. Ever since that night, I tried not to think of him, because all I could see in my mind's eyes was the horrendous image of him dead. I wanted to remember my father fondly and without fear so I took deep breaths and tried over and over again.

I remained there until I could see him laughing.

When I arrived home and saw the cop car outside the apartment waiting for me, I almost didn't want to get out, but Dante's words on how exposed I was to an attack popped into my head. I jumped out of the car and ran all the way up to my apartment. I could breathe a little bit then but just as I arrived at the elevator, I heard my name being called.

I was reluctant to stop, but the voice was all too familiar so even though the elevator doors slid open I reluctantly turned around and faced my real estate agent. Dorothy was dressed as though she had specifically come for an 'official' visit and my heart immediately sank.

"Miss Leone." She smiled but it was more troubling than if she hadn't. "I was hoping to get a word with you. There are cops and reporters lurking around too …"

She said it as though she was looking for me to confirm her speculation. I shrugged. "And?"

She looked offended. "There's no need to be rude. I know you're going through a difficult time, but we have rules here that must be obeyed at all times."

"What rules have I broken?"

She frowned. "Actually, I have something very important to tell you from the building tenants and your landlord as well."

I nearly rolled my eyes. "And what is that?"

She got straight to the point. "We're going to need you to find a different place to live. It's unfair that the other tenants have to be the ones to move out because they don't want to live in fear. This is a good area and we'd like it to remain so. Here is a letter from your landlord."

She handed over the letter and all I could do was stare at it.

"What exactly are they worried about?" I asked even though I could take a good enough guess.

"Their safety," she said.

"It appears your father's ... case is still ongoing and according to the news, it will not be resolved soon. And with random news media dropping by and ... the cops ... they just don't feel safe anymore. They would really appreciate it if you found another place to live in for the time being. You are always welcome to return when all this fuss dies down."

Without a word, I headed into the elevator.

It wasn't a shock given what had happened at the office today, and human nature. However, it didn't mean it didn't hurt. I put the key in and opened my door.

"What's wrong?" Antoine asked, and I could see the fear in his eyes. A fear, no doubt, he tried hard but unsuccessfully to hide from me. My decision to leave solidified even more. Beyond myself, I needed to protect those who were around me.

"Nothing." I gave him a little hug of apology and headed into the apartment to see a cop waiting for me.

"He just arrived," Antoine said.

"What is this?" I asked.

"Subpoena," he replied.

"They really need to get the trial back on track. Please notify your place of work that you won't be able to come in on the stipulated days. Given your testimony might take several hours or several days and you might be called back to court multiple times, please do all that you can to be available."

Then he gave a little nod of his head and bid me goodbye.

His departure left the apartment with an eerie silence. Antoine turned to me with a smile ready.

"Why are you home so early?" he asked. "It's the middle of the afternoon."

"I was kicked out of the office," I said and headed over to the sofa.

"What?"

"I pose too much of a safety risk for them to tolerate," I explained briefly as I let my body drop onto the sofa.

His mouth fell open. "Wow, those bastards. Can we sue them or something?"

"It's paid leave."

"Oh. But still, we could get more money suing them,

harassment, loss of face, mental distress ..." he suggested cheekily.

I smiled. "Their concerns are valid. Things might seem quiet right now, but as I've been told over and over again by people who know better than me, danger is still lurking and could strike at any moment so I need to be on guard. You too."

He huffed but it couldn't quite hide the nervousness in his face. "They don't have any business with me and neither do they have any with you for that matter."

I thought back to that night. "I saw one of them. He was going to kill me," I said and almost flinched as I recalled the kick that had sent me flying across the room.

"He has a tattoo," I said. "I grabbed his leg when he was kicking me, and I bit down into his ankle. He cursed and pulled back. That's when I saw it. The tattoo on his arm. I can't remember the exact details, but if I saw it again, I would recognize it."

"Did you tell the prosecutor about this?" he asked.

I shook my head. "I haven't told anybody. The memory just came to me now."

"You can tell them in the morning."

"That's the dilemma. If I keep quiet then they might hunt me down and kill me because they think I know more than I do. If I speak up, they are going to be furious at me and they might kill me too."

He frowned. "What are you going to do?"

"I've decided to join the witness protection program."

He stilled. "That doesn't sound good."

"None of this is good," I said. "But I think it's time for a new start. I don't have any relatives apart from my father so I guess it might work. Start all over ... maybe I'll feel safe."

A wave of sadness came over his face. "Noooo ..."

"It's for the best."

"Does that ... does that mean we'll never see each other again?"

I shook my head slowly. "You're safer that way. I don't want to put anyone I love in danger so it's better that I'm out of here."

He headed over to the couch, tossed away the cushions and we took their places. I leaned my head on his shoulder.

"None of this was even within the sphere of our imagination last week," he said.

I nodded. "Life, right?"

"Yeah."

"I'm going to testify honestly. I'm going to say all that I know. I can't let the bastards who did this to my father go scot-free. I'm going to fight as much as I can, but I have to do it alone."

"So, you came to say goodbye?"

I smiled grimly. "Actually, I've already been asked to get out."

His eyes widened as I passed over the eviction notice I received from the agent.

He tore the envelope open and, after reading through it, looked at me with a flabbergasted expression.

"That bitch. Is this even legal?"

"Who knows? At this point, nobody seems to care what is legal and what isn't. Everyone just does whatever they want. Hurt whoever they want. Me, I'm going to bring my father's killers to justice without injuring anyone around me. But first I need a lawyer. A really good one, but with what happened to my father I just don't know if any of them will be willing to take on my case."

"You have to try," he said.

"I intend to," I said, and he pulled me into a very uncomfortable hug.

Chapter 12
Dante

"When did she start loading the vehicle?"

"About an hour ago, Boss."

"Follow her," I said and ended the call.

She was running away to keep those she cared about safe. The next trial date would be coming up soon. Unfortunately, she was refusing to reach out to me for help which probably meant she was considering getting into the program. That was possibly the worst thing she could do.

Luca rang with an update. "Boss, she's just arrived at her father's home."

I frowned. "What?"

"She seems to be moving in there permanently."

I was surprised. After the trauma of her father's murder, was she really planning on living in that massive house alone?

"Do we have any cameras in the house?"

"Mr. Leone only allowed us to install them around the perimeters. There are none inside of the house."

"Confirm they are all working and that you have access

to all of them. And watch for every single movement in the grounds and for any visitor that comes to her door. No matter who it is, inform me."

"Alright, Boss."

I felt rattled so I switched on the video feed outside her father's house and immediately saw the pizza delivery boy standing outside her door. He rang the doorbell. I frowned and peered closer. Was he a threat? Was he an assassin in disguise? I was heading home, but I had no choice but to change directions.

"To Mr. Leone's house, Aldo," I instructed.

"Yes, Sir," Aldo said with a nod.

I immediately called Luca.

"Do you see the delivery boy?" I asked and he responded in kind. "We have a gun trained on his head. One wrong move."

"Good."

On my phone screen, I saw that the door was never pulled open. I saw the delivery guy squat down and I realized she had slipped his payment underneath the door along with a little note that he opened up to read.

He left after setting the box down on the front steps. After his motorbike left, she pulled the door open. Her head peeked out and she grabbed the box. As quick as lightning, she disappeared back into the house.

With a sigh of relief, I leaned back against the cool leather.

Chapter 13
Zola

It took a while for my heart to calm down after I had shut the door. My father's housekeeper had sensibly cleared out the fridge and pantry so I had no choice but to order a takeout.

I leaned against the solid wooden door, hoping that a bullet wouldn't pass through. But the windows on the other walls in the entrance were a constant source of worry to me.

In short, at this point, I was convinced the escape space underneath my father's desk was where would be best for me to hide, but it had already been discovered. Plus, there was the fact that the shattered window on the day of the murder remained unrepaired and simply covered up with some temporary material.

I was still trembling from fear as I moved towards the kitchen, but then changed my mind and darted up the stairs leaving all the lights on. I went straight to my father's room as his windows faced the front of the house and I could have a better view of the house entrance. I switched on the bathroom light and left the door open to illuminate the room. I didn't need any attackers knowing exactly what room I was in.

I thought I would be too terrified to stay in my father's room, but being in my own room was for some reason even more terrifying. Through all of my years of growing up, I'd always run here to Papa's room even when he was at work and physically unavailable.

I settled down on the floor with my extra cheese, extra pepperoni pizza, and my father's familiar smells surrounding me. His scent somewhat calmed me and I opened the box and began to eat, but I realized everything tasted of nothing. I stood and darted over to the study on the top floor.

There was a little wine rack there. I could still remember evenings full of laughter with my father and mother as they shared a bottle. The memory was heartbreaking.

I found a bottle of my father's favorite wine and returned to his room. Locking the door behind me once again, I uncorked the bottle and filled my glass all the way to the top.

"This is for you, Papa," I whispered, raising the glass.

The first sip brought tears to my eyes. I bit my lip to stop myself from crying then I downed half the glass in one go. I took a bite of pizza and watched the news with the volume turned all the way down. I must have been on my third glass when breaking news on my father's case was suddenly announced.

The news stated the informant who had not turned up for his meeting with my father had been found dead in a motel room a few miles away from the city.

"How horribly cruel the world is," I murmured, but my words were slurred.

I drained my glass once again, knocked it aside, and grabbed the bottle instead.

I knew I shouldn't get drunk since I had to remain alert, and I didn't think I was yet, but all the strength did seem to have seeped out of my body. I could no longer sit upright so I laid down on the floor and continued to drink. But the wine spilled down my face and at first, I cursed, but then I began to laugh.

I laughed so hard that I began to cry. The more I laughed, the more I cried.

"What's so funny?" a rich, deep voice asked from the doorway, causing my heart to almost leap out of my body.

Chapter 14
Dante

Getting the keys to Marco's house had proved a feat that had taken about three months of constant badgering to succeed. I had finally convinced him it would prove beneficial in case of an emergency involving his daughter. He had given them to me to be used only in case of an emergency.

This, classified as one.

As I took in the drunk girl on the floor who seemed to be in the depths of despair, to my surprise something in my chest twisted. It had been a long time since I felt even the slightest twinge of pity for another human being. I had learned to distrust human beings. Even the ones that looked vulnerable. All snakes. All capable of turning around and biting the hand that feeds.

And this one was particularly dangerous to me. She awakened long-asleep desires. I could feel them powerfully and uncontrollably unfurling inside my body. I had to be careful that they did not consume me.

The last thing I wanted was to startle her but it was

unavoidable. I had softly knocked on the door, but she was in the throes of a laughing-crying fit and had not heard me.

Her reaction was surprisingly fast though, considering how drunk she was. She scrambled up, lurched over to her father's bedside, pulled out a gun and pointed it directly at me.

Her eyelashes were all wet and stuck together. I'd never seen her look so vulnerable and sexy at the same time. "Is that gun even loaded?" I asked as I walked over to the pizza and picked up a slice. It was loaded with cheese and quite greasy, but I was starving and it would do.

"What are you doing here and how the hell did you get in?" she demanded hoarsely. She was so drunk she was swaying.

I glanced over at the empty bottle rolling on the floor and a half-empty bottle still standing upright. "Your father gave me a set of keys a long time ago."

"He gave you the keys or you stole it?" she scoffed.

I didn't bother arguing with her. Not when there was a gun pointed at my head. I took another bite. "Doesn't your arm hurt yet?"

"Fuck you," she muttered and flung the gun on the bed.

"This is terrible food."

"I want you to leave. Right now, or you're going to regret it," she threatened adorably.

"You know I'm not going to hurt you. Why are you so panicked by my presence?" I asked calmly.

"What am I supposed to feel? Relieved?" She picked up her phone from the carpet. "I'm going to call the cops."

I shrugged. "If you do, the media will cover the story, and everyone will know you're back in this house."

"My life is a living hell and it's all your fault," she blurted out suddenly. Her lower lip trembled and she dropped her head to hide it from me.

"You wish I hadn't saved you that day, don't you?" I asked softly.

She didn't lift her head, but I knew she was listening. How I wanted to pull her poor grieving body into my arms, hold her close, and never let this cruel world hurt her again. But she would probably scratch my eyes out. I turned and stared out the window.

"Because of that incident, you sense your father felt indebted to me. And that was why he could never let go of my case even though it was dangerous."

"If you hadn't saved me, I would be dead," she whispered.

I turned to face her. She was staring at me and her beautiful eyes looked enormous. "Yes, but since I did your father is dead. Isn't that the dilemma you're struggling with to handle his loss?"

As if she could no longer bear her own weight she sank heavily to the edge of the bed and buried her face in her hands. A long silence ensued between us.

"Don't join the program," I said earnestly. "It's a bad deal."

"Don't try to tell me what to do," she replied. "I can still shoot you."

She was cute when she was being unreasonable. I turned away to hide my smile. "You've been subpoenaed so you'll need a lawyer."

She sighed heavily.

"It's too dangerous for you to find one yourself, and you

don't know enough about what you are up against to choose the right one. I'll find the very best one for you and send him over tomorrow. He'll be here around eleven to see you. Thanks for the pizza." I got to my feet then and started to head toward the door.

"What if they get me before the night is over?" she asked.

I turned around to look at her and at that moment I knew. I would protect her with my life. Not because I owed her father, but because ... because. What the hell was going on with me? Was I losing my mind over a girl? I shook my head to clear it. And when I spoke my voice was hard.

"Every inch of your home is under the watch of my men. Even a cockroach cannot get into the house without my men's knowledge. As for the window in your father's office, it will be fixed in a few hours ... so don't panic if you hear any drilling noises. We'll try to keep it brief. This is not the ideal location for you, but you are well protected. No one can harm you.

"When you wake up you have my office number. Call my secretary. She's at your disposal for anything you might need, including a lawyer to handle your father's will, the sale of the house ... anything. She will only send approved people your way. This is not the time to use strangers. I hope that you will heed my advice. Now try to get some sleep."

She was still staring at me speechlessly when I left.

Chapter 15
Zola

I stared blankly at the door for a good few minutes after he left, then I rushed to the toilet and was sick as a dog. Alcohol and I were not good bedfellows. I cleaned my teeth and got into my father's bed. Pulling the covers over my head, I shut my eyes and was asleep in minutes.

I slept well ... more than I had in a while.

When I woke up the next morning, it was with a slight headache and a heavy grogginess that I richly deserved. I felt too disgusted to go back to sleep so I stumbled to the bathroom and stepped into the shower. A little while later my hair was washed, my body clean, and my head somewhat cleared.

The events of the previous day and evening had already begun to come back to me. I felt a strange sense of guilt as I thought about Dante. I recognized that my father's death was ultimately not his fault and I should stop trying to blame or hate him, but if I did, then how on earth would I stop my body from responding sexually to him? Because my body had not got the memo that I was grieving for my father and it was noticing stuff about him. The way his hot eyes moved over my body, the way his sensual lips twisted into a mocking smile, the strong column of his throat, his manly wrist, his deeply tanned skin against my own ...

Don't go there, Zola! For the love of God don't go there.

Putting him firmly out of my mind, I changed into one of my father's oversized T-shirts. There was a time I'd made a habit of wearing his shirts, but not since I moved out. As I went down to the kitchen, I recalled how he would sometimes feign annoyance, especially if I wore one of his favorite ones, but never once did he ever forbid me.

The empty lemon-scented refrigerator reminded me the house was a food desert. Dante said he would take care of it, but it was only nine o'clock so it was probably too early to expect groceries. I returned to my father's room to check on my leftover pizza, but when I took in the two congealed hardened slices, I instantly lost my appetite.

A message pinged on my phone. It was from Dante.

Groceries are outside the front door. Don't hesitate to contact my secretary or me if you need anything at all.

I reread his message and wondered how long he aimed to keep this up. I needed to speak to him. I wasn't comfortable about the responsibility he was forcing upon himself in order to ensure my welfare. I headed over to the front door and through the peephole, saw three sturdy bags stuffed with food and vegetables.

Chapter 16
Zola

I took the bags with me to the kitchen, interested to see what he had gotten. It was a bonanza of food: organic eggs, deli bread, specialty cheeses, farm-reared pork sausages, handmade pasta in a box, apples, melon, strawberries, bars of dark and milk chocolate with pieces of orange rind, hazelnut cookies, orange juice, and basically everything I could need to cook myself a big breakfast. I tried but couldn't find any reason to reject the gesture.

I quickly sent him a new message.

Thank you. Please send me the receipt so I can pay you back.

I set the phone aside and got to work quickly whipping up some scrambled eggs and toast. After losing most of my pizza in the toilet last night I was very hungry, but when the meal was cooked and I'd sat at the table to eat, my appetite suddenly deserted me. The sound of the fork scratching on the plate echoed and stopped as I put it down.

Around me was a strange stillness and silence gathered. My father's big, vital presence was gone. There was no longer any life in this place, only ghosts, and it made me realize just how alone I was. All I had was a big, empty house and absolutely no one who loved me.

I swallowed the lump in my throat. I didn't want to cry ... this was too devastating an event to cry over so I held back my terrible sorrow and began to eat.

But I couldn't.

As I moved my food around my plate, I recalled vividly the sound and sights of my father heading out to work, or even the housekeeper Catalina keeping busy, my eyes burned with unshed tears. I stopped picking at my food and tossed it into the bin.

I knew I should put the groceries away, but I didn't have the energy for that. I left the kitchen and went up to my old room. There was some familiarity and warmth to it in the daytime. As I lay on my bed, I came to the conclusion I needed a new beginning or at least, a change, or else I was going to lose my mind.

I called my father's secretary, Rosa's cell phone.

She immediately picked up, sounding surprised but relieved to hear from me which made me realize I hadn't even found out if she still worked at the firm.

"How are you doing, sweetheart?" she asked.

"I'm doing okay. Um ... I'm sorry I haven't been on top of things lately and I also wanted to thank you immensely for helping me organize the funeral."

"You're welcome, sweetheart."

"Do you, um ... still work at the firm?"

"Yes, I do. I was reassigned to a different department, but I'm still in charge of your father's affairs until I've passed everything over to you."

"Oh, I'm so sorry," I apologized. "I've delayed things, haven't I?"

"Not at all. Take your time and when you're ready, we can resolve what we need to. I got a call by the way from Mr. Moretti. He explained the situation to us and asked us to send the estate lawyer over to the house and arrange all meetings there for safety purposes. Is that alright with you?"

"It's fine, but don't I have to come in personally for any reason?"

"Our doors are always open for you, but if you prefer, I can send his things to his home."

Once again, I choked up, but I managed to hold on for a few minutes longer. "No, I'll come and pick them up. I want to be in his office one last time," I replied.

"Of course, honey."

"When will be best?"

"Just let me know when you're ready, sweetheart, and I'll make it happen."

"Thank you, Rosa," I said and ended the call.

I stared ahead for quite a while not knowing where to start or what to begin to tackle first. I remembered one of the last words my father said to me involved a mention of an email.

I hadn't looked at it yet. The very idea of once again looking at words directly written by my father for me made me almost start to tremble. So, I pushed the thought out of my head and got up. I felt I could no longer bear to remain in that empty house, but Dante had pounded into my head that I couldn't leave the house alone and remain safe.

Despite the burn to my ego, I found his number and placed a call.

Chapter 17
Dante

I was on the way to the airport when I received her call. I knew she was in no danger so I picked it up and waited to hear what she wanted to complain about.

"Ciao," I answered, but I didn't hear anything from her, which set me on high alert. "*Zola!*" I called, my tone rising. "Are you alright? Hello?"

She cleared her throat and I was so tense that I spoke before I could stop the words.

"Don't do that again," I admonished.

"Do what?" she asked.

With a frown, I turned my gaze toward the window. "Is there a problem? Do you need something?"

"I need to get out of here," she said. "For a little bit. And since you've repeatedly mentioned I technically can't go anywhere ... I'm wondering, can someone go with me? Or do I go alone and they just have their eyes on me?"

She would never know how happy she made me with these words, but her next words sucked the joy right out of me.

"Before I enter the witness protection program, I want to sort out my father's affairs and just spend time out of this house."

I knew better than to remind her of my advice not to join the program, so I simply focused on her request to have some time away from the house. I knew how to play the patience game.

"I'm going to the airport right now," I told her.

"Oh," she said. "Never mind then."

"No," I said before she could cut me off. "I'm headed to London for a meeting and I'll be there for two days. Is that enough time away for you?"

"You want me to go to London with you?" she asked incredulously.

"Why not? I'll be busy and you'll be practically on your own for most of the time. The change in scenery will do you good," I said. "All you need is to get your passport and be ready in thirty minutes. Can you manage that?"

"Okay, but you're not going to take me out of the country and kill me somewhere, are you?" she asked quietly.

"Be ready in thirty minutes," I said and ended the call.

Half an hour later and as I sat drinking a glass of whiskey in the plane while waiting for her arrival, I was still strangely unsettled. She had almost sounded resigned to the possibility of her death on the phone. The usual fire and life in her voice were completely gone. Even the anger and loathing that had been directed at me at the funeral was no longer there.

The Guardian

Through the window, I watched the arrival of the two cars I'd sent to pick her up. The second SUV was pulled open and she got out of the vehicle. She was casually dressed in jeans and a T-shirt and in her hand was a small suitcase.

She came on board and kept her sunglasses on. I nodded at her and she nodded back then she headed to the seats in the back.

It felt good to have her with me. To know she was safe. I closed my eyes and slept well for the first time since the nightmare of the last two weeks had begun.

Chapter 18
Zola

I stared out of the window at the fluffy white clouds.

It was more relaxing than I had ever realized. For one, my nerves were not shot to pieces and I actually felt safe which was quite a contrast to the constant background anxiety I'd experienced for the last two weeks. I didn't realize the weight of it as over the days it had begun to feel normal.

I felt heartbroken and empty and with no sense of how to go on. And Dante ... well, he was the only person who offered refuge so I guess now I couldn't help but look at him. I looked at him and his eyes were closed and his features were relaxed. He looked softer and even more beautiful, but I reminded myself of his deep involvement in this entire situation and resolved not to let my guard down.

The truth was, until further proof, I was travelling with the enemy.

My father's unread email came to mind and I decided to read it.

One of the flight attendants came over with refreshments and appetizers. I pushed my glasses up to sit on the top of my head. I wasn't hungry and was about to decline, but when I glimpsed the appetizing looking finger sandwiches and accepted a plate, I took a bite of a smoked salmon sandwich, wiped my hands, and opened my laptop. My hands were shaking as I navigated to my inbox and clicked on his familiar personal email address. In it he furnished me with another email address and told me that password to access that email was the answer to the question:

"Who saved you on your 16th birthday?"

My eyes nearly popped out of their sockets. "What?" I said out loud.
"Is everything okay?" Dante asked.
I thought he was asleep, but he was looking at me with such alertness he could not possibly have been sleeping.
"Yes," I whispered, and he closed his eyes again.
I almost couldn't look, the grief was crippling, but I followed Papa's instructions. Using Dante's name as the password I entered my father's secret email inbox. There was only one item in it. It was a letter addressed to me. It bore the date of my sixteenth birthday.
I took a deep breath, lowered my head and began to read my father's email to me from beyond the grave.

Chapter 19
Dante

I remembered that first night I met her. Her father had warned me beforehand that it would not be a pleasant meeting.

"It's not that she's grumpy," he had said. "She's just a little bit upset at me for stepping out on her birthday. We were baking a cake together before I had to go pick you up."

I had nodded, still uncertain of the man who had appeared out of nowhere to fight for me. His daughter and whether or not she would be friendly was not even an issue. I was fighting for my life.

Until I met her.

Until I saw her pale still face against the tiles.

I could recall that night as vividly as if it happened yesterday. My heart had been pounding so hard as I began to administer CPR.

When her father had rushed over, he pushed me aside and took over. He seemed surprisingly calm as he worked on her until he turned to me and roared at me to grab his phone and call 911. When I returned, she was coughing out spurts of water.

Her father was crooning something unintelligible to her over and over again. With fascination, I watched him. It was as if I was seeing into his very soul. He loved that girl so deeply he couldn't, wouldn't accept losing her. I knew that day he would give up his life for her. I knew no one like that. No one who loved like that.

"Have you called them?" he yelled again, holding her in his arms.

"They're almost here," I replied.

He kissed her forehead and cheeks. "You'll be alright sweetheart. You'll be alright."

I might as well not have existed.

She was rushed to the hospital and I remained in that unfamiliar house waiting for him to return. I called him once to ask if he needed me at the hospital but he refused.

"You can't be out and about. Stay in the house and be safe. I've instructed the staff not to let anyone in. If there's anything at all that makes you suspicious, call the cops immediately. Zola is okay. She'll be fine. Thank you, Dante. Thank you. For as long as I live, I will never forget what you have done for me. Perhaps one day, I will be lucky enough to have the opportunity to pay back this debt."

The next morning, she returned and for the next few days, I saw what it meant for a father to completely pamper his child. It had endeared me so much to that man. I held him in reverence and was almost jealous of her. I'd have given anything to have a father like that. Our relationship grew deeper.

But the way my trial was going indicated Ugo was going

to lose, and I knew him well enough to know he would definitely lash out when he lost. I became terrified that my presence in Marco Leone's home would bring harm to him and his beloved daughter.

I left one night and never went back ... until a few months back when Marco began to follow and ingratiate himself into my legal troubles.

Now here I was; suddenly shaken awake by his daughter's troubled voice. I kept my eyes closed, but I knew something was not right. I cracked my eyes open to slits and watched her surreptitiously. She seemed oddly restless and distressed.

Then she buried her face in her hands and began to sob softly.

Chapter 20
Zola

The staff were all probably watching me making a fool of myself, but I didn't care.

Reading the letter ... my father's words ... made me realize what hurt the most. That I had just lost someone who loved me like no one else probably ever would again.

A part of me wanted to be grateful I had at least experienced being so unconditionally loved, but then another part was angry they had been snatched away from me so early. I felt a presence next to me and opened my eyes. Dante was crouching next to me and I suddenly couldn't take my eyes away from his. I felt as if I was drowning in his blue eyes. I gasped for air.

"Hey," he said worriedly.

And just like that I was able to see him in a different light, away from the twisted way I'd viewed him before. I felt so confused and vulnerable I quickly pulled my sunglasses down to put a barrier between us and he moved away slightly. I grabbed at the first thing that came into my head and blurted it out.

"When did you lose your parents?"

"I never met my mother," he said quietly. "As for my dad ... that's a long story. I was raised by my grandfather. He died when I was nine and I was put into the system." His eyes were blank as he rose and went back to his seat.

Before I could respond one of the flight attendants arrived with a menu. I wanted to refuse as I didn't have any appetite, but I had no idea how long it would be before we reached London so I smiled politely and thanked her.

I chose the fried rice and roasted duck. It looked great when it arrived, but I couldn't taste a single thing and the rich sauce actually made me feel sick. I stopped eating and grabbed the salad instead. It was pretty with brightly colored vegetables and fruit and promised to be more refreshing, but after just one bite, I was forced to abandon it. I was too sad to eat. I pushed the plate away and leaned back against the chair.

"If you don't like those dishes, they can bring something else for you," Dante said.

"I'm making space for dessert," I lied with a small smile.

An attendant swung by to spirit away my barely touched plates. It bothered me that I was blatantly wasting his resources although I tried to talk myself out of it, I had to state my offer to cover my own expenses.

"I'll pay you for all the expenses I incur during this trip, except the plane. There's no way I can afford that."

He didn't answer so I pulled the window cover down and settled deeper into the seat so I could attempt to get some sleep.

It didn't work. All I could think about was my father's letter, and once again I found myself opening my laptop and rereading it.

My darling Zola,

If you're reading this, it can't be good news. Hopefully, you're receiving this message a very, very long while after me writing this. However, I will keep updating it as frequently as possible. This is a strange thing to write since I'm still very much here. In fact, right now, I'm at the hospital with you, sitting by your bedside.

You almost drowned tonight.

And I can't believe it. My hands are still trembling. I think I'm in shock. I can't even understand how it happened. You are such a strong swimmer. Never mind. Main thing is you're fine. I've been told there will be no lasting damage. While I'm incredibly relieved and glad you are fine, I think I'll be traumatized by this for a very long time. Now more than ever I am glad of my decision to bring Dante to our home. If not for him I would have lost you tonight. I'll be grateful to him for the rest of my life because if I had lost you then I would have been done with.

No more reason to live.

But today showed me how fragile this life is. And this is supposed to be my letter to you in case I am the one who has to leave you, hopefully not too early.

I guess I want to tell you I love you, but just putting down the words is not enough. I want to tell you that a few minutes ago I cried like a baby. In a way, I haven't in at least fifteen years. I didn't even cry this much when we lost your mama. It's not because I didn't love her as much as you, but because I had time to get used to the idea that she was leaving. I could see the vitality leaving her day by day. I had time to prepare myself.

Seeing you lifeless tonight, Zola, it took me to a place I never want to go again. So please, even when you're reading this because I'm no longer here, don't hurt yourself like you almost did tonight. Don't hurt me, because I'll feel it. Wherever I am, even if I'm no longer with you.

I love you with all my heart, and I also want to say if you are indeed reading this letter then I'm glad because it means I left before you.

I know you'll feel very sad and alone, but I haven't always been the most present father either. I'm going to try my best to change, but always know there is nothing or no one I think about as much as you.

It was my biggest blessing to be your father. You are amazing, wonderful, kind, and adorable and I'm so sorry I'm no longer with you.

But I know you. I know you'll pick yourself up and keep going. You'll be stronger than ever before, I guarantee it. Hopefully, I'll join your mama and we'll watch over you, so please try your best not to be sad for too long. And know that even if we're not physically with you anymore, we will always and forever be in your heart.

You can talk to me anytime and I'll listen so never hesitate.

I love you, baby.

Okay, that's it, enough of the mushy stuff.

Now onto the boring stuff. I'm going to leave all the information about every material asset I own for you and my recommendation for what you should do with it. I will update this regularly through the years, but I don't think I'll touch this letter again.

Anyway, be strong, stay safe and I'm sorry for using Dante's name as the password. It's just that I currently can't think of any other shared info between us that won't be easily revealed like birthdays or anniversaries.

Dante though will be hard for anyone to guess.

I hope you two become friends someday and I hope you don't forget him. He's a bit cold but he's been through quite a lot. Anyway, if we're still on good terms with him when you're reading this letter, then please give him a chance to be in your life. He has a good heart and I'm sure you'll always be able to turn to him for help. However, if I am not on good terms with him when you read this then do not go anywhere close to him. He is as dangerous as he can be loyal. But I really do care about him. And now I am forever indebted to him for saving your life.

This letter has now gone on for too long. I'm sorry for my ramblings.

I love you, sweetheart.

Papa

I set up my laptop and turned to look at the man seated across from me. He was gazing out of the window and seemed to be deep in thought. I hesitated to interrupt him. There were quite a number of things I wanted to say to him, but one kept circling, so I didn't hold back.

"I don't think I ever thanked you back then ..." I murmured. "For saving me."

He turned to look at me. His eyes were guarded. I guess, I had never been anything but bitchy towards him.

"Thank you," I said sincerely. "Officially."

"No problem," he said quietly.

"And I'm really sorry for being so rude and ungrateful. I was just out of my mind with grief and I needed someone to blame. You were perfect."

"No apologies needed. Don't give it another thought." He turned back towards the window.

"Papa left me a letter."

Dante turned and met my gaze curiously.

"He said if he was still on good terms with you by the time I read his letter that was my permission to not be wary of you. But if he wasn't then I should beware because you could be extremely dangerous."

"He was right," he said shortly.

I watched him. "Haven't you always been somewhat dangerous though? I've always wondered why my father wasn't guarded around you?"

"I don't know," he said. "But I have lived a violent life and should be considered dangerous."

Chapter 21
Dante

"Good. Because I need you to be dangerous. Nothing matters to me anymore except for getting the bastards that killed my father," she declared bitterly. "That's all I care about now."

I felt the exact same way but it wasn't a sentiment we needed to share.

She spoke again. "About the informant from that night? The news said he was killed. I assume you're aware of this. Can you tell me all that you know about it?"

I was pleased. It was the first time she willingly requested any information from me. Being stuck together thousands of feet above the ground in the clouds was not a bad idea after all. I softened my expression and tone, let down my guard as much as I could, and relaxed my posture. Then I held her gaze and spoke.

"I don't know much about him. What I do know from your father was that he worked at the lounge where the woman was killed."

As I spoke, she stared at me intently. Her eyes were slightly swollen and red and ... I started to feel a deep urge to feel her body against me. The urge was so strong that I was stunned. I had never felt that way toward anyone in my life.

"The case your father was working on for me involved a lucrative olive oil export deal. Not many people know but almost all the olive oil sold in supermarkets and delis around the world have been touched at some point by the Mafia. I'm well versed in it because it was how I began under Ugo." I paused. "Do you know who Ugo is?"

"He's the mafia boss who's orchestrating all of this?"

I nodded. "Yeah. He wanted me to be in the inner sanctum of his organization, but I had to pass the test of loyalty. I had to obey him blindly, instantly, without question. We were invited to a top nightclub and shown to the VIP lounge. There were big bowls of cocaine and caviar on the table, and beautiful, willing, scantily clad girls had been hired for the evening. Bottles of the most expensive champagne waited in ice buckets. Everything was for us. All of it. But first the loyalty test. He urinated into a champagne glass and held it out for us to drink."

Zola shrank back with disgust.

"Again and again, he refilled the glass and all the other guys drank. Some of them gagged, but every single one kept it down and thanked him. Then came my turn. He held the glass out to me. Steam came out of the glass. I looked into his eyes. They were filled with a sick delight. He was enjoying this.

"When I did not take the glass, the expression in his

eyes changed. No one had refused until then and the narcissist inside him understood instantly. He had misjudged me. Yes, he had found me in the gutter, yes, I was burning with ambition to be successful, but I knew my self-worth. Drinking his piss was not how I was going to make it in the world.

"But now he was caught in a trap of his own making. He was about to be humiliated by a worthless street boy. It was the ultimate slap in his face. I turned around and walked out of that nightclub. He could have killed me, but he now hated me so much death was too good for me. He tried to pin a murder rap on me. His intention was to let the system throw me in prison so he could have me raped daily by his men.

"Unfortunately, his plan backfired. Your father took me on and shined a bright light on him and his organization, making it impossible for him to attack me openly. He'd been trying to get back at me every day since. He tried many times, but I can be more slippery than an eel. He's thrown his net again, but we'll see if he catches me this time."

"How? What kind of net?" she asked curiously.

"I'd been invited by a business associate to dinner at his private club. During dinner I needed to use the restroom. While I was in there one of the club's attendants came in. It immediately struck me as strange, because exclusive clubs don't employ women to attend to the men's restrooms. As she held out a towel, I noted her face and there was something vaguely familiar about her. Suddenly, someone came out of a door with something behind his back. He was directly in the line of sight of the woman, but she didn't seem startled or suspicious as she should have been. That was when I knew for sure. I was in danger. The man brought out a gun and as I reached for mine, the woman flicked the towel at my face and my gun went off. I heard two shots were fired, mine and another. By the time I had thrown off the towel, she was lying on the floor. Dead. The man was gone. The cameras only captured me and the woman going into the bathroom. The gun on the ground had my fingerprints on it and I had gunshot residue on my hands. I recognized it. An old one that Ugo had saved all these years. And the woman. I remembered her later, a prostitute who worked for Ugo. She didn't know she was the sacrifice. They found a wine glass with her prints on it in my apartment. Ugo thought it should have been an open and shut case ... until he found out I had already reported my gun stolen years ago and my security company had many months of CCTV video and no sign of Ugo's whore. At best, he would implicate me in something unsavory. It could have been bad PR, but my businesses are sound and I didn't fear it. Then your father found the whistleblower and Ugo began to sweat."

She stared at me and I could see by her expression just how hard she was contemplating it all.

"I feel as though there are a lot of details still missing, but I don't know where to start asking the questions."

"That's okay," I said. "Take your time. I'm always available to you."

"Tell me about the informant?"

"Right ... he worked for Ugo. He told your father he was willing to give information, dates, and names on Ugo's business practices in exchange for some money. He had it all in a little black book."

"But he's dead now?"

I nodded. "Yes."

"So everyone connected to the black book is dead except me."

"Yes."

Chapter 22
Zola

I woke up to a warm hand on my skin, tapping lightly, and at first, I almost ignored it, but the tapping was insistent and I reluctantly opened my eyes.

I was still half asleep and my half-asleep mind registered how close in proximity we were and how devastatingly attractive he was. His hair was a little disheveled. It was usually combed away from his face, but right now, the dark mass was falling in a blunt shock down his forehead and it made him look quite ... edible. Thank God, those piercing eyes seemed to be unaware of what was going through my head.

"We're here," he said and turned away.

After running a careless hand through my hair, I grabbed my huge sunglasses even though it was already getting dark outside and slid them back on. Quickly, I gathered up my things and stood. As we descended the steps of the plane, I saw two bullet-proof SUVs waiting.

"It's safe for me to be alone in London, isn't it? I can take a taxi to a hotel?"

I could immediately tell he was far from pleased with my words.

"What hotel?" he asked tersely.

We were on a tarmac, and I didn't know where to go. I began to squirm under his steady regard. It was annoying and I wished he wouldn't employ intimidation tactics.

"Get in," he said, sounding exhausted. "We can talk about it on the way."

I detested his tone. "No," I replied. "I'll find my way from here. Thanks for the lift."

"*Zola!*" his tone rose.

He stared at me and I glared back. "Am I some sort of prisoner or something?"

"We can't let our guard down," he said. "I'm not aware if Ugo operates in London, but men like him have contacts all over the world. It won't be hard to order a hit on you if they do find out where you are. In fact, it'll be easier here than back in New York."

My heart instantly began to race. "You are the master of generating fear, aren't you?"

"I'm not generating fear," he said. "I know these people and how relentless they can be. I'm not taking anything for granted. "

I sighed in defeat. "So, what's the plan?"

"We're going to go to a very secure hotel in Mayfair. It is run by a good friend of mine so you will be completely safe."

"Won't I be able to step out of it at all?"

"You will," he said. "I'll just make sure you're adequately protected. That's something I can't arrange right now or work out fully because I'm exhausted. Let's at least get to the hotel and then work things out."

His tone was cordial and his words made sense so I calmed down and went with him to the car.

To my surprise, he pulled the door open for me. I thanked him and got in. A few seconds later he got in as well and then we were seated side by side. His scent and presence once again filled my nostrils and in the quiet of the car, there was little else to notice beyond this.

"What's the name of your cologne? My father had something similar."

His response surprised me.

"Yes, it is very similar. I had both custom-made last year."

The depth of their relationship continued to surprise me. Gradually I was beginning to understand my father truly did care for him. He was the son he never had.

Soon we arrived at the hotel and there was no need to stop at the reception. We were immediately escorted to the elevator.

"I booked you a room across from me. If there's any emergency your key card can also access my suite. Do you have my phone number saved on your phone?"

I nodded. "Thank you."

The bellboy unlocked my door, and I walked in. The room was magnificent, the epitome of luxury. I had to admit, my troubles felt far away and I felt comfortable and safe here. Although, I couldn't help but feel as though I was racking up big bills that I would have to pay sooner or later.

It made me think about my father's wealth.

From the records he had attached to his letter, I could

see he had left me far more than I had imagined he possessed as he lived a modest humble life. And right now I didn't care to do anything with it. Perhaps it was because all of this was still too early and I'd never thought of his properties or wealth as mine in any way. I'd moved out the moment I could, determined to make it on my own. And so now it felt horribly weird that I had access to everything that was his. He was healthy, I thought he would live until he was in his nineties. He would, at least, see his grandchildren.

It made me feel bleak again.

With a long, somber sigh, I stared at the inviting bed before me. I was wide awake and the bed looked especially lonely. So I turned around and exited the room and headed down to the bar. I sat on the stool by myself, ordered a Long Island iced tea, and sent him a message.

I'm at the bar. In case you're searching.

Then I began to read all that was available about Dante's case online. Then I went further back and began to search for any news on Dante's case from when we had first met in our teenage years.

Chapter 23
Dante

I was unable to rest from the moment I received her message, but since she at least informed me, I wasn't as irritated.

"She's alone, Boss," Lorenzo said. "At the bar."

"Keep an eye on her and if anything's amiss or she starts getting too tipsy, call me."

I went straight to shower and worked for an hour. There were no messages from the men which was odd to me because I didn't expect her to still be at the bar.

I placed the call and found out she was.

"She's getting to the tipsy stage, Boss," Giotto said.

It was just gone midnight and although the lobby was still bubbling with activity, things had dwindled down and were a lot calmer. I headed straight for the hotel bar which was deserted except for her and my guys in one corner trying to look surreptitious and failing badly. Her head was lowered but her drink remained slightly elevated in her hand.

The Guardian

I sat on the stool next to her. She was the closest thing I had to family now. Marco's family was my family.

"Three and a half Long Island Iced teas," she mumbled. "That's what you want to know, right?"

"Alcoholism is the new habit you're taking up?"

She blinked as though she couldn't comprehend the question. Then she downed the last of her cocktail and ordered another.

"Cranberry juice," I mouthed to the bartender and his brows furrowed slightly in confusion.

Still, he respected my instruction when he saw she wasn't exactly coherent. He passed it over and I watched as she took a sip.

Her face wrinkled with distaste, but to my relief, she kept drinking. Then she set the glass down with a cute "ah". I couldn't help but admit seeing her this carefree, though it was alcohol induced, was a pleasant sight to behold. The only thing I'd seen her experience since her father died was grief and unhappiness, and if staying at this bar for a while longer would make her feel a little merry, I was willing to participate. After all, I was by her side so she would be safe.

I leaned away and narrowed my eyes at her. She did the same and for a moment it seemed as though she almost smiled.

God, she was beautiful.

"What are you doing here?" she asked.

It was going to be a long night for me. I called the bartender over. She continued to stare at me as I placed the order for a neat single malt whiskey.

"I've been reading about you," she slurred. "Did you do the bad things that Ugo jerk did too?"

"Yes. Yes, I did," I said.

"Oh!"

"I told you, Zola. I was a street boy. I stole cars, I robbed, I sold drugs, and if I had stayed with Ugo I would have over time gone on to kill people too. The only thing that stopped me was that night when he asked me to drink his piss. Everything came to a screeching halt in that nightclub. The girls, the drugs, the champagne, the glamorous lifestyle, it was all a lie. The inside was rotten and infested with crawling, wriggling maggots. I saw what I had allowed myself to become and what I would become if I drank his piss."

"I'm glad you didn't drink the piss," she whispered.

My drink arrived and as the barmen set it down, long slender fingers closed around it and snatched the glass away. I watched her lift it to her lips. I looked into her eyes and she looked into mine and my heart began to pound.

"It's time for you to go to bed?" I said and my voice sounded thick.

"I don't want to go to bed. I want another drink. A real one."

I signaled to the bartender and he ordered another cranberry juice.

"I'm not drunk, you know," she denied hotly.

I watched her hooded eyes, her dangerously swaying body, and knew she would be crashing to the ground very soon. I got to my feet and was just in time. She wobbled, tilted, and dropped right into my arms.

I knew she could walk but it would be faster if I just carried her. I did exactly that, but all she did was protest. The scent of her shampoo filled my nostrils as she wriggled against my body. God knew I wasn't into drunk women, but sexual awareness frizzled up my spine making my cock hard with need.

"Where are you taking me?" she demanded with a catch in her voice.

"To your room."

She sighed and rested her head against my chest. It was a sweet gesture and I felt something inside me melt. When I laid her on her bed, she opened her eyes and looked at me from beneath her eyelashes.

I understood instantly.

The air between us throbbed with thick desire. To say I was not tempted would have been a lie. I was. So tempted I had to force myself to turn away, but her hand reached out and gently curved around my wrist. I looked down at it. It looked so fragile and pale against my skin.

"I just want to forget," she murmured. "Just for a little bit. Can you really not oblige me?"

"You're drunk," I said, my voice sounding harsh.

She shook her head. "I'm not. Not really."

She was half-drunk, disheveled, and dressed in an oversized tracksuit, but at that moment she was the sexiest woman alive and I wanted her. How I wanted her. Unlike her, I didn't want her because I wanted to forget my pain for a while. I wanted her because I'd always wanted her. From the first moment I saw her. I swallowed hard. This was wrong. This was Marco's daughter and I could never take advantage of her when she was under the influence.

"Sleep on it. If you're still interested when you get up, come to my room." She had no idea just how much restraint I had to employ to reject her offer.

"Then can you stay with me for a while? We don't have

to do anything. When I fall asleep you can leave. Please, Dante?"

I took a deep breath. She was really asking for the impossible. Still, considering how much alcohol she had consumed it was a safe bet to say she would be asleep in no time. I was no animal. I could control myself for a few minutes.

Wordlessly, I unzipped my jacket and shrugged out of it. Then I lay down next to her, not touching any part of her, and waited for her breathing to become even.

Chapter 24
Zola

My eyes were fixed on the ceiling as I listened to his gentle breathing. A part of my brain tried to warn me this was a terrible, terrible idea ... horrible, but between my legs I was soaking wet.

I couldn't remember the last time I'd felt such a strong, almost irresistible desire for a man.

Was it the alcohol? Or maybe, if I was really honest, it was the simple, uncomplicated lust for an extremely delectable man.

Why not? He was attractive and I felt illogically safe with him ... It made perfect sense on paper, but I'd never forced myself on a man who didn't want me and I wasn't going to start now. Alcohol always made me drowsy so I let it do its work ...

I shut my eyes.

One hour later I was still wide awake. I turned to face him and the more I looked at him the more my appetite intensified.

Unable to hold back any longer, I tapped on his shoulder. "I'm hot. Are you hot? I mean you can take your shirt off."

He didn't respond, but it was highly unlikely he was asleep. I took my top off and threw it on the floor. My sweatpants followed. I was now only in a tank top and a thong, and it still felt like too many clothes.

I turned to my side and watched him. His hair fell over his eyes, and it made me want to reach out to tenderly brush it away. And that is exactly what I did. Still, he did not open his eyes. Because his eyes weren't open and piercing through me as usual, I found that I could properly admire and even appreciate the beauty and magnificence of his face. He was all chiseled angles and contours, yet with an undeniable sensual softness to his mouth that made me hungry for him.

Actually, famished was closer to what I felt at that moment.

Even if I got nothing else from this trip, I would have the memory of finally sleeping with my teenage crush.

"You're not really sleeping, are you?" I whispered.

His arm came over his eyes and one corner of my lips curled in a smile. I decided then I was done waiting or susceptible to any feelings of shame. The only thing I could think about was giving my full attention to the maddening pulsing between my legs. If I had been emotionally attached to him in any way, I might have kissed him, but since I wasn't, I rose up and positioned myself across his midriff. I tried my best to settle my weight on him as gently as I could.

My heart was racing so hard it was as though it would fly out of my chest, yet I persisted. Grabbing the hem of my tank top, I pulled it over my head and flung it away. It left me in just my bra which I considered leaving on, but when I considered what I ultimately needed to feel was the weight of him intimately pressed against me, I took it off as well.

Just a little push of the fabric of my thong to one side and his shirt up his torso, I had direct access to the warmth I desired. With both of my hands settled on his torso to stabilize myself, I slowly began to slide my wet sex against his abs. I knew he wasn't asleep, and if he was against what I was doing he could have easily thrown me off. But he didn't so I kept rocking against him.

My clit throbbed and found relief against him, but I needed more. I just wanted to be impaled and taken hard.

Funnily enough, he didn't feel like a stranger. Perhaps it was because I had naively and graphically imagined doing this with him many years earlier so it registered as a familiar scenario in my head.

"Mmmm...," I moaned as my pleasure intensified. I was so turned on I knew if I rode him for just a little while longer, I would climax. I kept up the pace when I started to get out of control. A hand grabbed my waist and I was forced to come to a stop.

My eyes shot open and met with his.

Just as I had predicted he didn't seem groggy or surprised that I was on top of him and nude for a scrap of thong, but what I could not ever have predicted was the expression in his eyes. I couldn't pull my gaze away from him. I had never seen him like this. His eyes were shimmering ... shimmering with naked hunger.

He angled his head to the side and studied me, his eyes roving over my lips, my throat, my shoulders, my breasts, my stomach, my open pussy pressed against his skin. I felt incredibly exposed but it did not make me want to get off him. On the contrary, my instinct was to shift my position and open my legs wider still to show him the pink inner core of me.

Wordlessly, he reached behind me to release my hair from my ponytail. It fell all around me, hiding the flush of my skin as fire began to lick underneath me. And I started to grind my sex once again against him.

His hand remained positioned on the sides of my hips. He watched as the pleasure began to simmer through my veins.

"Up," he commanded suddenly.

And I froze. He wanted me to get off him.

But to my relief, he didn't push me off. Instead, he shifted slightly under me, got rid of his shirt and flung it aside. The sensual movement of the muscles underneath his skin nearly sent me over the edge with need.

I had to admit, I was dangerously attracted to him. My chest was filling with so much excitement I was barely able to catch my breath.

His hand hooked into the waistband of his pants and in no time, he was stark naked. I could feel the hardness of his cock behind me, poking and seeking my attention. I turned to look. The hardened, flushed, upright shaft was gorgeous. It was slightly curved. His girth was one of the thickest I'd ever seen.

It was the perfect length, but before I could reach out to touch the raw glory the way I wanted to, he rested his hands on the curve of my hips and began to move the warm contact to the flat of my stomach and up my torso.

By the time his hands arrived at my breasts and cupped

the full mounds, I was nearly out of breath. He leaned forward with the speed of an athlete, captured a nipple into his mouth, and sucked hard.

I couldn't muffle my moan.

The tip of his tongue flicked and teased the engorged bud. It sent fiery sparks shooting through my body. Suddenly, he grabbed my waist and before I could process his intentions, my body was pulled forward toward him.

Moments later the string of my thong snapped between his fingers. I gasped at the slight sting against my skin as he yanked it away from my body.

My legs were now wide open and my pussy was exposed to his greedy eyes. I felt his face come between my thighs and gasped. This level of intrusion and dare I say intimacy always warranted a shock, but with him it … it was more. Far more.

"Sit on my face," he ordered, his voice thick with lust and greed.

I obeyed and the velvet rasp of his tongue as he pushed into me was so intense it was almost a shock. I'd never experienced that before.

"You taste like heaven," he growled.

I began to feel light-headed as he continued to lick and suck on my slick sex. The pleasure kept coming in waves that reverberated through my body. Then my clit was in his mouth and he was ravaging my sex in a way that it drained all the strength from my body.

I came suddenly, explosively, my mouth opened in a silent scream, my body arching, my muscles straining, my juices flowing out and dripping into his mouth and running down the sides of his face. I was shocked by the sheer force of my climax. My hands were gripping the headboard tightly and I was still panting harshly while he gently licked at my swollen sensitive pussy.

Inside me, a different kind of hunger grew. I'd seen his cock and I'd already dreamed of it in my mouth. I found myself turning.

"My turn," I crowed, as I curled my hand around his cock. I loved how he smelled and I couldn't help leaning closer to breathe him in.

He smelled wonderful.

I took my time and kissed every inch of him. My lips traced kisses up the underside of his balls and up his wonderful length and girth until I arrived at the head. It was already leaking with precum so I lapped it up and savored the taste as if it was the finest wine.

I heard a sharply drawn breath from behind me, After a while he suddenly jerked me up, and put me back on his mouth, sucking harder this time. I cried out, writhed, and tried to get away, but he held me in place and carried on the delicious sucking, driving me to the edge, right to the point I was on the verge of a scream the whole floor was sure to hear.

But just before I was about to fall apart, he released me and deposited me on my back on the bed.

Our eyes met for a brief moment then his lips swooped down on mine. He tasted smoky, of whiskey and me. The kiss was excitingly rough and passionate, almost a demand for my total submission. In the rush of sensations, I lost my mind. All I could do was feel: my heart racing in my chest, warmth flooding the pit of my stomach as the intoxicating scent of sex surrounded us both.

The Guardian

As I unraveled before him, he reached down and slipped a finger in. I tried to contain the mind-numbing pleasure that was rushing through my body as my muscles spasmed, and my pulse raced out of control. Another finger joined the first one, then his thumb began to roll against my clit.

And that was it.

I came so hard I screamed. Or perhaps it was an endless, pitiful whimpering, I would never be able to tell. I recalled grabbing onto him, in search of an anchor because it felt as if I was falling into a deep, unfathomable abyss from which there was no return.

Still, he didn't stop.

He continued to thrust his fingers in and out of me, firm and precise while his kisses deepened. Sensory overload was what it was and I savored every single bit of it.

Immediately afterward, I needed to move away from him, to give my heart and body the space they needed to recover. He let me and I found a cool spot on the bed and collapsed, an overheated, exhausted sprawled wreck on the bed.

I felt him come over to me. His presence and sensuality were just too much. He held my jaw and once again I was kissed senseless. This one was more sensual than the others and I felt like I would melt into a puddle by the time he was done.

He lifted his head, but before I could speak, I caught sight of his erect cock. I couldn't resist its call and found myself uncoiling my body and taking the length in my hand. Our eyes locked as I slowly and deliberately circled the leaking head with my tongue. His taste was wonderful ...

clean and intoxicating. I took the whole thick head into my mouth and sucked hard, but I felt as if I still couldn't get enough.

My hand began to stroke up and down the silky-smooth rod, my grip firm. His eyes became hooded and his breathing heavy. Soft groans came from deep within his throat.

They spurred me on. I must be doing something right. I continued to pump him, my head bobbing up and down while my tongue licked and lapped up as much of him as I could. It didn't take long before his hand was grabbing the sheets and he was almost wrenching them off the bed. With a fierce roar, he spilled into my mouth. A steady heated stream that I swallowed eagerly.

I basked in his taste and afterward, I couldn't help but lay my head on his broad chest to rest. I could hear the steady drumming of his heartbeat and felt cocooned in the warmth emanating in waves from his body. It wasn't long till exhaustion completely overcame me and I was unable to keep myself awake.

Chapter 25
Dante

That night I dreamed of Marco.

I was lost inside a crumbling ancient castle made of gray stones. Demons were chasing me through the maze of broken walls and spiderwebs. The air was full of the smell of sulfur and death and I was afraid. From far away came the sounds of women wailing. There was a dim light burning somewhere and I began to run towards it. When I got it, I found Marco. He was standing at a window holding a lamp. He turned and looked at me.

"She is my life. Take everything I have, but please, please don't hurt her, Dante," he begged sadly.

"Never," I promised.

Then I felt a wet claw clamp around my neck. The demons had caught up with me. I turned around to face them and I woke up with a jerk.

Zola was sleeping soundly next to me.

My heart was racing. I watched her sleep for a few minutes. She was so beautiful, my soul writhed inside me. I wanted to touch her, make her mine, own her forever.

But I could see Marco's face full of sadness and reproach.

And I was filled with guilt and regret.

What I had done was wicked. I knew it then. Marco had trusted me to take care of her and I should have known better than to let myself be tempted. She was young and innocent and I had taken advantage of her in her moment of vulnerability. It was wrong.

"I'm sorry, Marco. I will never hurt her. I will protect her with my life, the way you did. I won't let you down again," I said quietly.

Then I carefully slid out of bed and walked away without looking back.

Chapter 26
Zola

I woke up to the sound of my phone ringing. My arm flailed out and hit something unfamiliar. My eyes snapped open and the fog of sleep disappeared. Ah, I was in London, in a hotel room.

Last night I did ... um ... things with Dante.

I hadn't been completely drunk but at the same time I hadn't been completely sober so I could very clearly recall the extent to which we went. There had been no penetration though.

The phone continued its shrill ring. I ran my gaze across the room in search of it and realized it was probably in my jacket. I rolled out of bed and made my way towards it.

"Where the hell are you?" Antoine demanded the moment I picked up. "I was about to send the police after you."

"Don't do that," I said as I sat back against the headboard.

"What do you expect me to do when you suddenly disappear and refuse to answer my call?"

"You've only just called," I pointed out.

"And I've sent you a bazillion texts."

"I was asleep. Switch to video, I need to multitask," I said, taking the phone with me to the bathroom. His worried face filled the screen.

"Where are you anyway?" Antoine asked.

"London."

His eyes widened. "What?"

"It's a long story," I replied, as I positioned the phone against the vanity mirror. I put a T-shirt on and stared at myself in the mirror. I looked like a hot mess.

"Tell it."

"Let me brush my teeth first," I said as I grabbed a toothbrush.

"No, tell me, and then brush your teeth while I ponder on how to fix your bad decisions."

This made me smile so I obliged, and by the time I was done, he had both eyebrows raised.

"Hold on," he got up and took the phone with him as he went to the kitchen. "I need a snack for this."

He retrieved a tub of ice cream and jabbed a spoon in.

"That's communal," I reminded.

"It was two days ago, but not anymore now that you've run off to London," he reminded.

Grabbing my toothbrush, I began to squeeze toothpaste across the bristles.

"So technically, you didn't have sex."

"Isn't oral sex, sex?" I asked.

"Nope. Penetration is sex. Everything else is foreplay. For instance, this is the first thing I'm having since I got up, but is this a meal or is it dessert? The fact that it's going into my mouth the same way that breakfast will doesn't make it a meal."

"It's too early in the morning," I groaned.

But then he kept staring at me with an odd smile on his face.

"What?" I asked defensively.

"I'm glad," he said.

"Well, as you said, it is nothing without penetration," I countered.

"Are you going to return in his jet or go commercial? I still can't believe you flew in a jet or that you know someone who has one and I wasn't invited. I feel betrayed."

I smiled. "I'm sorry, but you can't be anywhere around me right now."

"But he can?"

"Yes. He has guns."

"And a thick dick apparently." He shoved ice cream into his mouth while I cringed.

"Please stop. My head is still a bit sore," I pleaded.

But he was having a blast. "Can you send a picture next time? You know I'm an expert at dick adjudication."

"You're ridiculous," I said and began to brush my teeth.

He laughed. "On a serious note, how are things going to be between you two from now on? I recall he wasn't exactly your favorite person."

"He still isn't," I muttered.

He shoved another spoonful of ice cream into his mouth. "But he makes you feel safe."

I spat and rinsed my toothbrush. "Yes. I don't know why, but he does, otherwise, I would never have allowed him to come close to me for any reason."

"I've always loved a good romance," he said dreamily.

"Look, I have to go," I said.

"Okay, honey, but keep me updated?"

I ended the call, ran a hairbrush through my hair, and headed into the shower. The warm water was soothing and I luxuriated in it a lot longer than I usually did. Wrapped in a big fluffy towel, I returned to my room, opened the thick drapes, and let in bright yellow sunshine.

Wow! How different the buildings outside were. There was a red phone booth below and people walking on the sidewalk. Suddenly, I was excited to explore this new city. Just then my phone pinged with a message from Dante.

I've sent one of my men up to your room to escort you down if you're interested in joining me for breakfast.

Before I could answer, another message came in. It was from Antoine.

Don't avoid him. He might be a good distraction for you.

I was still smiling at the message as I got dressed quickly. Indeed, one of his big burly men was standing outside the door as I emerged.

"Good morning," I greeted.

He nodded politely and silently began to walk so I followed closely behind. It was an old hotel with great charm and a far cry from modern hotels. We arrived at the hotel's restaurant, but to my surprise, we weren't having breakfast with the other patrons. Instead, I was shown to a private area dotted by his men. And over in a corner overlooking London's distinctive skyline was the current object of my distraction. With the sunshine behind him, he looked regal, his suit the color of cold steel, his eyes polished aquamarine, and his jaw stern.

There was nothing in his grim expression or mannerism that alluded to the memory of the whirlwind that happened between us last night. As I settled into the chair across from him, it was almost easier to convince myself it didn't happen, that I'd dreamed it all than to convince myself it did.

Except for the swollen state of my sex.

And the craving. The crazy, uncontrollable craving for him. I finally had to admit to the aching need to finish what we started, preferably before we returned because then everything would return to grimness and desolation again. And having to deal with the dreaded idea of leaving everything I knew and starting all over again.

I pushed the painful thought away and tried my best to relax as I spread the napkin over my lap and perused the assortment of food on the table and cart beside us.

"This is a lot," I said.

All of his attention was on me, and it was so intense my hand instinctively reached up to my hair. I'd changed my hairstyle into a half-up and half-down do. It wasn't in its usual ponytail. I'd put on red lipstick for some life and color, and applied some mascara.

"Good morning," he murmured.

God, even his voice made the air between us crash and burn.

"Good morning," I mumbled, as I grabbed a croissant and two miniature apricot jam bottles. I cut the croissant in half and spread so much jam on it, that his eyes widened with surprise

"You'll be heading out for some sightseeing?" he asked as he leaned back and lifted his cup of coffee to his lips.

"Yes, I was planning to. It should be okay, shouldn't it? We're in London and no one knows I'm here. Except Antoine."

He frowned and his eyes were suddenly sharp as they slid to me.

I took a bite of my croissant and shook my head. "Don't worry. I've known Antoine for years. He'd rather die than betray me."

"Everything is under control and I'd like it to stay that way. We don't want to put Antoine's loyalty to the test," he said, and the hardness in his tone sent chills down my spine.

I dabbed the corners of my mouth with my napkin. "So, can I, or can't I go?"

"You can. Just let me know where you'd like to go and my men will take you there and keep watch over you."

"Hang on," I said. "I'm asking this out of pure curiosity, but don't you need to be protected as well? Aren't you at risk too? Ugo can attack you too, right?"

"He can," he replied coldly, "but I can take care of myself."

"Ah," I replied sarcastically. "But I can't."

"Can you?"

Although my words had been laced with sarcasm, I couldn't deny he had raised a very valid point. The undeniable truth was I couldn't.

I pressed the croissant and watched the jam ooze out of it. "I hate the idea of being followed and watched, but if I have to be then could they not be too obvious? I'd really like to enjoy the city as much as I can since I don't know when or if I'll ever return."

He lifted his cup to his lips once again. "Yes, I can arrange for them to be as unobtrusive as possible."

"Thank you," I replied. "And how much will this protection cost? Whatever their service costs, I'd like to pay for it. As well as my stay here."

His eyes became chips of ice. He had retreated behind a cold wall, but his voice, when he spoke was even. "I'll send all the relevant bills to you at the end of the trip."

I felt confused. This was not the man who asked me to sit on his face. The man who let me come in his mouth. I took a deep breath. "Good. Thank you. I want to learn how to shoot properly. Take some basic lessons. Do you know any shooting ranges nearby?"

"There are none nearby, but yes it can be arranged," he said. "I'll test you when we return."

I almost spilled the juice I had been lifting to my lips for a sip. "What?"

"I imagine they can't really teach you what you need to know. So go ahead and hear the basics and I'll add to the lesson when I return tonight."

What he said made sense, but I didn't just want to agree to whatever he said.

I set the glass down and moved my attention to a chocolate muffin that seemed to have blueberries in it.

"Do you know where else you'd like to visit?" he asked.

"Not really," I replied. "I thought maybe, London Bridge and Madame Tussauds. Or maybe just some shopping."

I didn't really want to go shopping but it might be a

great way to pass the time. Maybe a coffee shop near Harrods?

"How long are we going to be here?" I asked.

"A week," he replied.

His phone rang and he looked at it and said, "Please excuse me, I have to go."

"Is there a problem?" I asked.

"No, there is no problem. Enjoy your day."

I watched him walk away and felt so confused. We weren't platonic strangers anymore, but his aloof behavior was as if last night never happened.

There was no way I could have made a dent in the food on the table. After tasting everything, I guiltily set my fork down. If only I could pack everything up and take it back to Antoine. With a sigh, I got to my feet and headed out to the entrance. Obviously, Dante had arranged security for me although I didn't have any details about it.

But as soon as I emerged out from the hotel entrance, an SUV stopped right in front of me. A suited man got out and introduced himself before he opened the backdoor for me.

"We'll take you to the gun range, Miss Leone," he said.

"Oh, thank you," I replied. I glanced back at the hotel, wondering if Dante had left for the day or if he was still around. I wouldn't mind one more glimpse of him, but he'd probably already left.

I got into the car and began my first day in London.

Chapter 27
Dante

"What's happening?" I asked.

"We're at the shooting range, Boss," Lorenzo said. "She's getting lessons from the instructor."

"How is she doing?"

He went silent for a few seconds. "She's doing okay, but..."

"But what?"

"She needs a lot of practice."

"Send me a video," I said and ended the call.

A few minutes later a video arrived.

The first thing I noticed was how unreasonably close he was standing to her as he instructed her on how to fire the gun. I stared with astonishment as the pervert's hand brushed her back. That was deliberate and totally unnecessary. Damn it to hell, the man was taking advantage of her.

Black fury filled my chest.

I flung my phone away and took deep breaths to calm myself down. I reminded myself of the solemn promise I'd made to Marco and told myself I was acting like a fool. This possessiveness was going to become a big problem if I didn't nip it in the bud right now. She was not mine to have or keep, only to protect. I was her guardian and I had to learn to stand aside and protect her even on her wedding day to the man of her choice.

I forced myself to pick up my phone and deliberately shifted all my focus to the technique he was showing her. Clearly, he had never shot anyone in his life. The way he was teaching her to hold that gun could get it kicked out of her hand in seconds. I shut my phone. I'd seen enough. I would teach her to shoot myself.

For the rest of the day though, and despite the fact I didn't explicitly ask for it, Lorenzo kept sending me videos of her as she went about her day. I didn't mean to monitor her but it was a guilty pleasure to watch her.

She took selfies with some of the waxworks at Madame Tussauds, she sat on a park bench and had something to eat, she fed some pigeons the crumbs, she strolled from Oxford Circus to Piccadilly Circus which was so full of crowds of people it made me slightly nervous, but I trusted my men. I watched her window shop. Sometimes she went in, but she never bought anything.

I wondered why. How much did interns get paid? I didn't think it would earn her much, though she did live in New York so it couldn't be that bad. Of course, Marco had left her considerable wealth but she hadn't sorted through any of it.

I phoned one of my assistants and instructed him to get one of my credit cards to her.

Chapter 28
Zola

"What is this?" I asked as the Amex black card was handed over to me.

"Mr. Moretti wanted you to have it. Whatever you need can be purchased with it. There's no limit."

I frowned. Why would he think I would need his credit card? Did he think I was penniless? Or did he think I was some kind of bimbo he had brought along for a dirty week in London?

I couldn't figure out which possibility annoyed me more.

I gave the credit card a dirty glare and ignoring it, went on with my window shopping, but I was now getting more and more annoyed. After the aloof way he had treated me at breakfast as if last night had never happened, this was a slap in the face.

I didn't need his stupid money. I had only hitched a flight with him and that was it. We weren't here on vacation together. Apart from the bodyguards which I planned to pay him back for, he absolutely didn't have to provide for me in any way.

My fingers flew furiously over my screen as I sent him a message.

What's the credit card for?

In truth, I had been itching for a reason to get a reaction out of him all day so this was the perfect opportunity. I had hardly finished sending the message when my phone began to ring.

"Zola?" his smooth unhurried voice filled my ear.

"Why are you giving me a credit card to use?" I demanded hotly. "I have my own money and it's not like you owe me anything."

If I thought my angry question would be a gotcha that he would have to talk himself out of I was mistaken. His explanation was calmly delivered and made perfect sense.

"It's for security purposes," he said. "We have to be as vigilant as possible. If you use your credit card it will be possible for them to track your location. Use mine and you become a puff of smoke."

"Oh," I said, my great anger collapsing around me. "Why don't we find a way to do this through cash? I could send you a transfer directly to your bank account and you could give me the cash equivalent."

"That would work," he agreed, and before I could say anything else he ended the call. I stared at the phone. I'd never met a more elusive man. I wanted more of him, but I didn't know how to go about it. Every time I thought I'd made a connection, he moved away, further than he had been before.

Suddenly, an inexplicable sadness came over me. I looked around at the throngs of people going about their normal, probably pleasant lives, and realized I no longer had one. There were no pleasantries to be found in my circumstance because not only had I lost the family I had, but I had also lost my own life.

What was I doing here? I slipped my phone into my pocket and continued to walk along the street. The longer I did, the more deflated and overwhelmed I felt until eventually, I found a bench and sat on it.

I couldn't believe it. Just a little while earlier I'd been celebrating the advancement of my career. A career I had chosen out of love and excitement and worked so very hard at, but now even that was going to be taken so abruptly away from me.

I was going to have to start all over again, under an alias that meant absolutely nothing to me. With no one to share my history or memories, and no one I could even trust enough to reveal it. I must remain hidden and invisible forever. What was even the point of living if I had to hide all the time?

My heart wrenched and I reached up to hold my chest. This was the closest I had ever come to having a panic attack. I took deep breaths, but I couldn't find the strength to leave.

Just then, one of Dante's men approached me. He held out a fat envelope. Stuffed with cash, no doubt.

"If you need any more," he said, "please don't hesitate to ask."

"Um ... okay," I said, taking it, and he started to walk away.

But I had completely lost any interest in sightseeing or whatever the hell I was doing. I got to my feet and called him back before he could go too far out of sight.

"I'd like to go back to the hotel," I called out.

He nodded and waited for me.

Chapter 29
Dante

I had back-to-back meetings all day and by the time the last one was concluded, it was nearly eight. I knew Zola was safe in the hotel, but she had not answered my calls so I decided to pay her a visit before I returned to my suite. I knocked and she opened the door a crack.

"I'm about to go to bed," she said.

"I have something important to talk to you about."

She pulled the door open fully and stepped aside to let me enter.

She looked unhappy. Her eyes were red and swollen and her hair messy.

"What is it?" she asked. "What did you want to talk to me about?"

I looked around the room. The bed linen was creased. She must have been lying on top of it. I also couldn't help but notice just how quiet the room was. The television hadn't even been turned on.

I turned to face her. "I tried to reach you several times but you didn't pick up my calls."

"Sorry, I was asleep. My phone was set to silent."

"You can't do that. There could be an emergency and I need to be able to reach you immediately at all times."

She sighed and nodded.

"Alright."

"Have you had dinner?"

She seemed surprised. "Dinner? Is that what you wanted to ask me about?"

"No, but have you eaten?"

"I don't have an appetite."

Her tone was firm and definite and a very clear message for me to take my leave, but I couldn't leave. Not while she was in this state. I turned away from her and headed straight to her bathroom.

"What are you doing?" she asked following me. "Where are you going?"

I pulled my jacket off and draped it across one of the chairs by the side. Then I rolled my sleeves up.

"I think a bath will be good for you," I said.

She stopped by the door. I turned on the faucet. I don't know the first thing about running a bath for a woman, but I figured it just had to be full, fragrant, and soapy. I looked around at a basket of supplies. There was mineral salt, gel, perfumed oil, and bath bombs. Not knowing which to use I dumped them all into the water. Almost immediately the water began to rise and foam. I considered my attempt successful. I turned around and saw her watching me, amusement in her eyes.

"To start with, I didn't say I wanted to have a bath," she said. "Also, you'd better shut the water off, you kind of overdid it with the bubble bath."

I shut the taps off. She was right. "Regardless it would be nice to have one, wouldn't it? It smells great, it's warm, and it will help you relax."

She met my gaze and for the next few seconds, neither of us said a word. I pulled my phone out of my pocket.

"What do you want to eat?" I asked. "Is there anything in particular you want from a restaurant in the city?"

Her expression showed me how disengaged she was before she turned around and walked towards the bed. I called the hotel service as I went over to the sofa chair. I heard their selection, made a variety of choices, and ended the call.

"I need to rest," she said. "I won't be able to do so if you're still here."

My defense was simple. "I ordered enough food for the both of us. I'll leave after we're done eating."

"You're forcing me to have dinner with you?"

"I ordered for two," I pointed out.

She sat up and leaned against the headboard and closed her eyes. A defeated gesture.

"Zola," I called softly. Maybe it was because of the unusual tone of my voice but she immediately looked up and met my gaze.

"Why did you come back to the hotel early?"

She shrugged. "Why not? I gave your men a chance to rest."

"You came here to find some sort of escape and relief, and to rest. My men are paid very handsomely to protect you."

A long stretch of silence followed, and then she said, "My father died on your watch."

Her words cut deep like a knife and it must have shown on my face because immediately I could see the remorse in her eyes.

"I'm sorry," she apologized. "I don't know why I'm being such a bitch. I know he asked you to divert your men to look for the informant."

"You're just still in shock. You haven't even started the process of grieving yet."

She drew circles on the bed with her finger. "Maybe ... When I get back and get into the program, they're going to send me far away from everyone and everything I've ever known. I'm going to have to start again and I can never share my true self with anyone."

I looked at her and understood where her unhappiness had arisen from. "Ugo is not going to be free forever. It is my personal mission to make him pay for what he did to your father. I promise you that. He will not go scot-free."

At my words, she turned to look at me. "Do you mean that in literal terms?"

"The less you know, the safer you will be."

"Are you going to do it immediately ... or are you going to wait for the court to try him and find him guilty?"

"Whichever occurs first," I said, which was not the truth. He had lived his whole life by the sword and must find his end on it.

I could feel her staring intently at me. "He's turned my life upside down. I don't know him, but I hate him so much I want to kill him myself. But even death is not enough for the hate I feel. It won't pay for what he has done to me?"

I couldn't help my smile. "And how are you going to do that when you can barely hold a gun correctly?"

The Guardian

At the slight jab, she turned toward me and I could see the clear offense on her face. "You were keeping tabs on me?"

"Learning how to defend yourself is of prime importance to me. I had to be sure the instructions they were giving you were accurate and effective."

"Will you teach me how to properly use a gun?"

It had been my plan all along but I wasn't about to tell her that. "Take a bath and eat something. Then we'll talk about it."

To my surprise, she got to her feet. "Sure, I'll bathe in expensively scented water and agree to eat really good food when I'm hungry anyway."

"I'm used to you rejecting every single suggestion I make," I said, but she was already disappearing into the bathroom and shutting the door behind her.

A little while later there was a knock on the door. As the three food carts were being wheeled in, she came out dressed solely in a bathrobe. Her hair was damp and falling all over her shoulders. She looked beautiful, clean and so impossibly sensual I had to look away.

"What did you order?" she asked as she went over to the carts. I got to my feet to join her. We sat across from each other and ate bits of all kinds of food. Muscles, steak, chicken, spaghetti carbonara. Nothing made sense. Only that she was naked under her robe and I wanted her, but I had promised her father. We ate silently until she turned and caught my gaze.

She went still for a moment. "You usually eat in silence?"

I nodded. "Always. Unless I'm out with friends."

"So ... when are you going to teach me to hold a gun?"

"After dinner."

She nodded again. After we had eaten, I stepped out to retrieve my gun. I set it on the table before us. She gazed at the gun, then she moved her attention to me.

"What kind of gun is this?"

"It's a 9mm Glock. It has relatively low recoil so it's easier to control and aim accurately."

"Oh," she said as she stared at it.

"Your father really never taught you how to use a gun?"

"No. Maybe he didn't think I was in danger."

"He must have. He had measures in place," I said.

She looked at me in surprise. "What do you mean?"

"From the time I came to your house until my trial was completed and even about two years after I think, he had at least two security personnel on you at all times. I assumed he would have taught you how to protect yourself. Maybe he didn't want you to be afraid."

"Yeah," she said, her gaze back to the window. "He kept a lot of things from me. I knew it and I had no problems with it. That was his world and I didn't really have an interest in it."

I knew it was time to leave. I grabbed my phone and jacket. "You're not alone. You have me. I'll help you ... in whatever way you need."

"For how long?" she asked.

"For as long as you need," I replied.

She leaned forward and picked up the gun. She turned it around, as though she was admiring the polished steel, and then she put her forefinger in the trigger hole.

"There are no bullets in here?" she asked.

I slid my hands into my pockets. "No."

"Why?" she asked, a corner of her lips tilting in dark humor. "Scared I'll shoot you?"

For a brief moment there I felt my heart miss a beat. She was gorgeous. I found myself admitting to myself once again, and it wasn't in a glaringly obvious way. Rather, her beauty seemed like something that occurred to you the moment you saw her but you needed quite a while to understand. There was innocence in her gaze, but at the same time mischief, and a whole lot of sorrow. It made me wonder if there was a time when she had been truly completely happy. If there had been, then more than anything I wanted to know what had caused it so I asked her.

"Why would you shoot me?" I asked.

She smiled. "I could find a reason."

This made me smile. "Like what?"

"We didn't go all the way yesterday," she said. "Shouldn't we finish what we started?"

"You are driven by pain and a need to escape," I muttered.

"Take off your shirt," she said.

My cock throbbed in my trousers. I knew I should go, but I couldn't move. I stared at her. She was forbidden to me.

I stood as still as a statue as she came forward and began to unbutton my shirt. She kept her gaze on me until all the buttons were undone. Then she pushed the shirt off my shoulders and gazed at my body. Her lips curved into a slow appreciative smile.

"You shouldn't do this because you want an escape from the hurt," I growled.

She smiled sadly at my words. "Can you take me back to the days before my father died?"

I stilled at her words.

"Because that's where I want to go, but I can't, can I?"

"I don't want to hurt you. I promised your father I wouldn't," I whispered hoarsely.

She pushed me down to the chair. "You're not going to. I'm a big girl now and this is what I want."

She stared pointedly at me as she pulled the robe up her thighs and before I knew it, she was astride me. She held onto my shoulders and lowered onto my lap and her warmth settled against the bulge in my pants.

My relations with women in the past had never been tumultuous. Obviously, I took enjoyment from their soft skin, their beauty. It was enjoyable, but I always thought of it as a passing excitement. Soon it would be over and they would go their way and I would go mine. And it was always so...

Until now, I found myself holding my breath. She brushed her hair over her shoulders as her gaze lowered to my lips.

My hands went to the shapely curve of her hips. She leaned forward to kiss me. I could taste the red wine we'd shared. "Don't you want me?"

"More than you know, Zola, more than you'd ever know, but I promised your father," I whispered.

"He's dead, Dante. He's dead. I don't think he would give a shit if you fucked me," she cried and began to sob softly.

The Guardian

I held her close to my heart and felt the terrible grief in her shaking body. "Let me dry your hair."

She turned her face away. "Do what you want."

"Stay. I'll be right back."

A few minutes later I returned and saw her seated in my chair with her glass of wine once again in her hand. She looked dejected as she stared out of the window.

I found an outlet nearby and plugged it in.

Chapter 30
Zola

The dryer came to life and drove away the strained silence of the room. I watched his reflection in the glass of the windows.

I found myself enjoying the sensual almost hypnotic feel of his hands moving on my scalp. It was very subtly done with no expertise, but with a tenderness that I would not have expected from a cold hard man like him.

When the hairdryer was turned off, I didn't turn to look at him. Our eyes met in our reflections.

"I'm not a sixteen-year-old girl, Dante. I'm a grown woman. No one is going to get hurt. It's just sex. Nothing more. My father loved us both and he would never deny either of us this brief fling before we go our separate ways."

His body stilled, and for a few seconds, he did nothing. Then I turned and he reached out and touched my bottom lip as if he couldn't believe I was real.

"I know I shouldn't, but you're so beautiful I can't help myself," he whispered more to himself than me.

"Don't think of me as Marco Leone's daughter. I'm just a woman in a hotel room in London."

His eyes moved from my lip up to my eyes and we stared at each other. I thought I saw something like pain cross his features. He remained still and shut his eyes as if he was praying to his God.

When he opened his eyes, he was different. "Just sex?"

"A brief fling before we go our separate ways," I confirmed.

Turning around he walked towards the bed. With his back to me, his hand pulled at his belt as he began to undress until all that was left was his briefs.

My breath caught in my throat as he pulled them down, revealing his perfectly shaped butt. I'd felt the tight cheeks the previous night, but seeing his nakedness in this way was far more erotic.

He pulled the covers back and sat on the bed.

"Come here," he said. Two simple words, but the command was unmistakable.

I got to my feet. My freshly dried hair bounced as I went to him. Stopping in front of him I loosened the sash of my robe. He seized the edges of the soft fabric and gently pulled me toward him. My body tingled with anticipation. The warm glow from the lamps cast a romantic glow over him and made his eyes seem soft and sensual ... and the silence was the perfect complement to the tension and heat we both felt.

Or maybe it was just him ... the longer I stared at him the more convinced I was that there was something about him that completely captured my senses and made me so acutely aware of him it was impossible to think of anything else.

I lifted my hand and slid it into his hair.

I was unable to resist the silky feel and the sense of power it gave me to see the intimidating man lean into my touch. There was a connection here and whether it was the grief we both shared or something beyond it I couldn't tell. But what I did know was this felt too beautiful, too precious. Too much like ... making love and I didn't want it to continue in that way. I didn't want him to care. I didn't want to care. I wanted him to be a touch brutal when he took me.

I pulled my hand out of his hair, placed it against his chest and pushed him backward hard, but it was like pushing a granite wall. He cocked his head as if he was wondering what I was doing.

I put both my hands on him and pushed him again, but still, he didn't budge, and it became a challenge. The third time, however, he caught my wrist, and I looked up to see the slight frown between his brows. I was almost tempted then to reach forward to kiss the crease away, but I stopped myself just in time.

I tried to pull my hand away but he didn't budge and kept staring into my eyes.

"Don't make love to me, Dante. Fuck me hard."

"How hard?" he rasped.

"Do your worst."

For a while, he continued to stare into my eyes, his expression searching, and then he moved, so fast I squealed with shock as he caught me by the waist and dumped me on the bed as if I weighed nothing.

"Your scent has been driving me insane all fucking night," he growled.

My robe had come open but before I could take it off, he loomed over me.

"Open your legs," he snarled.

I spread my thighs.

"Wider," he ordered and his eyes were blazing with deep desire. I could hardly believe this was the same man who had dined with me. I never knew this beast lived inside the expensively suited man.

Excitement coursed through my veins as I obeyed, but it was not to his satisfaction. Roughly, he jerked my legs wider still so I was completely exposed, and looked down at my flushed, open sex with naked hunger.

He swiped his finger through the wet curls of flesh and smeared the slickness he had gathered onto my lips. I was so shocked I froze.

"Lick it," he commanded.

I slipped my tongue out and did as he instructed.

He gathered more juices and smeared my lips again. He dipped his hard fingers into my mouth and made me suck my own juices off them.

"You look beautiful like that," he growled, his eyes were glazed, half-closed.

I tried to sit up and was rewarded with a punishing kiss. His mouth crushed as his tongue demanded entry into my mouth. I sucked it and instantly forgot anything else existed other than our joined mouths.

By the time he released me, I was gasping for air.

His body pressed me relentlessly into the bed and the

strength that he exuded was something I knew to never again take lightly. I couldn't move an inch.

I got what I wanted. I was his prisoner.

His hands closed around my breasts and he began to massage the full and heavy mounds. Suddenly, he seized my right nipple and pinched it cruelly between his finger and thumb. An involuntary hiss of pain tore out of me. He pinched the other engorged bud and I cried out sharply, but I didn't tell him to stop. Again and again, he pinched making me clench my teeth as my nerve endings became more and more sensitive. My nipples felt as if they were on fire when he pressed my breasts together and his lips closed around each hardened aroused peak.

The pull of pleasure made my sex clench, and my body arched, pushing my breasts out. My nipples, obscenely hard and wet, were pointing at him, begging for his cruel mouth. They were so swollen I squirmed even when his hot breath struck them.

"Don't stop," I begged.

As soon as the words left my mouth, he stopped. I had crossed the threshold from pain to pleasure and his job was finished.

He moved downward and began to run his tongue down my body. I broke out in goosebumps as the wet trail inched down towards my sex. My heart was beating like a drum and my toes curled with anticipation.

It was pure torture.

I couldn't hold back my cry when his velvet tongue finally reached the most private part of me. Without an ounce of gentleness, he thrust his large hands under my ass and, lifting me up, began to eat me out. I grabbed onto his hair and ground my pussy against his greedy mouth. He sucked my clit and my body shuddered at the sweet pleasure.

I let him do whatever he wanted with me and made noises I'd never made before, satisfied, inviting, animal sounds. I arched my body, spread my legs even more, wriggled, and thrust desperately against his mouth.

"Yes," I hissed. I was so close. So close.

Pleasure, too much pleasure began to course through my body. I never wanted it to stop. I writhed uncontrollably in it. My body strained. I was choking. I couldn't think. It felt so damn good.

"More, Dante. More."

"Come in my mouth," he ordered, and his voice was rich and dark.

My head swung from side to side. My breath stuttered. Then I came so hard, so explosively, I'd never have believed anyone could come like that. The waves of pleasure came and came. I screamed into the void and let it take me.

As I came back and my vision cleared, I saw Dante standing over me. His massive cock was already sheathed and it was bobbing between his muscular thighs. He grabbed me by my waist, flipped me over, and threw me on the mattress. Grabbing me by my hips he yanked me to my knees. Then he grabbed my hair and pulled my head back so I could see the blazing desire in his eyes.

"Still want me to do my worst?"

"Yes."

He let go of my hair and pushed my head down so my hips and pussy were raised and totally exposed to him. Then he thrust his huge cock deep into my gushing pussy.

He stretched me so much I felt as if he had split me in half. He didn't stop until his pelvis slapped my ass. He growled as he rammed into my body, again and again, the wet slap of our skin echoing in the room. I was gasping, panting and whimpering as he manhandled me.

"I've been wanting to do this ever since I saw you," he muttered as he pounded into me.

My answer was a guttural grunt. It was all I could manage.

His hips sped up and he began to fuck me as if he was taking all his rage and frustrations out on my poor pussy ... and I liked it.

I felt a twinge deep in my sex. My belly warmed. And the twinge happened again. A shiver ran through me. Something was happening to me. I was going to climax again. I rode the state between ecstasy and pain until my orgasm claimed me.

A howl escaped my open mouth.

It was wild and beautiful. By the time his release came, I could barely maintain consciousness. I struggled to push against him. He ground himself against me and curled his body over mine, rubbing my ass cheeks with his groin.

Finally, my brain came back to me, the tension dissipated and it was a great relief, but there was a vast emptiness left behind. All that stuff about 'just sex' and 'being adults' was horseshit. He wasn't mine. He would never be mine.

I pulled away from his shrinking cock. Papa knew. This man was going to hurt me.

Chapter 31
Dante

https://www.youtube.com/watch?v=XHMFFIzGHFk

She rolled away from me.

It was just sex for her, but not for me. I didn't want to let her go.

All I wanted to do was hold her tightly. I'd vowed to protect her, but I never thought it would take me over in this way. Hell, I wanted to make her mine and keep her forever.

Every fiber of my being yearned to take her in my arms and never let go.

I got off the bed and headed to her bathroom. I flushed the condom in the toilet and looked at myself in the mirror. Something very special had happened between us. Just sex? That was not just sex. It was a level of connection I had neither imagined existed, nor ever hoped to find.

My cock was still rock solid.

Just sex, huh?

I left the bathroom and found her lying on her side with her back to me. I picked up another condom from my trouser pocket, sheathed myself and got on the bed. She didn't turn to look at me.

She gasped as I roughly pushed myself deep into her pretty little pussy. She was tight like a fist, but well lubricated. "I can't believe how much cock is inside me. I thought it would hurt. But it doesn't. It feels amazing to be so full and stretched," she whispered.

I began to take her from behind, thinking only of my pleasure. She panted and moaned before her hips bucked in orgasm. The motion took me over the edge as I spurted and bathed in pleasure.

Chapter 32
Zola

I woke up late the next morning with hunger pangs. I was alone, but my thighs were sticky and the room reeked of sex. My body felt sore. Nothing a hot long shower couldn't fix.

My phone pinged with a text message from him.

I'm having breakfast. Join me in my suite?

My heart skipped several beats as I considered the invitation. I decided I wanted to talk to him so there was no reason to refuse, although I wondered if it would be awkward after last night. I had behaved in such a shameless way. I actually asked him to fuck my mouth. I'd never done that with any man before.

I was hard, but I had to learn to be like him. Just sex. Nothing more.

I dressed casually in sky-blue jeans and an off-the-shoulder blouse and a pair of low-heeled sandals. My hair was in a top bun because it was an absolute mess from the last night.

His men were hanging around outside in the corridor and I was a bit self-conscious as they must know that Dante had spent most of last night in my room, but luckily, they were extremely professional and showed no expression as they opened his door and let me in. I saw he was on the phone so I took a seat opposite him and began to butter a piece of toast.

He was probably very busy so I didn't expect to stay long, but to my surprise, he concluded his call quickly and turned to me. He was dressed in a dark suit with a beige necktie and looked fresh, alert, and drop-dead handsome. Nobody looking at him would believe he was the same man I was with last night.

"Good morning," he greeted brightly.

"Hi," I said and I coughed.

"Are you alright?" he asked.

I nodded and swallowed the piece of toast. I was aware he was watching me.

"Everything okay?"

I managed to work up a smile as I nodded. "Yeah, fine, thank you."

"Good," he said. "I have a very busy day ahead so I'll catch you later."

"Wait. I need to talk to you."

"Is it urgent?" he asked. "We can talk when I get back."

"When? Tonight?" I asked and he nodded. I didn't think I could wait that long.

"Can I have five minutes?" I asked. "I don't think it will take longer than that."

"Okay," he said, and leaning back looked directly at me.

I was so affected by his direct regard that my throat felt suddenly parched. It became even more cemented in my head that I had to sever my ties with him quickly. He was dangerous to my peace of mind. Last night had been good, more than good, mind-blowingly brilliant, actually, but if that were to continue, it wouldn't be long before I was hopelessly hooked on him.

And that was the last thing I wanted.

There was no way this was going to end well. I leaned forward, determined to keep the conversation short.

"I want to know what plans you have for Ugo," I said.

"What do you mean?"

"How do you plan to handle him? Are you going to let things play out according to the law or are you going to take any extra measures? I need a definite answer."

He stared at me, and to my relief didn't bother pretending as though he had absolutely no idea what I was talking about.

He straightened and arranged his jacket. "At first I was willing to allow the law to handle it since I wasn't all that concerned about my safety, but now that you're involved, I will not be comfortable if it's dragged out."

At his words, a cold chill ran up my spine. Underneath his fine manners and his fabulously expensive suits, he was a mobster after all. I looked down to hide my expression.

"This is why I don't want you to go into the witness protection program," he said and my head shot up.

"I don't think I have a choice," I replied.

He shook his head. "The government can't keep you safe."

"But you can?'

"Yes," he said. "You have to trust I will keep you safe because it is the truth."

"Thank you, but I think I'll have to go my own way from now on." Even as I said the words I felt pain in my chest. The thought of leaving him was already difficult to accept.

"Let's talk about this a little bit more when I return tonight," he said, and I could hear the frustration in his voice.

"I'll be returning to New York before then," I told him. "I'll fly commercial. I'll be safe. I'll call Detective Hudgens and he can arrange for someone to pick me up at the airport."

"There's no need for you to fly commercial," he said. "I'll have Giotto arran-"

"There's no need," I cut him off. "I'm going to be in public places and–"

"Stop fucking arguing with me!" he suddenly roared.

My heart jumped into my throat. I was so shocked all I could do was stare at him. I barely ever heard him raise his voice so for him to suddenly yell at me made my brain screech to a halt.

He took a deep breath and when he spoke his voice was level. "I understand you don't want my help and I won't force you to take it, but I brought you here and at the very least I'm going to get you back into the States the same way I took you out. Then you can go your own way, but until then you remain my responsibility. Is that understood?"

The Guardian

I didn't even try to argue. Taking his private jet and being completely secluded and protected every step of the way was incontestably the best option.

When I nodded, he rose and walked away. I retrieved my phone from my pocket and placed a call to Detective Hudgens.

Chapter 33
Dante

The rest of the day was stressful for me. As it wore on without any word from her, it dawned on me that she had made up her mind. It hurt, incredibly, and kept me on edge but I knew enough about her by now to know she wasn't going to budge. It wasn't as though she wasn't aware of the dangers her decision held, but she was still willing to go down that senseless path. It was clear that she shared the same stubborn streak as her father.

I had done my best to talk him out of handling my case. The last thing I'd wanted was to put him in the line of danger. Yet he had insisted and one mistake had brought us here. I could see history repeating itself all over again and I didn't know how to take it. How would I be able to bear the weight on my head and in my heart?

There was a knock on the door and Giotto entered.

"You know what Leone meant to me and by extension his daughter. She is his only family left so I hope I'm communicating to you how crucial this is."

He nodded and then raised his head to look me in the eye. "We're ready, Boss. We got this."

"Ugo will be ready too," I said through gritted teeth.

He looked down at his shoes.

"What time is her flight scheduled?"

"At seven," he said.

I nodded. It was almost five so it wasn't too late for me to head back.

"Get the car ready," I ordered.

He made the call as we left the office.

As I arrived back at the hotel I went straight to her door and rang the bell. I lifted my gaze to stare directly into the peephole.

She opened the door a crack. "I'm running late."

"You're not," I said, and she had no choice but to let me in.

I walked in to see that her bags were packed. She walked to the window and watched the city descend into the evening. She appeared calm, untroubled, but I knew that internally she must have been troubled and afraid.

"Here to say goodbye?" she asked.

I told her the truth. "I'm here to try to convince you to stay."

"That's not going to happen." She sighed. "If you're so worried that the government won't be able to protect me then why don't you protect me as well? Or can't you do it? The moment they have me you won't be able to find me?"

That was exactly what I was going to do, but I couldn't

admit it to her. My new plan was to allow the government to mess up first so she would be willing to consider a different route. This was extremely risky because too many things could go wrong and not being in direct control of her well-being was frustrating, but I had no choice.

"Be careful," I said to her. "Anything could go wrong at any second, so you need to be prepared at all times."

She nodded and continued staring out of the window.

It was time to leave, but with every step I took away from her and toward the door, something inside me died. She meant something to me. This much was now incontestable. Beyond her father, no one else had any hold on me whatsoever in as long as I could remember.

I heard the door click behind me.

Walking away and relinquishing control of her safety to others was one of the hardest things I'd ever done. I couldn't go back to work so I returned to my room. I sat on the bed with my head in my hands.

Chapter 34
Zola

As soon as we landed, his men had driven me straight to my father's house and waited around until Detective Hudgens's officers arrived.

The officers sat me down in the living room and briefed me on the process and how my life would go from now until this trial was over and I entered the witness protection program. I could only blankly listen and try my best not to miss the most important things. I would be protected and given the time to get my affairs in order while they set up a new identity for me. For the moment I would be taken to a safe house.

I began to feel regret from then on.

Things turned even bleaker when we arrived at a nondescript house. It was small and covered by vines and trees and suitably inconspicuous.

I walked in and almost had a panic attack.

I tried listening to one of the agents who had been assigned to around-the-clock surveillance but I didn't hear a word. I looked around in horror at the dark stained beams of the house, the drab decor, and the musty vomit-colored rug. The dark musty vibe and musty scents of this house were going to compound my misery. It was a far cry from the neat, bright little apartment I shared with Antoine. My face must have shown my distress.

"Are you alright?" Sarah asked.

"How long am I going to have to stay here?"

Matthew and Sarah shared a look before they turned to me.

"Until the case is concluded," Matthew said.

What? The house looked and smelled like death. I stared at them and felt tears begin to burn at the backs of my eyes. "Where's the bathroom?"

"Right down the hall next to the kitchen," Sarah said.

I went into it and locked the door behind me. The urge to call Dante was overwhelming, but that would be like going from the frying pan into the fire. Losing Papa was enough heartbreak without adding unrequited love for Dante to my troubles.

Suddenly, I felt exhausted. I went over to the only bedroom in the house, but the moment I opened the door and saw the patterned sheets and the dark room, I found I couldn't go in.

I returned to the agents. They were making coffee in the kitchen. They looked up at me expectantly.

"Um ... Is there anything white in this house?"

"Huh?" Matthew said.

"I mean bed sheets and fabric. Everything's so dark and musty."

"Oh," he said and took one look around the house as

The Guardian

though he was just seeing it for the first time. "I don't know. I'll find out."

He turned around to take his leave, and I had a feeling I wouldn't be hearing from him any time soon.

If I was stuck in this house day in and day out with nothing to do it was certainly going to drive me crazy.

Chapter 35
Dante

The more of Giotto's report I listened to the angrier I became.

As I punched the bag over and over again, each hit getting more and more vicious, his speech faltered and eventually slowed. I stopped and turned to face him, sweat dripping down my body.

The scowl on my face was more than enough to relay my annoyance. "The fuckers really didn't even take her out of state?"

He shook his head.

"If we managed to follow them so easily Ugo would have as well."

I thought of the warm hazel eyes of the most obstinate, contrary person I had ever met. Her mulishness had landed her in the middle of nowhere with no friends or family to communicate with.

I could picture just how horrible that would be for her, but I couldn't do anything about it except watch from afar. She had made the choice, she believed, was best for her. At first, I was so frustrated and furious I wanted to forcibly lock her up somewhere safe, but now I understood better. Given my relationship with her father, coming to me for refuge, I understood now, it was too difficult for her to do. Perhaps all would be fine. I would take out Ugo before she came to any harm.

I grabbed a towel, wiped the sweat off my face and rose to my feet.

I turned to Giotto. "Make sure her agents don't catch you guys lurking around. If they think you're Ugo's you know how deadly that will turn out."

"Yes, Boss."

Chapter 36
Zola

The day I would give my testimony in court was still some time away, and already I found myself becoming even more jittery than usual. I realized there was not much I could do about it. This was what I had chosen against Dante's wishes and warnings.

"Can I fix up my room? I'll be sleeping here for a while longer, won't I?"

Sarah looked confused. "Fix up your room?"

"Yeah. With paint ... maybe change up the furniture a bit. Get rid of that hideous ceiling fan or at least clean it?"

She considered my words and then frowned, and I could see that I must sound like an idiot to her. I didn't know how to explain to her that the house had a strange effect on me. Perhaps it was from the old wood, but I constantly felt like I was surrounded by death and I couldn't take it.

It was going to drive me over the edge.

"Please," I said when I saw that her contemplation was

taking longer. "Maybe I can give you a list of what I need and some money so you can buy it for me?"

She smiled. "Okay."

I smiled back and went to sit on the veranda in the backyard. I wished I could reach out to Dante. I missed him terribly. I had thought I would forget him, but as the days passed the longing for him became more and more intense.

Those two nights in London replayed endlessly in my head.

Chapter 37
Dante

I couldn't get Zola out of my mind.

I couldn't reach her, or see her, and night after night, I couldn't push away the memory of her in my arms. I woke up in a heated sweat with the memory of her skin and its taste on my tongue and my heart racing out of control. She *mattered* to me, more than any woman probably ever had. So much more was at stake. It felt as though I had carelessly given up control of my family's well-being to the government and it wasn't something I could stomach. Yet there was nothing I could do.

My men had sent me long-range photos of her painting her bedroom. Given the sorry state of the house they had put her in, she must have taken it upon herself to handle it.

The program had always been known for its low budget, but the less-than-stellar effort got on my nerves. To start with they shouldn't have moved her to a house in the middle of nowhere. It would have made far more sense to hide her in a high-rise where security could be monitored at all times and access could be easily restricted.

Where she was, and without my men guarding her, she was a sitting duck.

Ugo had always lived in a fortress-like home, and since the announcement of the trial, he hardly ever left his residence and had made the security around him even more impenetrable. We were two adversaries circling each other. Both could not survive this battle. It was either him or me.

One thing I knew for sure. While he was alive Zola would never be safe. I was certain, just like me, Ugo knew exactly where she was, but he was biding his time. He was one of the most patient men I knew. He never forgot an insult and he always got his revenge.

His preferred strategy was to wait in hiding and then strike with a single, fatal blow. One day, when she was least expecting it, he would attack and no matter how many detectives were guarding her, he would kill her.

Chapter 38
Zola

"Could you please order me another tin of the sunny yellow paint?"

Sarah put her ham sandwich down and smiled broadly. "Actually, how about we drive you over to the local store and you can get it yourself?"

I stared at her. "What?"

She shrugged. "It's not far and it's a small, family-owned business. We'll be able to take you there and make sure nothing happens to you."

I frowned at her, certain she was joking.

"I know you're nervous but we have things under control. We have extra reinforcements and are ready in case anything goes wrong. It'll be good to do a test run before your day in court."

Put like that it didn't seem as crazy as it had when I had first heard it. A drive out would do me good. After they finished their ham sandwiches I got into the back of the SUV with them.

We were about fifteen minutes into our trip when the

nightmare started. Our vehicle was suddenly and violently slammed off the road. The car spun around as if in slow motion and I began to scream. Matthew and Sarah were shouting something in a panic.

Then the sounds of gunfire started.

My heart started racing. It was Ugo. Without a doubt, I knew it was Ugo. He had found me. Matthew and Sarah were pulling out their guns and radioing their colleagues. I stared at their panicked faces. How lazily confident they had been when they were eating their ham sandwiches and how horribly terrified their white faces were now.

I couldn't believe what was happening. I felt as though I had been dunked underwater, the world around me turned into a haze of chaos and despair, but suddenly I was pulled right back out to the surface.

The car crashed, hit something, and turned to its side, which caused me to slam against the door. Everything in the car that wasn't tethered had fallen on top of me. My neck throbbed with a sharp pain. A hissing sound was coming from the engine. Grasping the handle hard I raised myself up from a twisted position into one where I could think. Matthew and Sarah had exited the car. They were probably keeping the gunmen at bay until help arrived.

Seconds felt like hours and every gunshot fired seemed oh so close to my head I burrowed deeper into the footwell. I was sure it was only a matter of time before it was over for me. Before someone shot a bullet into the car that went through me or jerked the door open and put one in my head.

For the last few weeks, I had romanticized the possibility of my death as the ultimate relief, but now that I was faced with the very real possibility, I felt anything but relief. Instead, I was a crying, fumbling mess, my hands shielding my head.

In those crazy moments I thought of Dante and suddenly knew. It was almost a revelation, like one of those religious disclosures.

I was in love with him.

From a distance, I heard screams and the screeching of tires. I had never felt so weak and powerless. I began to pray I would come out of this attack without harm and I could be rescued and taken far away from danger.

An eternity later or perhaps it was just a few seconds later, the shooting stopped. Obviously, one side had been annihilated violently. I heard men's voices coming closer and closer to the car. Was it one of Ugo's men or was it one of the supporting agents that Sarah had mentioned? I sat frozen until I heard an Italian accent.

Jesus! Oh, sweet Jesus.

It was any second now ... any second now and a bullet would be shot through me ... and it would be the end. I would be gone.

I righted myself and, in a panic, started pulling on the door's latch, but it wouldn't budge. I pushed and kicked at it till tears rolled down my eyes in frustration, but something had jammed it from the outside.

I was just a few seconds shy of screaming with pure frustration, but my fear wouldn't let me. I continued to push on the door with all my strength.

Suddenly, the door on the other side was pulled open. Screaming with terror I hit even more fervently against the door.

The Guardian

"Zola!"

I gave up then. With my eyes tightly shut, I waited for the pain, but I was grabbed by a strong hand and pulled upwards.

The grip was so hard that no matter how I struggled to get my arm free, I couldn't because the person's strength was phenomenal. Despite my protest, I soon felt the grass beneath my feet and the sun on my face. The person's voice and scent weren't familiar to me so there was no way I could calm down.

There was a screech behind us and then a black car drove onto the grass.

I tried to crawl away on my hands and knees as fast as I could, but I was grabbed around the waist as though I weighed nothing and lifted off the ground. Then I was thrown into the vehicle that had just pulled up and in the next second, we were being driven away.

I was deposited on the opposite side with everything in my body aching so bad that it left me disoriented. I was finally able to calm myself down enough to notice the men in the car. They were all speaking rapidly in Italian, but I recognized one voice. The voice that was coming from the speakers. Instantly my brain and heart recognized it.

Dante.

Dante's men had come to help me and not hurt me. In a flash, I saw that the man by my side was bleeding profusely. Half a scream left me before I was able to slap my hands across my mouth.

I watched as one of the other men inspected the wound. His face was contorted in pain as he pressed a torn T-shirt to his wound, but he shut his eyes and rested the back of his head against the headrest.

Dante continued to communicate with him from the car's speakers and the man responded with as much strength.

I wanted to help but didn't know how. Plus, I suspected I would just make things worse so I kept quiet, rested my head against the window, and watched as we sped away from the scene.

I couldn't control the tears that ran down my face. I was still so shaken that I found myself trembling, and even when one of the men gently called out to me my voice quivered unnaturally.

"Yeah?" I asked.

"The boss wants to speak to you," he said.

"Are you alright?" Dante asked.

His voice sounded so soft that I couldn't help but break down in tears again. I tried to respond but when I couldn't, I handed the phone over. I heard the man's report in Italian, low and controlled, and then the car was once again silent.

I continued staring out of the window. I watched us head out of the city and continue about sixty miles south. About an hour later, I could feel the vehicle which had thus far been going at an incredible speed begin to slow down. I sat up and saw a dark green Mercedes waiting by the side of the road.

The SUV parked in front of it and all the men disembarked. Before I could panic the door to my side was jerked open and I was caught just in time by firm, sturdy hands.

Chapter 39
Zola

I was still shaking and in shock, but his scent was instantly familiar. I stared up at my lover's concerned face as if I were seeing a ghost. Relief started seeping into my terrified body.

At first it was a slow trickle as it began to dawn on me that I was safe. And then it overwhelmed me when I realized he and only he represented safety to me. I wasn't alone. My pride, inhibitions, and reservations disappeared. I flung my arms around his neck and sobbed with sheer gratitude.

I still didn't know what had happened, but in all of that uncertainty, he was the one solid thing I could hold on to. I held on tightly and didn't let him go and what was even better was he didn't try to push me away. He let me cling to him until it occurred to me that we were still quite possibly in danger. I pulled myself together and tried to move away, but the pain in my neck returned and caused me to wince. He was instantly alarmed.

"Are you hurt?" he asked, his hand gently cupping my

face. It was so warm and strong that I felt disappointed and unhappy when he pulled away.

"I'm fine. I think it's just a muscle thing."

He frowned. "Can you walk? Do you want me to carry you?"

"No. I can walk."

I tried to stretch my neck hoping the sprain or muscle pull could be resolved if I stretched, but it was not to be the case so I had no choice but to ignore the pain and keep moving.

"You're limping," he muttered and I was forced to notice this as well. I had been wearing a pair of low sensible kitten heels, one of which I had lost and had only now noticed. The cause of my limping however was a bruise to the side of my knee, yet another injury that hadn't registered during the rush of fear and adrenaline.

There was so much to inquire about and get answers to, but all I wanted was to get into his car and be gone ... back to the anonymous room in London. His driver pulled the passenger door open for me but then stepped aside and Dante helped me himself.

Once I was gently tucked in, he went around to the other side and slipped in beside me. The doors were locked and we were pulling back onto the highway.

I leaned against the window away from him and thought of my father. All of this was starting to feel normal to me. Not the attack, but the fear and close calls and expectations of harm.

"Ugo tried to assassinate me?"

"Yes," Dante replied, in his unhurried assuring low tone of voice. I could listen to him forever.

The Guardian

I turned to look into his beautiful eyes. It felt strange. I was so in love with him and he had no idea. "How did you find me?"

"At no time were you out of the sight of my men."

My eyes widened. "You've known where I was? All this time?"

"Yes," he said simply.

I looked down at his hands. They were big and capable and I was filled with immense gratitude and then ... wrecked by terrible regret for the way I had treated him. Yes, I was grieving for my father, but did I have to be such a bitch to him? I kept lashing out and he kept on being the good guy. Always protecting me, always never giving up on me.

I swallowed hard and decided that I would never again be rude or horrible to him, but I would never let him know that I had fallen for him because that would put him in an awkward situation. He was only keeping his promise to my father. I cringed to remember how hard I had to persuade him even to have sex with me.

"Thank you, Dante. And I'm truly sorry I've been so difficult and rude to you. I owe you everything."

His eyes narrowed. "Don't apologize. You had just lost your father. It was to be expected. He was a great man. A big loss. I would have been the same if I was in your shoes. You owe me nothing. Whose idea was it to take this trip?"

"Uh ... Sarah."

"Hmmm..."

I stared at him. I had become quite close to Sarah. I thought of her as my protector. "Why do you ask? Do you think she was a dirty cop working for Ugo?"

"Maybe," he replied. "In any case, my men were expecting an ambush of some sort, so they were ready and well prepared."

"Sarah and Matthew ... are they alright?"

He looked grim, but he didn't mince his words. "I believe they didn't make it."

I gasped with shock. I felt sick to my stomach. Both of them had been gunned down. I remembered them eating their ham sandwiches. So full of life. So young. So sure tomorrow would come. They were dead because of me. Guilt flowed into me.

Dante had warned me about the program from the beginning and expressed his displeasure at my intention to join it, but like a headstrong fool, I hadn't listened. I would have died today if he hadn't remained adamant about remaining by my side to protect me. All my life I had denied people's help, but that was over now. I clasped my hands together tightly and said a silent prayer for their souls.

"It's not your fault," he said softly. "They chose that line of work. They knew the danger."

"If I had listened to you, they would never have died."

"Don't do that," he said. "If they hadn't died protecting you it might have happened when they were protecting someone else."

"'I should have listened to you," I whispered.

"That's life. You can't go back. Only forward. How's your neck?"

"It's fine. I'm fine," I mumbled and smiled at him even though the pain was getting worse and worse. I didn't want to trouble him any more than I had to. Already, he had taken on such a big burden to protect me.

He was silent for a little while and then he said, "It's going to get worse."

"Where are we going... is it far?"

"Somewhat, but we'll stop soon. You must be hungry."

I listened to his words and found them strange. Eat? Food? I had no appetite for food at all. "No, I'm not hungry."

In a few minutes, we were pulling into a gas station.

"Sure you don't want anything?" he asked.

I shook my head.

"Be back soon," he said and got out of the car.

We were in an unfamiliar town, which made me want to remain in the car, but at the same time, I couldn't stand to be away from him. I watched him walk to the store and waited, hoping to calm my nerves, but no chance. A few seconds later I opened the door and scuttled out. I was so terrified about being out in the open and exposed to a bullet that I half-ran, half-limped to the door.

The bells chimed in response to my arrival and Dante whirled around. His eyes slightly widened and he waited for me to come over to him at the in-house food window. My looping, panicked dash to the door must have straightened out my neck because it didn't hurt as much.

"Changed your mind?" he asked.

I didn't, but I didn't want to admit that I couldn't bear to be in the car without him. My gaze ran through the sweets and snacks, but I didn't care for any of it so I kept looking around.

"I got you a bag of cashew nuts and a cheese sandwich. Is that okay?"

"Just great," I said gratefully. "I do like cashews."

"Yeah, they were what you reached for most frequently in London."

"Really?" I was impressed he had taken such close notice of me and what I liked.

"Really," he teased and went to pay for the stuff.

Chapter 40
Dante

I knew she wasn't asleep.

She had barely touched the sandwich. She had taken a bite and looked like she was about to gag. I knew she wasn't at peace. Her feet and arms moved constantly as if she was trying to find a comfortable position but just couldn't.

It made my heart ache to see her in this way, but there was nothing I could do for the moment, so I waited until we arrived at my well-guarded estate in the Adirondacks.

The house had been built on a massive stretch of land that was separated from the other lake homes. The view of rugged mountains and lakes I was certain would help to calm her down and make her feel safe.

The car pulled to a stop and instantly her eyes opened. Raul got out of the car and gently shut the door behind him.

"This is yours?" she asked.

I nodded. "Yeah. It's a little hideaway."

She continued to stare at it. "I don't think there's anything little about it."

I smiled as I got out of the car and went to her side. She was already opening the door so I held it open for her.

I saw her wince and knew the neck sprain was probably going to get worse. We were greeted by my housekeeper, Marie.

"Go with Marie and settle down in whichever bedroom takes your fancy. The ones that face the water are the best," I said.

Zola smiled tiredly and I watched her follow Marie up the stairs, her movements stiff.

As long as she remained safe and protected under my watch, she would slowly heal. Giotto came with me, and the moment I sat down we began to work on how to deal with the mess that the bastard Ugo had created this morning.

"How's Tony doing?" I asked.

"Doc has stitched him up. He'll make it. It went clean through his chest, but didn't hit anything major."

"Hmm," was my response. "Call his wife. Make sure she has everything she needs. And get a new phone for Zola."

"On it, Boss," he said as he walked out.

My phone rang. It was Detective Hudgens.

"Where is she?" he demanded aggressively.

My blood was boiling, but I kept my voice neutral. "Who?"

"Don't play games with me, Moretti. I know we didn't live up to expectations, but you can't keep her. She's a witness in your case. The court can use this to discredit her testimony."

"I didn't say I had her," I said calmly. "Why would I have her?"

"So, she's missing? And you're okay with that?"

"It's your case. I'm sure you'll find her."

"You're going to ensure this entire process is a hellish one for me, aren't you?" he asked belligerently.

He'd fucked up. She would have died under his watch and he dared to take that tone with me. Before I said something I would regret, I ended the call.

I was still reeling from how close to death she had come. I called Marie to ask which room she had chosen.

"She asked for the room that was next to yours, Sir."

Marie's words brought a song to my heart even though I was still very aware of the fact that at any point in time, I could be gone, and if she became too attached she would fall apart. I decided to take a stroll to her room.

The door was opened to reveal her in a towel with her hair piled on top of her head. Our eyes met and I couldn't help the rush of desire that ran through me. She bit her bottom lip.

"I was going to take a shower," she said.

"I just wanted to check on you and make sure you're ok."

"I'm fine."

"I'm getting you a phone," I said. "Giotto will bring it over."

"Thank you. What about you? Will you be ... around or ... will you leave?"

I smiled. "I'll be around. Actually, I'm heading to the gym. Got to release some energy."

She stared at me. "Okay."

"The compound's safe. You could go on a hike if you want. There's also the lake. You could go for a swim."

"A swim?"

"Yeah. It's warm today so the lake should be lovely. If it isn't then we have a heated indoor pool in the gym. I'll be taking a swim there later."

She looked at me. "A swim sounds appealing, but I still have visions of drowning."

I smiled. "Not on my watch. I'll be there."

She considered this and then she nodded.

"Just call me when you're ready to come down."

She nodded and I walked away.

Chapter 41
Zola

A swim with Dante?
The more I thought about it the more appealing it became.

I opened the closet doors and found it stocked with female clothes and all in my sizes. There were dresses, casual clothes, a couple of swimming costumes, and even pretty underwear. For a fraction of a wild second, I considered perhaps this had been put here for me, but it didn't make any sense.

There was no way he would have known an attack would happen and the government would be unable to protect me. Or that I would choose this room from the many others.

But then I saw the white swimsuit that looked identical to the one I was wearing when he saved me from drowning all those years ago ... and I knew. All this stuff was bought for me.

I sank down in shock as my eyes took in all the clothes.

All of it was my style. He'd put time and thought into it. I stood at the window. I would never have believed he could be so thoughtful. He was part of the Mafia, for God's sake. No wonder my father loved him so much.

I became determined to make it up to him.

I dressed in the white swimsuit, put a pair of shorts and a T-shirt over it, then made my way to the door. When I opened it, I found a box waiting outside the door.

I opened it and inside was a phone that when turned on seemed to already have been set up. I checked the contacts and found there were two names. Dante's name and Giotto's who I recognized as one of his men. I sent Dante a message and a few seconds later he sent back a response.

Him: **I'll send someone to get you.**
Me: **No need. I'll find my way there.**
Him: **Okay. Come to the basement.**
Me: **Cool.**

His house was beautiful. A perfect blend of texture and luxury. From the paintings on the walls to the unique accents and furniture pieces it felt like a top designer's dream home. It all fit together perfectly and like a magazine show home.

I followed his instructions and started to head down until I was back in the huge foyer. It was tall with windows that spanned the entire height of three floors. Hanging from the ceiling, was a glistening chandelier with green crystals. I was staring at its rare and stunning beauty when I heard movement behind me.

I turned around to find his housekeeper, Marie. She was advanced in age, but still elegant with kind eyes. She added to the feeling of warmth and safety my mind was beginning to attach to this house.

"Miss Leone," she said, "Mr. Moretti has asked me to escort you to the pool."

"That would be great, thank you," I said and went with her.

The gym was huge. I could see Dante in a corner lying on a bench and lifting weights. I couldn't take my eyes off him. He seemed so strong and beautiful. He set the weights down and stood. The raw strength and virility in every part of his body were incontestable, and once again it turned me on.

When I reached him, he stood and towered over me. Suddenly, he reached out and brushed my hair over my shoulder. I froze and so did he. I realized, he too had been taken aback by his own gesture. He had probably done it unconsciously.

Needing a distraction, I looked around the space. "This place is huge."

"Yeah. Ready for your swim?"

"No, finish your workout. I'll run for a little bit," I said, spotting a treadmill nearby.

"You don't have the right shoes."

I kicked off my sandals and stood barefoot on the treadmill. "It's fine. I won't run."

I pointed at the large screen TV against the wall. "Can we put it on a news channel?"

"I don't think that's a good idea. There's nothing they're saying that you're not already aware of."

I considered his advice and decided to take it.

I kept walking, going slow at first, and then slowly increasing my pace. Surreptitiously, I watched him as he continued lifting weights until he came over to the treadmill beside me. I smiled awkwardly at him. He began at a normal pace like me, but quickly increased his speed until he was running fast.

It was soothing to have him by my side. When he got off and headed to the showers next to the pool, I actually missed him. When I heard him dive into the water I got off the treadmill. I turned and headed to the refrigerator to grab a bottle of water and watched as he swam from one end to the other. His strokes were calm but powerful as he cut swiftly through the water.

I decided to join him. I took my shorts and baggy T-shirt off and I got in carefully using the steps.

The water was at a wonderful temperature and I immediately relaxed. I remained in the corner, kicking my legs underneath the water. I held my breath and went under, appreciative at how out of sight and safe I felt. My lungs soon began to hurt, but I didn't pay attention to it, wanting to remain underwater for as long as possible.

A few more seconds passed, and I started to come up but before I could, my arm was gripped and I was pulled up with immense force. As the water sluiced off my face I was startled to see Dante's scowling at me.

"What the fuck are you doing?" he yelled, his face pale with worry and fear.

I stared at him unsure of why he was so furious with me until it occurred to me that seeing me stay underwater for longer than was necessary had made him think I was drowning.

"Oh," I said. "I'm fine. I wasn't in any danger. It just ... it felt good down there."

It was an honest comment not meant to be dark in any way, but of course, he didn't take it that way.

"Are you suicidal?" he asked incredulously.

"No," I mumbled.

He moved me with his body and I didn't realize he was caging me in until my back hit the side of the pool and I couldn't move. The air around us became charged. My breathing lost its pattern and became harsher.

"Your dad will be pissed as shit if you did, you know that, don't you? He gave up his life for you. I know it's hard, but you'll get through this. I promise you."

"I know," I said.

He started to move away but I didn't want him to. My hands curled onto those thick arms of his and he stopped and looked at me. I couldn't look away from his eyes.

He pressed against me and I could feel the hardness of his shaft. He was as turned on as I was, and that knowledge filled me with excitement.

His gaze lowered to my lips and as I lifted my head, a pain shot through my neck.

"Awww," I yelped.

He frowned. "Your neck?" I thought he would kiss me, but he pulled slightly away to once again look into my eyes.

Gingerly, I touched the side of my neck. "I thought I had got the kink out, but obviously not."

"Come, I'll give you a massage and some painkillers with food," he said. "You've had nothing to eat for hours."

He got out of the pool and gently pulled me out, before placing a call to Marie for some food.

* * *

"Do you come here often?" I asked as we headed upstairs.

"Unfortunately, no," he replied. "I wish I did though. It's probably the only place in the world where I can fully relax."

"It is?" I asked as he ushered me in.

"Yes," he replied. "It's my safe house and almost no one knows about it."

I looked at him in surprise.

"Really?"

"Yeah." We'd arrived on the top floor and he stopped in front of our rooms. "Yours or mine?"

I was already familiar with mine, but I did want to see his room. "Yours."

"I found this place when I was looking for somewhere to recover."

"To recover?" I asked as he closed the door.

He stopped to look at me and I realized I was being intrusive. "It's alright if you don't want to answer."

He shook his head. "I want to, it's just how I've always been. I'm not really open to divulging information about myself."

I smiled. "I understand. My father was exactly like that."

"He was," Dante said. "He made you feel so comfortable around him, but when you think about it, you realize he is actually very closed-lipped and guarded. I think it had a lot to do with you. Not many people were even aware he had a daughter."

"You're right," I replied. "He kept me completely out of it. I rarely felt the impact of his work on our lives apart from the fact he was gone a majority of the time."

Dante sat on the bed and stared up at me.

Chapter 42
Dante

She had put on her shorts before we'd left the pool, but it did little to make me forget the sight of her in that swimsuit. All those crazy memories of her from that fateful night came crowding back into my head.

I thought of all the women I'd been with since that night. It was no wonder none of those relationships stood a chance. They were all beautiful in their own way, but none could compete with the image of her in her white swimsuit.

She was a dream in my head.

I couldn't look away.

The more I tried, the more seductive the dream became.

Here she was, my dream, in my bedroom. I was thrilled. My body trembled with emotion.

She looked around, taking note of the surroundings and I wished I could hear what she was thinking.

"I love this room. The safe house I was in was dark in the worst of ways. Everything about it was just terrible. It actually smelled like death. Obviously, I couldn't renovate the house, but I had to at least renovate the room I was in, otherwise, I would be haunted by my nightmares."

Any other time I would have been amused by her cute chatter, or the way her nose wrinkled, but not now. I had dreamed of seeing her for too long. I could have lost her today, but in the middle of the chaos, we were together, alone and safe. My cock throbbed.

"Neck massage then shower for you," I said as I hooked my hand into the band of her damp shorts and pulled her slightly closer to me.

"Sounds good to me." Her voice was a whisper and her eyes were shining. Then I did something I never did: I let my guard down.

I knelt in front of her and leaned my forehead against her stomach. I could hear her blood and smell her sweet juices. She lifted her hand and settled it against my neck ... softly ... delicately. She stroked my nape and then moved to my hair and my heart swelled. Her touch was so gentle, and filled with affection. Or perhaps it was all in my head, but what I did know without a shadow of a doubt was that apart from her father she was the only person I'd ever cared about.

I hooked my hands into the band of her shorts and pulled them down. She let them fall and I leaned forward to pepper kisses on her white swimsuit. She was my goddess. I would want her forever.

I stood and brushed the soft tendrils around her forehead away from her face and lightly stroked her cheek. Taking her hand, I lead her to the bathroom.

I found a massage oil in the cupboard, poured it into the

palm of my hand and warmed it by rubbing my hands together. I turned her to face the mirror and instantly our eyes met. Hers were trusting. I'd never seen them so until today. I placed my hands on her neck and began to softly massage it. She closed her eyes and moaned a little.

"Guide me?" I instructed.

She nodded and her hand came on top of mine and led me.

"Down here ..." she said. "It feels like something twisted or knotted."

Gently, rhythmically, I smoothed it out. Then I retrieved a towel from the cabinet, folded it, and put it around her neck.

"Bend your head to the right ... no jerking," I told her.

She did it slowly and intentionally. I made her repeat it to the opposite side and by the end of it, her eyes came open. She met my gaze and nodded.

"I think it feels better."

"It'll get worse before it gets better," I said.

She smiled. "You're so pessimistic."

"Not pessimistic," I replied. "Just experienced."

I turned around and headed into the shower. I turned on the water, adjusted the temperature, and stood under the spray. The water flowed down my body. I turned when I heard the glass door open and pulled her to me. I held her neck as delicately as I could and slanted my head to kiss her.

Her body sagged with relief and pleasure. Her taste was incomparable. I felt sweetness and peace fill me. It felt like I was home. I grabbed her ass, soft and full, and began to grind her sex against my hardness, sensually, tenderly. She moaned into my mouth and held onto my biceps. Her grip was hard as she tried to contain her arousal. I was so turned on that it took all of my self-control not to pull her back to me and take her roughly against the glass.

I knew what she needed the most was to be consoled and gently stimulated. I stepped away from her and watched the water flow down her hair and her body, her pussy. I couldn't look away as she parted her legs.

I saw the pink slit and I ached to once again taste it, but my head kept telling me it wasn't the time. I had to focus on getting her relaxed; I picked up my shampoo bottle from the shelf against the wall, pumped a healthy amount into my hand, and began to gently massage her scalp. Shampoo suds ran down her glistening body. Then I switched to a body wash and set about soaping every inch of her body.

I couldn't hold back then, and I kissed her.

She responded in a way that I had only dreamed about. I forgot myself. My hands molded to the silky wet surface of her breasts, and my hand moved even further down until it came to the junction between her thighs.

I slid my fingers between her slickness. I tried my best not to go too quickly, but as I continued to rub and stroke her swollen bud, her breathing quickened and unable to bear the stimulation, she ground her pussy against my hand mindlessly.

I was no saint, and at that point, there was no way I could hold back. I turned her around, grabbed her hips and lifted her up. Her hand came behind her to grasp my cock and glide it along her ass to the pulsing folds of her sex.

I flattened my palm against the wall.

She spread her legs even wider and pushed her hips

back and my cock slipped inside her. I started to move my hips.

I went slow despite how fast she urged me. It took all the strength in me not to give in, but at the end of the day holding on tightly to her and rocking both of us to oblivion was beyond special. It felt as though she was an extension of me. The steam, heat, and wetness had melded us together. Where her skin ended and mine began could be known.

"It's fine," she breathed through her ecstatic haze. "I'm ... The pill. It's fine."

It was crazy, but I had not even thought about it. It felt so right. Nothing, not even the thinnest condom should come between us. She came with a cry while I felt the effect course through my body like the softest, sweetest blow to my guts.

I poured my thick cream deep inside her body. She turned and threw her arms around me.

"I think you're right. My neck's gonna hurt," she grumbled into my chest.

I almost laughed, but I didn't like the thought of her in any kind of pain. I moved us out of the shower and got a towel. She stood submissively as I dried her down like a child.

She looked tired. I threw the towel aside, gathered her into my arms, and headed straight to bed. There was no question now that she was going to spend the night with me. I watched her naked on my bed and felt my chest swell with emotion. I made myself a promise. One day I'd put a ring on her finger. And she would be mine. All mine. And only mine.

Her eyes were closing.

The Guardian

Marie had left a tray of food for her and wanted to try to get her to eat something before sleep could take her.

"Sure you don't want to eat before going to sleep?" I asked.

"No," she replied softly, and completely naked, snuggled deeper into the pillow.

Chapter 43
Zola

I awakened to a pain in my neck and unfamiliar surroundings and a warm and solid body behind me. Ah, Dante. I smiled at the memory of our time in the shower. I tried to turn my head and look at him and winced at the stiffness. As soon as I moved he opened his eyes. They were so startlingly blue they made me blink.

"Gosh, your eyes are so blue," I exclaimed.

He grinned. "The better to see you with, Zola, my dear."

I giggled. The idea of him as a wolf was too delicious. I couldn't help myself. "Oooo ... what perfect teeth you have, Mr. Wolf."

"You shouldn't have said that," he warned.

I screamed and tried to escape, but he had me in his grip.

"Wait, wait. I have to go to the toilet," I pleaded.

He let me go and I quickly wriggled out of bed and went to the bathroom. I looked at myself in the mirror and tried to move my neck. It was uncomfortably stiff just like

Dante said it would be. I took in my appearance. My hair was a complete mess. I glanced at the spacious shower room, and my knees went weak with the memory of the way he had fucked me so passionately.

Knock, knock.

"I'll be right out," I said and ran his hairbrush through my hair. I opened the door and found him deliciously bare-chested, but the playful look was gone from his face. It was etched with concern.

"You're in pain, aren't you?"

"I'm fine," I lied.

"No, you're not."

He took my hand and dropped a couple of tablets into my palm. Then he held out a glass of water.

"Pain reliever," he explained briefly.

He stood in front of me and watched me down them.

"Breakfast?" he asked

"Breakfast sounds good.

"Let's go find some clothes for you to change into," he said. "I'll help you."

"I think I'll be fine," I told him. "I don't want to become completely reliant on you."

"It'll just be for a couple of days. Three days tops."

"Still." I smiled.

"Off you go then," he said.

I hesitated and chewed my bottom lip. "How could you be so sure I'd choose the room next to yours?"

He laughed. "I didn't. I believe you have clothes in all the other rooms too."

My jaw dropped with shock. I stared at him speechless. This man was an enigma. I didn't deserve him. The old me would have said, I'll pay you back. The new me was filled with gratitude.

"Thank you," I said softly.

"No problem," he said. A cheeky look came into his eyes. "Are you going to ask me for a bill so you can pay me back?"

I shook my head. "No. I'll never say that again. I could never pay you back for everything you've done for me even if I spend the rest of my life trying to."

A message pinged on his phone.

He frowned and picked it up. As I watched him read the message I could see and sense his emotions change.

"Is everything alright?" I asked.

He lifted his gaze and nodded. "Yes, but I'm afraid I won't be able to join you for dinner."

"What's wrong?" I asked nervously.

"Nothing is wrong. I just have to personally see to some issues at the office since I wasn't available yesterday. I'll be back in no time."

Suddenly I felt clingy and overly dependent, and it wasn't a good feeling. I always remembered my grandmother saying nothing scares a man more than desperation in a woman so I stepped back a little.

"Ok." Before I left I allowed myself to just touch his arm ... for assurance.

But he grabbed my wrist and entwined his fingers with mine. "See you later."

"See you later, alligator," I quipped, and he laughed.

It was a good sound. A very good sound.

Chapter 44
Dante

The two private investigators standing in front of the suburban house in Brooklyn nodded when they saw me. After exchanging salutations, we walked in. I took my seat behind the desk and addressed them.

"What makes you think this guy's death is connected to Ugo?"

They shared a look with each other, and then Derek responded. "The only connection he has to you is, he's an employee in one of your companies. We had our people search into his history to check for links to the Mafia to explain why he was gunned down in front of a restaurant in a deliberately Mobster style. Which makes it a very juicy story for the media. Obviously, they don't slander you outright, but they intentionally make the connection to you. What they haven't mentioned though ..."

He took a file folder from Jacob and handed it over to me. I accepted it and began to flip through the report.

"Is the fact that he was one hundred and sixty-five thousand dollars in debt. Money that wasn't borrowed from the bank."

At this, I looked up.

"We're not completely sure what the source of the money was since the story just broke a few hours ago, but we suspect a link to Ugo."

I listened to his theory as I flipped through photos and police reports.

"The only thing I don't understand," Derek said, "is why he would want to draw any attention to himself just before the trial?"

"He's not drawing more attention to himself," I replied. "He's drawing more attention to me. I wond-"

Just then my phone began to ring. I would have ignored it, if not for the ID of the person that flashed onto my screen. I brought the phone up to my ear and swiveled my chair to face the window.

"It's been a long time Hell Fire, hasn't it?" a blast from the past asked.

The harsh face of Ugo's second-in-command came into my mind. It was a long time since anybody had called me by my old nickname. Hell Fire. In some ways, he was crueler than Ugo and had been a bigger source of hell for me than anyone else. I'd always said I'd repay the favor to him one day, but that day hadn't come yet. I said nothing.

"I take it you got the gift I prepared for you this evening?"

"You still doing your own wet work, Tony?" I drawled.

"Fuck you," he spat furiously. "I don't do my own wet work you gutless piece of shit. What a fucking disappointment you turned out to be. You were like a son to me then you fucking stabbed me in the back. You stabbed all of us in the back and you're still fucking doing it. But you're not going to get away with it. That idiot was just the first. There are more sweet tragedies coming your way ... all linked to you."

I chuckled. "You're still wanking off to fantasies of catching me?"

"Very funny. Laugh while you still can. You just made a big mistake today."

"Why? Because I snatched Leone's daughter from under your noses this morning?" I taunted.

"No, because we lost Benjamin and Elias today," he said. "You know how the boss has always felt about Benjamin. You're in deep shit. He's not going to play fair anymore."

As if he ever did.

"The only way this is going to play out from now on is for you to return the girl. If you do not do this then ..." his laugh was dry and bitter. "We've been given free rein to release all the contents of hell at you."

"Thanks for the heads up," I said. "I'll look forward to your unimaginative idea of hell."

I ended the call and I set the phone down.

A war had been declared and by my words, I had promised to eagerly participate. Was I truly ready to indulge in a bloodbath with those crazy psychopaths?

Yes. For Zola, I would fight to the death.

"Sir?" I heard the call from behind me. I turned around to face Derek and Jacob.

"They're going to kill at random," I said. "Don't bother trying to trace which of them had any connections to the mafia. As long as they're associated with me, they are fair game."

The two men went completely silent with shock. I dismissed them and I sat alone in my office.

If I didn't get this rampage under control then no one would care whether I was guilty or not. There would be too many dead, too many families devastated. All they would want was to see me gone.

I got to work.

Chapter 45
Zola

Without switching on the TV, I had no clue how my disappearance after the attack was being presented in the media. It was sure to have embarrassed Detective Hudgens, and his team must have been trying to search for every way possible to get me back to save face.

Marie came in to serve me breakfast; French toast, bacon, and some fresh juice,

"I hope I'm not stepping out of line," she said. "But are you Mr. Leone's daughter?"

"Yes, he was my father," I said sadly.

"I'm so sorry for your loss my dear. You must miss him greatly. I do," she said in the kindest, sweetest way imaginable.

"Thank you," I said.

"I heard about you from him. You're working in publishing, right?" she asked and I nodded with a smile.

"Yes, I was."

"Your father was very proud of you," she said.

I felt emotion choke my throat so I just nodded.

"Mr. Leone was very special to Dante. He was the only guest here and sometimes he would come over when Dante wasn't here too."

I was surprised to hear this. "Really? He did?"

"Yes, she answered. "He was so comfortable here that sometimes he would spend the weekends here."

"He liked peaceful places," I said. "So, I'm sure he liked it here."

"Oh, he did," she said. "Especially during late autumn. All of the trees along the lake would be that striking burnt orange and he would come all the time just to settle down and relax there. He never stayed long, but whenever he came, Dante would always find the time to come over to see him."

Her smile was sad.

"Anyway," she said as she resumed her chores. "I have access to anything you need so just say the word."

"Thank you," I said and turned around to exit the kitchen.

I decided I liked her. She was soft and sweet. I started to head back to my room, but I was sidetracked by a huge living room that led out to a massive outdoor patio. I took a seat out there and looked out at the lake and the sky.

My father sat here and I never knew.

I sat there until sunset. Staff came to light the storm lanterns and start up the fire pit. It was very beautiful, but suddenly, I became nervous. Where was Dante? The longer I sat, the more frightened I became; I couldn't stop myself from calling him.

His phone rang and rang and then it disconnected.

doors. There's a computer there if you need it, Wi-Fi ... books. And it's comfortable, I hope."

"Okay, I'll check it out."

"Good."

"Please be careful," I said.

"I will," he replied and the call came to an end.

I rose and went in search of the library.

It was easy to find mainly because of the huge double doors. They were impossible to miss and the moment I walked in, I began to feel something close to excitement.

He had seriously undersold the grandiosity of the library. Bookcases filled with books lined the walls from the floor to the ceilings while the windows that gave a magnificent view of the lake were equally as huge and elegantly carved.

I didn't want all the lights on, so I selected a few lamps and after turning them on, turned off the main lights. The space was bathed in golden light and I felt even more motivated to put in some work for the night as Dante had suggested.

I turned on the computer and began to write what came to my head. Twenty minutes later I only had a single word written on the page.

Murder.

I stared at it for a long time. When I couldn't look at it anymore, I got up and headed over to a nest of sofas in a corner. It was the perfect place for me to relax and think. I put a soft pillow under my head and before I knew it, I had drifted off to sleep.

Chapter 46
Dante

"I didn't have the heart to wake her, Sir," Marie said. "I figured she'd wake up when she was good and ready. Plus, she looked like she really needed the rest."

I opened the doors and walked in as quietly as I could and saw her curled up like a cat, fast asleep on the couch. The window blinds were open, the room warm and filled with a soothing silence. As I watched her, I felt a sense of great peace fill my chest. She made everything worth it.

Her features were so delicate, that she almost didn't seem real. Her lashes, soft and long, rested on her cheeks, and her nose had a little flush at the tip. And then her lips, so soft, with the bottom one plump and slightly protruding out. I loved kissing her, but right now an image of her lips wrapped around my cock came into my head. There were very few sensations that could compare to her having my cock buried in her face and her looking straight into my eyes.

Unable to stop myself, I brushed her hair out from the sides of her face and she stirred in response.

Then her eyes fluttered open and she was staring directly into my eyes.

"You're back," she said sweetly.

I nodded.

"Everything under control?"

"Yeah," I replied.

She reached forward to touch me affectionately on my arm. "You should get some rest. We can talk later, after you wake up."

She looked at me and I could tell she was hesitating. "Do you want to have a bath? Afterward, you can fall asleep. It'll be wonderful."

"Sure," I said. "I have to be back in the office in a few hours but a bath and a quick nap sounds great. Join me?"

She smiled shyly at me. "Okay. I guess I could use a bath too."

We headed straight for my room.

While I undressed, she ran the bath. I watched as she untied the robe she had on, leaving her naked. She hung it on the railing and went over to the tub to sink in.

"It's really warm and lovely," she said invitingly.

I pulled away my towel as well and joined her.

I couldn't remember the last time I had a bath. She was making me slow down and it was strange. Slowing down had never been a consideration in my life. There was no chance for it. From time to time I would need to take short breaks but that was only after the storm had passed. But to slow down in the middle of it? I watched her begin to pull all her hair up and wrap it into a knot on top of her head. Something about the fact she was right here with me, so close ... made every other problem seem inconsequential. She was safe. Nothing else mattered.

I couldn't help but look at the swell of her breasts above the water. We shared a small smile and then her leg began to slightly stroke against my upper thigh under the water.

I kept staring at her and when my hand reached out to stroke her, I realized we were too far apart from each other.

"Come over here," I said.

"I thought you didn't want us to spend too long in here?" she said.

"I've changed my mind," I replied.

She moved closer to me.

I held the side of her face gently, slanted my head and kissed her. The kiss was soft and sweet, almost platonic, but when I pulled away and our eyes met I could feel the atmosphere change from lighthearted to one that was incredibly charged and tense. She leaned forward and kissed me, but hers was nothing like mine. It was deep, passionate, even desperate.

I relished the feel of her tongue as it glided along mine, and the slight pull of her lips as it sucked on mine. I loved everything about the way she kissed me. She took her time, as though she were savoring a glass of fine wine. I lost myself in it with no reservations. We were both so connected it felt as though nothing could ever break it.

In the silky water, she shifted her body and settled between my legs, and as a result, my rock-hard, aroused cock was directly pressing against her sex. She rocked her hips sensually against the throbbing shaft.

I moved my hand to my cock, positioned it between her

soft folds, and slid into her until I was sheathed so tightly inside of her, I couldn't hold back a groan. Her breathing was harsh and ragged as she shut her eyes to savor the sensation. When she opened them back up to stare at me, I wondered what she was seeing. What she saw and thought as she looked at me.

Still staring at me she began to ride and take her pleasure from me.

Water splashed out of the tub and onto the floor. Knowing her, later she would fret about what Marie would think or how much extra work she was giving the staff, but right now, she didn't even register it.

I could feel the tremors in her body and the composure slowly slipping out of her grasp. I adored her little moans and gasps especially when my lips found her earlobes and lightly nibbled on the soft flesh. The way she clung to and moved against me felt so deeply intimate.

Eventually, the pleasure became too intense, and I needed relief. I was filled with an urgency that was driving me crazy. I needed to hear her cry out my name and I needed to hear her ass slapping hard against my groin as I fucked her senseless.

Grabbing her around the waist, I got to my feet, the water dripping all around us, and positioned her against the wall with her hands high over her head and pressed against the tiles.

I thrust into her sweet heat and she cried out. The sensations storming my body were nothing short of incredible. I took a few moments to savor how tightly her walls gripped my cock and then I wrapped my arms around her and buried my face in her hair. I inhaled the scent of her shampoo. She arched her back and we were completely lost in the moment.

She was special in my mind, had always been and would always be.

"Dante, look at us in the mirror," she gasped, as I brutally pummeled her little pussy.

I turned my head and couldn't tear my gaze away from the image. We were perfect together. Her body fit like a hand in a glove to mine. I wanted to remember the way we looked forever.

I memorized the beautiful curvature of her back, the long length of her shapely legs, the flare of her hips, the curve of her neck, the bounce of her hair. I memorized it all. Every last detail.

My heart soared with every thrust into my beauty.

The erotic sounds of flesh slapping incessantly against flesh filled my ears and resounded in the room.

Then she was climaxing, her walls clenched tightly around my cock, and it spurred my own release. I came without holding back. I had found my safe harbor. I'd found home. I pumped her body with my seed until I had wrung out every last bit of pleasure. Until she collapsed against me. Gently, I lifted and put her on the little corner seat. I had never understood the need for it. Silently, I thanked my interior designer.

I kissed her gently and turned on the shower.

The water came cascading down on me. I turned my face up to it and shut my eyes.

"You're something to watch," she said dreamily from behind.

"I am?" I asked.

Her breasts, full, and perky were calling out to me once again to go over and suck hungrily on the pink peaks.

"Yeah," she replied as she reached out to run a hand down my body.

Smiling, I turned to retrieve the bottle of shampoo, squirting a few drops on my head and began to lather up.

"Come over here," I said.

"Nope. I just washed my hair," she said, shaking her head. "I don't want to be bald."

I smiled at her. I was happy. If I could be this way with her for the rest of my life I wouldn't ask for anything else.

"It's weird," she murmured. "But I feel so comfortable with you now. I never thought it could be like this with you, but the way you always speak your mind has brought my guard down. Being with you is like being instructed to add a cup of black coffee to your chocolate cake batter and thinking, Ugh ... this is not going to end well, but then being very pleasantly surprised because that cup of bitter coffee actually makes your cake even more chocolatey and wonderful. Now, I finally understand what Papa saw in you. Why he told me to trust you."

I couldn't stop smiling.

The more she spoke the more I smiled.

I must have looked like a love-struck fool, but I didn't care. I was home.

I was finally home.

Chapter 47
Zola

It was almost lunch when I awakened. I had dreamed of Sarah and Matthew. A confused dream that I couldn't remember properly, but I felt guilty for their deaths. Not so much for Sarah, especially if she had betrayed me, but definitely for Matthew. He had been tough, quiet, and kept to himself and I had felt reasonably safe in his presence. But then a single bullet shattered that all to pieces.

I wouldn't even be alive if not for Dante. I turned to look at him. A few weeks ago, I would have been hard-pressed to find anything favorable about him, but now his strength had become a pillar for me to lean on.

I watched him.

There was a regality about him that couldn't be denied. I couldn't help but also note his vulnerability. And if I looked even deeper, a strange innocence and purity. Like the lotus plant that grows in filth and yet its flowers rise above the mud, spotless and unsoiled.

When he was awake the force of his presence prevented me from seeing him as anything other than intimidating, but now, in his unguarded state, I could see traces of the man/boy I first met years ago. The deep urge to touch him arose but I didn't want to wake him.

A crazy thought occurred to me and I froze with fear. I don't know why I never thought of it before, because it was the most obvious thought. No one else had a bigger target painted on their back than Dante did.

Without thought my hand went to the strand of hair falling over his eyes.

His eyelashes fluttered in awareness and I could almost feel the change in his body.

"Sorry," I whispered. "Go back to sleep, don't mind me."

We looked at each other.

"Are you alright?" he asked. "How's your neck?"

"It's completely better."

"Then what causing the crease between your brows?" he asked.

"I was frowning?"

"Mmmm."

I got to the point. "Ugo wants to kill you. How can you remain so calm?"

He looked straight into my eyes and his voice was cool and detached.

"A man can die many times or he can die once. I decided long ago to die only once. I learned to make peace with the idea that in the blink of an eye, I could lose everything. Even my life. So, what's there to be scared of?"

I looked at him and could feel my heart rate picking up, a very clear indication I hadn't made peace with losing him whatsoever.

Chapter 48
Dante

I had a plan. It would be no small feat and the risk it carried was that Zola could lose me. If that happened, she was free game for Ugo, and he was sure to shred her to pieces. I was ready to die rather than remain with Ugo and now I was ready to kill to protect Zola.

Larry, my operations manager, walked into my office. I nodded towards one of the chairs in front of my desk and he parked himself in it.

"Seven employees quit today," he said. "And another eighteen applied for a sudden leave of absence."

I shrugged. "I'm surprised it's not more."

"If another murder happens, our operations will be in serious jeopardy, and I can imagine that it will be very difficult to recruit employees for their replacements."

"Another death will happen," I said. "It's only a matter of time. Ugo will be sure to make it happen to disorganize and humiliate me."

He seemed taken aback by what I said, but quickly

recovered and gave a suggestion. "Do you want to speak to them? I could arrange a conference meeting now."

"No," I shook my head. "The video is sure to leak out and then it'll be all over the news. I'll send a memo. What I need more than anything else at this time is very limited visibility. Remember that Zola is still technically missing. Detective Hudgens has been trying to get a hold of me all day and has threatened me with an arrest."

Larry's eyes widened. "Will he actually do that?"

"He can, but he won't. He's just playing the waiting game. He has nothing to lose and I have everything to lose. But if the next death happens, I will be immediately called in for questioning. They will have no proof, and anyway, they know it's not me so they won't hold me for too long."

He nodded in response.

It made me realize I needed to prepare Zola for this. I had to tell her about all the dangers we were facing so nothing would come as a surprise and she wouldn't be frightened or lose hope.

My secretary called to say, my lawyer, Foster, was outside. Larry left and she showed Foster in. I nodded at him as I picked up the phone and called Hudgens.

"Moretti!" he greeted with feigned chirpiness. "Ready to turn yourself in?"

"Yes," I replied. "You're going to arrest me soon anyway if anything else should go wrong so let's just get it over with now. I have a crisis to deal with in the company."

"Let me guess, people are quitting."

Of course, he already had that information and I was certain sooner or later it would get to the news as well after being sold to the highest bidder.

The Guardian

"You're silent," he said. "That can't be good. For you at least."

I ignored his immature taunts. "When do you want me there?"

"When do I want you here? Wow! You seem quite eager to get me off your back. How are you so sure I don't have what I need to keep you here for as long as I want?"

"If you have a valid reason to keep me there then I'm even more eager to come to see what it's all about."

"Well, does kidnapping a witness sound feasible to you?" he asked aggressively.

"Kidnapping? A witness? Does this mean that Miss Leone is still missing? There's no mention of this in the press."

At my very blatant threat, it was his turn to go quiet. Then he chuckled. "You have a sharp tongue, Moretti."

"How long do you think you can keep this away from the public?"

"Until I retrieve her. Here's what I propose, no matter how bad things get for your camp you don't have to get arrested. All you have to do is offer me an invitation to your office and we can discuss how we can get Zola back into witness protection."

My response was calm. "I don't know where she is."

"The guy your men left alive at the ambush scene. Remember him? Oh yes, he's already sung like a canary. He has sworn that a black SUV took her. With all this stacked against you, do you still want to hold on to her? You already have enough charges against you, Moretti. Even if you get cleared of this, kidnapping carries at least twenty years. I swear, if you don't help make my job easier, I will find a way to double that fucking sentence."

Talking to him was exhausting. "Do whatever you want, Hudgens. I don't know where she is."

And with that, I ended the call.

"What's the update?" Foster asked.

I smiled grimly. "Never let a good deed go unpunished. One of Ugo's guys that we left alive at the ambush site seems to have switched sides, and is now collaborating with the cops."

Foster scowled. "That's not good, but then again, he is one of Ugo's guys. His words aren't worth shit."

"Exactly," I replied.

"The girl ..." Larry started and I waited for this question. "You do have her, right?"

I nodded.

"That's not good," he said nervously.

"I'm not giving her back to them. That'll be the same as serving her up to Ugo on a silver platter. Hudgens's team is made up of incompetent fools."

"It could severely affect your case."

"I don't care," I said and I damn well didn't. Playing by the books never works. Not when you're dealing with monsters like Ugo.

Chapter 49
Zola

"Another employee died."

"What?" I turned around at Marie's voice, my heart in my throat. With a horrified look, she nudged her head toward the muted television set in the kitchen. I read the bold text scrolling across the bottom of the screen.

I caught the update that employees were quitting in the droves. I didn't know if this was an exaggeration or not, but it sounded troubling. Clearly, Dante must be well aware of this and occupied with finding a way to control it.

I forced myself to return to the peaches I was slicing up for jam.

I had seen Marie and another housekeeper carrying in a basket of fruits and couldn't help but beg to participate in preparing them. Making pastries and sweet condiments was a long-lost hobby that I had pushed aside for my career. I thought it would be a comforting thing to return to.

But the fragrant smells of the fruit and sugar cooking couldn't hold my attention. My mind was alive with worries. Uppermost was Dante's safety. Without him, everything would be pointless.

I waited impatiently until Dante returned home. I tried my best to hide the strain in my neck but being ever vigilant he caught it.

"It still hurts?" he asked.

I shook my head. "It's fine." I was more concerned about him. He looked exhausted. I rushed to him and gave him a tight hug.

He embraced me just as hard and I could feel the exhaustion and the stiffness of his body.

"You're back much earlier than I expected," I said.

He pulled away and nodded. Looking down at me he tenderly brushed my hair out of my eyes.

"I need to speak to you," he said and my nerves slightly tightened.

"Uh-oh, that doesn't sound good."

He smiled. "I think I'm going to be arrested. At least, I expect to be in a few hours. They don't know about this place so there's no point giving them the opportunity to find it so I'll be in my apartment in the city for a bit."

"Oh," I said, now thoroughly panicked.

"Why would you be- I mean ..." I couldn't string a sentence together.

"They're pretending they need me to cooperate with their investigation, but they'll be using it as a chance to try to extract some information about your whereabouts. They're getting desperate to find your location so they'll try to intimidate me as much as they can."

"How?" I asked.

"Doesn't matter," he said. "I've come back early to give

you a heads up and to explain the state of things. You're not to worry. We'll get through it."

I could do nothing but nod at his words, but then as I watched him rise to his feet and proceed to leave, I couldn't help but get up as well.

"What about me?" I asked, my heart pounding in my chest. "What can I do to help? I mean, shouldn't I surface and tell them you rescued me?"

He shook his head. "If you surface now, you're as good as dead ... and Matthew would have died for nothing."

Chapter 50
Dante

"They're here," Giotto said as he got off the phone. I didn't need the announcement. I could hear the sirens all around the building and with the force of it one would think they had come to pick up a terrorist.

I had expected the deliberate provocation. Was waiting for it even. If he thought he could intimidate me into giving up Zola he could think again. I took my time finishing my drink until eventually there was a loud knock and a bang on the door.

Giotto gave me a look and then went over to open it. I set the glass down and watched as a team with guns and of course, Detective Hudgens came in.

"Oh, you're waiting for us I see," he said, and I stared at the man that had always been a pain in the ass to me. He had never been a nail that I needed to pull out, but with his current eagerness and disturbances, his existence was beginning to grate on my nerves.

I rose to my feet.

"What's the point of all this? Were you expecting me to resist?"

He smiled. "You're not the most accommodating of men, Moretti," he said. "We had to be prepared." He looked at his men and a few came over with guns cocked and pointed at me as well as a pair of handcuffs. They turned me around and recited my Miranda rights.

"You could have made this much easier hours ago, Moretti," Hudgens came over to speak to me while the other men backed away. "Why do things always have to be so fucking hard with you mafia guys?"

I didn't have anything to say to this so after giving him a look that I hoped he was able to interpret for his own safety, I complied as they turned me around and led me out of the apartment.

Chapter 51
Zola

I was sitting at the lake before one of the most beautiful views I had ever encountered, yet all I could think about was Dante and how everything was falling apart and closing up around us.

And there was not a thing I could do about it.

All I could do was sit around being pampered to death and feeling guilty as hell for pushing him out to fight my battles. I wanted to provide the same degree of comfort and assurance to him that he was giving me, but this seemed impossible.

I spotted a familiar figure in the distance. Marie was coming with another platter of food.

"Thank you," I said as she set the platter down before me. On it were an assortment of crackers, fruits, nuts, some sort of Mexican fried snacks and dipping sauce.

"I'm going to get so fat if you keep feeding me like this," I said.

"It's just to take your mind off things," she said. "If your mouth is busy then perhaps your mind will give you a break as well."

I doubted her method would work but I smiled and reached forward for a blackberry. When I lifted my gaze to hers, I noticed she didn't appear to be at peace either.

"What is it?" I asked, searching her eyes desperately.

She forced a smile. "It's nothing. Mr. Moretti's lawyer just called."

I shot to my feet. "Why? Did he want to speak to me?"

"Yes, but he'll be coming over. He didn't want to tell you over the phone. Maybe Dante told him to do so before he was-"

She caught herself in time, but there was no way I was going to miss what she almost let slip out.

"Before he was what?" I demanded.

She pressed her lips together. "I'm sorry. I didn't mean to worry you, but ... he has never been arrested before."

"He's been arrested?" I croaked. My heart felt as if it had stopped in my chest.

She nodded gravely and I could see the sheen of moisture in her eyes.

I had to remind myself to stay calm. Dante had warned me about this. He had also insisted that he would be fine. There was no need for me to panic. But right now, I had to question if this was actually true, or if it was just another way he was protecting me.

I took a deep breath and impulsively hugged her. "He expected this, Marie. He said he'll be fine."

She nodded, but I could tell there was more she was withholding.

"What is it?"

"He was not arrested because of his case," she muttered.

"What do you mean?"

"He was arrested for kidnapping."

My eyes widened. "What? Kidnapping?"

She nodded worriedly.

I took a deep breath. Once again, he had warned me this was coming. That they would play dirty. The organization would do anything to absolve themselves of blame for my disappearance. They had decided to pin it on him instead. This was exactly the kind of mess that had haunted me so far. I knew there was no way in hell Dante was going to admit to anyone he had me because doing so was sure to inform Ugo as well.

It was a checkmate for Dante.

Just then we heard a call. I looked up to see one of the staff with a man in a suit heading over. I assumed it was Dante's lawyer and it brought me a deep sense of relief to see him. Marie took her leave while the lawyer introduced himself as Foster Fuentes and shook my hand. His palm was cool and soft and he seemed calm and professional. Unfortunately, that did very little to assure me. He did not care. He did not care the way my father did. He was an excellent lawyer being paid to defend his client. He was no more and no less.

He smiled smoothly at me. "Nice to finally meet you, Miss Leone."

"I just heard Dante was arrested."

A momentary look of surprise and annoyance crossed his face before he could hide it. "You saw it on the news?"

"No. Marie just informed me."

The Guardian

"Oh! Good," he said and smiled suavely. He was relieved I had not seen it on the news.

"How is he?" I asked anxiously. It was the only thing I wanted to know.

"He's fine. I'm here because he told me to personally come over and speak to you. He said he had already warned you that things could get complicated, but he expected you to still worry, so he sent me to assure you there is nothing to be worried about."

My eyebrows rose. "Nothing to worry about?"

"Absolutely," he said with great assurance. "I would have gotten him out already, but one of Ugo's men has turned informant, and as a result, I can't get him out before twenty-four hours elapse. But rest assured I will get him out. There is absolutely nothing to worry about."

His words should have comforted me, but something felt off. Wrong. I frowned. "So he'll be fine ..."

"Of course," he confirmed instantly, assertively, but I knew. He was not telling me the whole story. It was not as simple as he was making out. Dante was in danger.

"Well, then." He got to his feet. "I should be going. I'll call you tomorrow and give you an update. Don't worry you should be seeing him in no time."

"Alright," I said, and once again he gave me his hand. It was slightly sweaty. I watched him walk away until he disappeared out of sight.

One of Ugo's men had turned! That didn't sound like 'nothing to worry about'. That was a game changer.

Now, I was 100% certain Dante had only given me one of two pieces of the whole picture. No doubt he was doing it to protect me. I was beginning to realize he truly would do anything to protect me.

But I didn't want that.

I didn't want him to take on more risk because of me. Already, his business was affected, and now his personal safety was. While he was being at the government's pleasure, he didn't have his own protection service. He could be in danger. What if Ugo had his men inside the force? They had corrupted Sarah, what if they were others in the police force? I loved Dante too much to put him in danger. I couldn't lose him. Not him. Not now. I had to protect him with the same selfless dedication with which he protected me. I knew exactly what I must do. He won't like it, but this was my decision. I had only met her once, but I memorized her number. She was the person who had stood in once for Sarah. She had been kind to me and I liked her. I dialed her number.

"Detective Mellor?" I asked when her phone was answered.

"Yes," her voice was wary.

"It's me, Zola."

The line went completely silent for a few seconds. "Are you alright?" she asked urgently.

"Yeah," I said.

I heard a deep sigh of relief. "Thank God," she said. "They said Moretti had taken you, but I didn't know what to think."

"I'm very sorry about Matthew and Sarah," I said.

"There's no need to be. It's not your fault. We know the risk we take when we sign up. It was our job to protect you and we failed. Thank God for Moretti."

"Yeah," I said awkwardly. I wasn't sure how much I should tell her about Dante's involvement.

"You are with him now, aren't you?"

"I just wanted to ask a few questions," I said, evading her question. "I really don't know what's going on but I want to know enough so I can make an informed decision."

"What do you want to know?" she asked. "I'll tell you whatever I can."

"Okay. Is Dante in trouble?"

"I'm afraid so."

"Oh," I said.

"On top of kidnapping, I'm pretty sure they're planning to throw in tampering with witness testimony, obstruction of justice. The list could go on. You're meant to be testifying against his enemy so you're not exactly supposed to be in his custody. It could make your testimony completely unusable. You need to bring yourself in, otherwise, things could get a lot uglier for Moretti."

"I know."

"We can help you and we can help Moretti. All you need to do is come in."

I thought about this and had never felt more confused.

"I'll consider my options," I said. "And then I'll let you know."

"You only have a few hours at most, Zola," she said. "The window's closing up fast."

"Sure," I said and ended the call.

Chapter 52
Dante

"How is she?" I asked the moment Foster walked into the interrogation room.

"Doing good," he replied. "At least, she was when I spoke to her."

His words gave me no comfort and I lifted my wrist to look at my watch. "Fucking four more hours."

He nodded. "Hudgens is a chump. He knows he's not going to get anything out of you so why go through the trouble?"

"He's not trying to get anything out of me," I replied.

Foster paused for a moment and he looked up, the hot coffee in his cup had steamed his glasses. I looked at him with irritation. He was good, but he was no Marco Leone. Zola's father had foresight and an intuitive intelligence that was almost impossible to find in anyone else.

He set the cup down and cleaned his glasses with a white handkerchief.

At that moment, the door was pushed open, and Hudgens came in along with another stoic-faced agent. He dragged out a chair, turned it backward, and sat before us while the agent stood by the door and acted tough. I watched him closely and looked forward to the performance he was about to put on.

"How was your night?" he asked. "It's no county jail, but I think we did our best. No blankets, but you didn't need one, did you?"

I lifted my wrist and pretended to look at my watch.

"You're impatient to leave, I get it, but it's not going to be that easy for you."

"It is going to be that easy," Foster said.

Hudgens turned to him. "I'm in a lot more control here than you think."

Foster smiled. "Sure, that's why you had to fabricate some nonsense to keep my client here for twenty-four hours. We let that one slide so you could at least save some face, but any longer and you can kiss your career goodbye."

Hudgens feigned an exaggerated shiver. Then he stared at Foster menacingly. "You need to excuse us."

Foster smiled pleasantly and took a sip of his coffee. "Sorry, but you don't speak to my client without me being present."

"That wasn't a suggestion," Hudgens said before he turned to me and looked at me meaningfully.

I knew what was happening. I knew the kind of officer he was. I had encountered him so many times in the past and we had our dealings and I guess now was the time to speak off the books.

I locked eyes with Foster and gave a nod. He stared at me, his eyebrows furrowing into a frown, making it very clear he wasn't happy at all about being dismissed.

"Don't worry," I said. "It'll be fine."

He didn't like it, but he understood that he didn't have a choice so he silently got to his feet and took his leave. I returned my attention to Hudgens, and he smiled at me.

He switched off the tape recorder. "Let's talk off the record."

I could sense the trap from a mile away. "Nothing is ever off the record," I said, glancing at the hidden surveillance cameras in the corners of the room.

"Look," he said with fake friendliness. "We've had our run-ins several times in the past, but things have always been cordial between us. I'm hoping it can be the same this time around."

It was the same conversation over and over again and frankly, I was getting sick of it. He saw my irritation but still waited for a response.

"Loss was nothing to me back then. Only monetary but not this time around."

"What do you mean?" he asked eagerly. "There's more at stake? Like a person?"

"Yes," I replied.

His eyes glittered. "As far as I know you don't have any family. So ... it must mean ... a woman."

I stared at him and thought of the truth and falsehood in his words. "I did have a family. Marco Leone was my family, which is why the lie your organization is trying to put forward that I would do anything to hurt his daughter is so ridiculous."

"We never said you would hurt her," he said. "All we said was you might have kidnapped her."

He pushed his chair closer to me and stared deep into my eyes.

"I've always considered you an ally because you've always made things easy for me. Throw me another bone, will you? Let's both get out of this unscathed."

I stared right at him. "Can you guarantee her safety?"

He lifted his right hand and swore. "You have my word."

I smiled with amusement.

"You don't believe me?" he asked.

I had nothing else to say and knew that one slip of the tongue and he would officially be sending me into custody, so I kept my comments to myself.

"If you don't cooperate you will jeopardize your case. I'll make sure of that," he threatened. "But cooperate and I'll give you a way out. The DA will be itching to give you nothing less than twenty years, but I'll put in a good word and get you ten. Good behavior means you'll only do five years."

I turned to him then and shook my head in wonder. "You're trying to get an innocent man to take the fall?"

He laughed out loud. "Ha! Ha! Innocent man. Come on, Moretti. I didn't fall off the turnip truck yesterday. I know more about you than I know about my own son."

"In that case, you should know you're wasting your time right now."

The ringing of a cell phone reverberated in the room and I was happy for the reprieve. Listening to him was beginning to give me a headache.

His colleague, who had been silent all that time,

answered the phone, actually grunted into it, and then returned it to his pocket.

"There's news," he said.

Hudgens kept his gaze on me, a sick smile playing at the corner of his lips. "What news?"

"Leone's daughter," he said in a dull voice. "She's just been sighted going into her old apartment building about five minutes ago."

There was surprise in Hudgens's eyes at the information, but there was no way I could hide the shock and annoyance in mine.

"Jackpot," Hudgens gloated with delight.

Chapter 53
Zola
An hour earlier

I couldn't believe it had come to this.

I was waving a gun riotously at Dante's men, but they seemed unfazed even though they watched me closely, like hawks on prey. They were certain I was either bluffing or didn't even know my gun was without bullets. Giotto had removed them before giving it to me. What they didn't know was that I had found some in Dante's room.

In order to let them know I wasn't joking around, I turned around away from all the people present and fired the gun. It resounded in the air like a bomb, almost forcing me to cover my ears with the unexpected blast. One of the female staff screamed, but all I could think of was the hole I'd put in Dante's gorgeous wall.

Anyhow, that's solved my problem. The men no longer looked unfazed. I saw their shared looks of concern.

"Get out of my way," I shouted wildly.

"Calm down, Miss Leone, please. Why not talk to the boss first, huh? Let him come home. What can it hurt to wait a little ... hmmm?"

I shook my head. "No, my mind is made up. If you all don't get out of my way, I'm going to shoot. Starting with you."

"You're making a mistake, Miss Leone. This is not a good idea. You are safe here. You won't be out there."

"I said, get out of the way."

"The boss will be angry with us if we let you go."

'I swear I will shoot you if you don't," I warned.

Reluctantly, they stepped out of the way and I ran to the car in the garage that responded to the key fob in my shaking hand. I had just opened the door when a vehicle screeched to a stop in front of me.

"Get in," the man who had tried to persuade me said. "We'll take you where you want to go. You can't go on your own. It's too dangerous."

I hesitated. I didn't trust them. I didn't trust that they didn't have a trick against me up their sleeve.

"That car you're trying to steal has a jamming mechanism," the guy in the passenger seat said in a thick New York Bronx accent. "It's not going to start unless we decide to let it."

I stared at him in frustration. It looked like I didn't have a choice so I got into the SUV and we drove away.

"Take me to my former apartment please," I said and they complied without any arguments.

I kept the gun pointed towards the front and my eyes on the two men via the rearview mirror. I felt terrible. They had saved my life and protected me, but I knew of no other way. If everything worked out the way I planned I would tell them that they were never in any danger. There had only been one bullet in the chamber and I had fired it at the wall.

When we arrived, I waved the gun at them again. I was sure they would try to stop me but they didn't. Instead, they jumped out and fanned out around the car, their eyes looking all around for signs of danger. I got out of the car and hurried over to my apartment. I didn't stop until I got to the elevator. I put the gun in the pocket of my jacket and rode the elevator up to the twelfth floor. I knew Dante would be furious with me, but by my reckoning, my plan carried less risk.

"This will help Dante," I whispered to myself as the elevator doors slid open. I ran towards my apartment. I had no keys so I rang the doorbell. The door was pulled open, and Antoine stood before me. Behind him, I could see Detective Mellor.

He looked at me, shock in his eyes, and then he pulled me in for a huge hug. My mind registered the familiar warmth and I couldn't help but completely sink into it.

"They said you had been kidnapped?" he accused and I held onto him even tighter.

"I'm sorry," I apologized.

He pulled away and looked at me with a confused expression. "For what?"

"For dragging you into my mess. I couldn't think of where else to meet her."

He made a face. "Ugh! She's horrible. Imagine having to sleep with that."

My eyes widened. "Hush," I whispered.

"Zola," Detective Mellor called.

"Yeah, I'm here," I said and moved into the apartment.

"Don't leave without talking to me first," Antoine said just before he disappeared into his bedroom.

I stopped in the middle of the place that used to be as familiar to me as breathing, but now it seemed so strange to me, it was as if I'd never lived here. For one it seemed incredibly small and way too bright. Had it really always been so bright?

"I'm happy you contacted me," Detective Mellor got to her feet.

"Please sit down," I said.

She smiled and did as I had asked.

"Do you want something to drink?"

"Some water will be fine," she said.

I retrieved a bottle from the refrigerator.

"With ice and lemon?" I asked.

"Those would be nice. Thank you."

When it was ready I brought it to her. In another glass, I had Antoine's famous persimmon iced tea for myself. She acted like she didn't have a single care in the world and suddenly, I knew I'd made a mistake. I swallowed.

"You wouldn't let me leave here even if I wanted to, would you?" I asked.

She shook her head and smiled. "No. You'll either leave here as a participant of the program or in handcuffs."

"For what?"

She shrugged. "We'll figure something out, but we need you in our custody and not where Ugo can easily reach you."

I was so incredibly annoyed to hear that bastard's name.

"Moretti isn't aware you've left ... is he?"

"I never said he had me."

She chuckled softly. "Understood. He's sure to be pissed though."

I drained my glass, eager to move on to the matter at hand. "So ... how are we going to do this?"

"It's just like we discussed," she replied. "We'll take you into custody as a part of the program. The story will be that you managed to escape from the crash and returned to a place familiar to you and then you called us to come pick you up. Stricter measures will be put in place to protect you."

"And if Ugo should attack me again?" I asked.

"We'll be more vigilant this time around, trust me," she said. "We already lost two of the best, so like I told you on the phone this is no longer just about Moretti. Ugo has severely offended us as well and we will not let him get off. This is not Mexico where you can get off with blatantly attacking the police force. He will be brought to justice. You are very much a key witness in Moretti's case as you are in Matthew's and Sarah's. By the end of all this, there will be no prison time for Ugo. He'll face the death penalty and I'll make sure of it."

At the bitterness and conviction in her tone, I felt myself relax just a little bit more. "Okay," I said. "I'm ready."

Just then my phone began to ring and I was almost afraid to look down at it. I knew exactly who it was, but I didn't have the courage to check or even to respond. I knew he would be furious with me.

"What's happening to Dante right now? Has he been released?"

"He should have been," she said. "Isn't he the one trying to call you?"

At her words, I pulled the phone out of my pocket. I couldn't postpone talking to him especially since I would be taken into custody by the U.S. Marshals soon.

I got up and left the room. I stood at the door to my former room but was unable to go in. Instead, I headed over to the bathroom and shut the door behind me.

I pressed the phone to my ear and for a moment I doubted he was on the other end of the line. There was nothing but silence. He was fuming, but I had to do what was best for both of us. Not just me, but him too. What was the use of me being alive if he was dead?

"I'm sorry," I apologized.

"Why?" His voice was low and controlled, but I didn't think if he had yelled, I would have felt his anger any more intensely.

"I think it's best," I said. "I couldn't let them fabricate some vile charges and pin them on you. Given your background, a jury is more likely to convict you than not."

He was so disappointed and angry with me he couldn't even speak.

"Dante," my voice softened. Tears burned in my eyes.

"You don't understand anything," he said harshly. "You've given away the only winning card I had."

I thought of him washing my hair and hot tears began streaming uncontrollably down my face. My heart hurt. All the warmth and joy I'd felt, I felt as if I'd killed it.

"Why couldn't you have trusted me just once?" he whispered.

I could have dealt with him raging and livid, even

sarcastic and indifferent, but that defeated, hoarse whisper. It broke me. I felt so distraught I nearly blurted out that I loved him and couldn't bear to see him suffer even for one moment.

Then I heard Detective Mellor call out to me and it snapped me out of my shallow pity party. I had taken this painful decision because I loved him and wanted to do something truly selfless for him, and now I must face the consequences, whatever they may be.

"I'll be fine," I said. "I wasn't kidnapped by you and I'll be sure to let them know. I won't let them pin that on you. Please take care of yourself, Dante."

As I ended the call and switched off my phone, I felt sick. I had defeated him. No one could have defeated that magnificent avenging angel, but me. I bowed my head with sadness. The familiar crushing pain of loss gripping every corner of my chest came back with a vengeance.

There was nothing I could do but welcome it back as an old friend. I returned to the living room and saw that two more men had arrived. Were they U.S. Marshalls? They had watchful eyes, but they nodded at me politely. Detective Mellor was on the phone with her back to me and facing the window, but she turned around when she heard me return.

She put the phone away and smiled at me. "Are you ready to leave?"

I looked at the two burly men. "They're from the U.S. Marshalls, right?"

"Of course," she confirmed.

I was led to the underground parking lot and put into their SUV and soon, we were on our way. Detective Mellor came with us which I found peculiar but I couldn't really say anything. In the past, she never came with Matthew and Sarah, but perhaps because of the ambush they were taking things more seriously. My only wish was that wherever they were taking me would be safe enough.

Chapter 54
Dante

"They shouldn't have let her go," I muttered tiredly. I felt drained of all strength. I felt betrayed by my men who agreed to take her to the apartment, betrayed by her that she didn't trust me. I couldn't understand why she would risk her life. What was she trying to prove? Of all the mule-headed idiotic things to do ...

"Maybe it's for the best," Foster said.

I glared at him.

"You hired me to defend you. Antagonizing the police was a bad strategy. Not having her in your custody will make your case more winnable," he explained.

I looked away from him.

"Anyway, after the damage to their reputation, I'm pretty sure they will be extra vigilant in protecting her now."

I listened to his words but it was as though we were on two different worlds. Didn't he understand? I wasn't going to walk away. I was going to get her back and it was going to be so much harder. I picked up my phone again and called Giotto.

"You have eyes on her, right?" I asked.

"Yes, Boss."

"Whatever you do, don't lose her. They know we'll tail them so ensure you don't lose them. Where are the guys that were looking after her roommate?"

"They're still there," he replied.

"Have them join you in trailing Zola from a different direction if possible. We can't lose her. No matter what."

I ended the call and leaned into the seat completely drained of strength but too terrified to fall asleep.

"You should get some rest," Foster said.

I considered his suggestion and then opened my eyes to see Luca watching me from the rearview mirror. He was waiting for instructions. A few minutes later, I made up my mind.

"No," I replied. "No rest."

"To the office then?"

I stared out of the window at the police station we had just exited. "No, let's go after them."

The car was silent for a little while but then Luca put the car into motion.

"What do you mean by go after them?" Larry asked.

"Zola and the U.S. Marshals," I replied. "Ugo is smarter than the average mafia boss and extremely strategic. If I have this many eyes on her then no doubt he has something cunning up his sleeve so I can't take any risk. I can't just go back to sit and wait either, so let's go after them."

The Guardian

Foster looked unhappy, but I ignored his sulkiness until we came to our first intersection.

"You're welcome to get off here." I turned to him. "It might get dangerous. I'll contact you later."

He gave this a thought while looking ahead. "No," he refused. "I'll go."

Chapter 55
Zola

We were leaving the city of New York and heading toward the outskirts and slowly I was becoming even less familiar with my surroundings. We were going toward Westchester County, but that was all I could tell. Something bothered me. What had me alarmed was the fact more security wasn't present. It was only the two guys in front and Detective Mellor seated by my side and none of them were speaking to each other. Detective Mellor had been courteous with Matthew and Sarah, but now she didn't seem very familiar or friendly to the men in front. Were they just being somber and vigilant because of Matthew and Sarah's passing?

Regardless, I felt uncomfortable, and I didn't know what to attribute it to. Something was wrong. I felt it in my bones.

"Where are we going?" I asked Detective Mellor.

"Don't worry. We'll be there soon," she said with a smile, but I'd never seen her smile like that before, and it made my skin tingle. Something was definitely wrong.

"Are you alright?" she asked.

I managed a tight smile and nodded.

She turned to stare outside the window and I did the same. I recalled I still had my phone on me. I was tempted to call Dante and tell him where we were, but something about Detective Mellor made me think I shouldn't do it in front of her.

We pulled into a gas station. The driver got out and began filling the gas tank while the man in the passenger seat stayed in the SUV.

"I'm going to get something to drink. Want to come with me?" Detective Mellor asked.

"No," I said instinctively.

"Suit yourself," she said and got out.

I watched as she walked towards the store. I knew I had to call Dante in private. Before I could talk myself out of it, I pushed the door open and went after her.

She looked behind her, saw me and gave me a peculiar look.

"I'm a bit hungry," I said.

She forced a smile, but it wasn't as friendly as it once was. My skin began to tingle as I headed over to the fridge to get a bottle of water.

As I pretended to stare through the glass at the multiple choices, I surreptitiously pulled out my phone and started to dial his number. It began to ring and I put the phone to my ear, but a disapproving voice behind me made me nearly jump out of my skin.

"What do you think you're doing?"

I spun around and stared at Detective Mellor. She looked very displeased.

"Um ... I wanted to make a quick call."

"You can't do that," she snapped.

"I can't? Why not? We're not at the safe house yet."

"It doesn't matter," she said. "From the moment we left your apartment you're not allowed to be in contact with anyone, especially Moretti."

She came forward and snatched the phone from me. For a couple of seconds, I was so shocked I just stood there like a statue.

"Hey!" I called out, but she didn't respond.

She just kept going and I had no choice but to run after her. She disappeared into a hallway, and I immediately assumed she was going to destroy my phone in the toilet, so I ran after her.

"Detective Mellor!" I called out desperately, but there was no one in the hallway. It was dim, illuminated only by the light from the store.

"Detective Mellor!" I called again, but there was no response. Sudden and paralyzing fear filled my chest and I immediately began to back away. I turned around to run and slammed straight into what could have been a huge boulder. But it was no boulder. It was a hulking man. The impact jarred up my spine and sent me flying to the floor. I hit my head and literally saw stars. For a few seconds, amidst the blinding pain, I had no idea where I was or what was happening. I raised my head and felt something wet trickling down my neck.

Blood. My blood.

The details didn't matter, but I knew for sure. I had made a terrible mistake. I had trusted the wrong person. Dante was right. Without him, I was dead meat.

I tried to get up.

I tried to fight the pain and the blackness, but it was impossible. After I tried to pull my body up and stand, I realized I couldn't. My legs felt like jelly. All I could do was cower in a fetal position.

"Dante," my heart breathed as I squeezed my eyes shut. In my head came images of him washing and drying my hair in London in the warm yellow light of the bedside lamps. How beautiful it had been. Oh, if only I could go back. I love you, Dante. I really, really love you.

Then everything went dark.

Chapter 56
Dante

I looked at the ringing phone in my hand in surprise. A call from her? How was that possible? I expected them to have confiscated her phone by now.

I immediately tried to take the call, but even as I hit accept the call was cut off. I went on high alert instantly. This was not good. I tried calling back, but the call went directly to voicemail.

Fuck! Fuck! Fuck!

I called Giotto.

"Where are they?" I asked urgently.

"Bedford," he replied. "They're in a gas station."

"Who's they?" I asked.

"She went in with the woman, but the guys are hanging around outside."

"Send me their exact location," I ordered. When he did I realized we were only about ten minutes away from them. "Alright, watch her closely and tell me the second she comes out of the store. I'll be waiting."

"Got it, Boss," he said and ended the call.

The Guardian

A few minutes passed and there was no response. I called Giotto back again.

"What's going on?" I asked.

"They're not out of the store yet."

I knew instantly. It was a trap. "What do you mean they're not out of the store? How long has it been since they stopped there?"

"About ten minutes."

"She's fucking gone," I shouted. I heard Giotto throw the phone down and dash out of the car and start running on the asphalt.

"Fucking step on it," I yelled impatiently at Luca. My driver obeyed instantly and the tires screeched as he accelerated to a crazy speed. A few minutes later another phone call came through from Giotto.

"Where the hell is she?" I roared

"Boss, I went in and ..."

My heart stopped in my chest. "And what?"

"There is no trace of her. The detective came out though and we're tailing them right now, but they're now aware of us."

"Why the fuck are you tailing them when she's not in the car?"

I cut the connection. Before the car had even come to a stop at the gas station, I was already out of it. Like a madman, I ran in, grabbed the attendant, and pressed my gun to his head.

"Where is she?" I asked, but he threw down his phone and raised his hands in the air.

His eyes were wide with terror. "Where is who?"

It was obvious the hapless kid knew nothing. I released

him and looked around for the back exit. I found the hallway and ran down it. On the floor, I saw blood. Quickly, I sped toward the back door. It was unlocked. I pushed it and was out into an empty space. There were a few chairs and empty beer cans next to them. It was late evening and there was no one around. I had come to terms with what had happened.

"Check the dumpster," I said to my men.

One of them hurried to look. "There's nothing here."

I felt my knees give way and I dropped to the ground. My fist hit the ground repeatedly. I wanted to roar with frustration.

I had failed.

I had failed her.

And I had failed Marco.

Chapter 57
Zola

I came to in pain and complete blackness. The absence of any light was terrifying.

But it was the incredible cold that got me. It seemed to have infiltrated my very bones and turned them to ice. My teeth were chattering and my body shivered uncontrollably. I didn't think I was tied up, but it didn't matter because I couldn't move. I knew I couldn't survive this much longer.

The smell of something meaty in the frozen air and the hum of a motor made me think I was in some kind of walk-in freezer.

In the haze of pain, cold, and despair, Dante's face when I had stayed too long underwater in his pool came into my head.

I remembered the vulnerability I had seen in his eyes. It had been poignant then, but now I realized if I was unable to survive this he would be left alone. I felt my throat close up with emotion at the very real probability I might die. My great sacrifice had come to nothing.

All I had done was disappoint him.

My head ached and it hurt even to cry, but I closed my eyes and felt the hot tears cool as they rolled down my cheeks. I couldn't tell how much time passed. I was so cold I felt myself losing consciousness. I knew then I was dying in a freezer with slabs of meat.

I tried to fight the darkness that was descending, but it was getting harder and harder. The darkness seemed soft and welcoming. An escape from the merciless cold. My eyes fluttered and closed.

In the distance, I could hear some faint voices, but it was impossible to make out what they were saying. But it seemed as if they were calling to me. Then I heard my father's loving voice say, "No. It's not time yet, *bella mia*."

A sound so loud, it was like thunder, filled the air, and a shaft of piercing bright light hit me and burned my eyes. I screamed. Someone had opened the door. A wave of warmth blew over my frozen body. I heard gruff men's voices. They were speaking Italian. Why did my father never teach me to speak it? I wished he had. My eyes became more accustomed to the light. I squinted and saw metal drums on the floor and huge pig carcasses stripped of skin hanging from ceiling hooks.

I wondered what was in the metal drums and felt so disgusted I felt the urge to puke. The stench seemed unbearable now that my brain registered what it was.

Rough hands picked me up and carried me away. I tried to speak, but no words would come out. I was still shivering uncontrollably. There was laughter and then I was deposited into the back of a large truck. The doors were closed behind me.

The engine roared into life and the truck began to move.

Flattening my hands against the floor I tried to pull myself up. After exerting such an excruciating effort, I was able to slightly lift up my upper body. Unfortunately, the vehicle came to a stop and I lost my balance and fell back to the floor.

Then we were moving again and I wondered where I was being taken to.

Chapter 58
Dante

So it was not Sarah who was the dirty cop, but Lisa Mellor.

I picked up my ringing phone and heard Detective Hudgens's sheepish voice.

"Any updates?" he asked.

"Shouldn't I be asking you that?"

"I don't know what else to tell you-" he said.

I ended the call and threw the phone across the table. Talking to him was a useless waste of time.

My foot was tapping against the floor. I looked at my watch. I picked up my phone once again and placed a call.

"What's the location of the boy right now?" I asked, and the response came.

"He's still in school, but his bodyguards are outside."

There was no other choice. Ugo left me with no other choice.

"Take the boy," I said.

"Today?"

"Yes," I replied.

"Yes, Boss," came the response and I set the phone down and sat at my desk to wait. One hour later I received a phone call.

I looked at the number. Unknown. I picked it up.

"I understand you had to get my attention. And it worked. It was good. You did it promptly as well, but you won't get away with it," Ugo said. His voice was low and cold, but I could feel the fury pulsating through it.

My lips twisted into an ugly smile. "I already did. If you hurt one hair on her head you can say goodbye to him right now."

"Only a fool plays chicken with me. Do you really think I won't go further than you? Hmmm? That even though you have my only child, my pride and joy, my five-year-old son, who I'd carefully hidden away in Matera, I will hack Leone's daughter to pieces and send the pieces one by one to you. How would you feel, Dante? To receive a toe, a thumb, a hand, a whole arm, a severed bloody head ..."

I felt the first prick of fear. God, I'd forgotten what a monster he was. Then I told myself he was bluffing. Of course, he wanted his only son back. Who would give up their son for the sake of an old feud?

"So, are you ready to play my old friend?" he drawled. "I'd love to see just how fearless you've become over the years. If I remember correctly, gore was difficult for you to stomach. You couldn't even drink a glass of piss, but if you're ready, I am."

"You understand, don't you, that her death automatically means yours as well as everyone you care about. It doesn't have to be that way. All I want is a straight exchange. Her life for his."

He laughed softly. "How I miss having you around …"

He was enjoying this too much. My grip tightened around my phone, but I forced myself to keep my cool and kept my voice firm. "Where can I pick her up?"

"Not so fast." He chuckled. "I haven't decided if you get to see her again. Now that I know just how much she means to you, I need a little time to think this over."

I couldn't believe him. "Your son or her? Really? These are your considerations?"

"You know me," he said.

"Yes, yes, I do. People mean absolutely nothing to you. It appears not even your own flesh and blood do."

"You're not going to kill my son," he scoffed. "We both know it so quit the ridiculous tough talk. I'll contact you when I have made up my mind on how to make the exchange."

And with that, the call came to an end.

I got to my feet, restless and unable to remain still. It had all been fruitless. All efforts to get to her and determine her location had been fruitless and it was driving me crazy. I didn't know what to do anymore and neither could I contain it for one more moment. I felt suffocated. I swung my arm and phone at the wall. It hit with such force that it shattered into tiny pieces. I watched the pieces fly apart, and words popped into my head.

"Not if but when everything falls to pieces, call me. If you contact me before that moment I won't respond. Come to me only when you are ready to completely get rid of Ugo."

I turned around to meet Giotto's gaze. "Do you know Tommy the Blade?"

His eyes slightly widened. "One of Ugo's underbosses."

"I need to speak to him. Now."

"I'll get you his phone number, Boss," he said and strode out of the room.

Chapter 59
Dante

"I'm going to assume you remember my stipulation about contacting me," Tommy said.

His voice was familiar though it seemed deeper than I remembered. It was twelve years since I'd last spoken to him or seen him but still, I would never forget the man who had nearly beaten me to death after my first altercation as a recruit with the *famila*.

"I do. Do you still mean what you said?"

"Yes, I never say what I don't mean."

"You know why I'm calling, don't you?"

"Yes, but the timing is wrong. This is the worst possible time to fight him. He is on high alert."

"Well, that's where I come in," I said. "You don't have to fight. All that I'm asking is that you get her back to me safe and sound, and I'll take care of him for you."

He went quiet and I waited to hear what he'd say. When he responded, I wasn't surprised one bit by his words.

"The way I see it, I don't have to do anything at all.

The Guardian

You've been at each other's throats since you were seventeen. The way I see it neither of you will be left standing and I'll be free anyway. Why bother getting my hands dirty?"

"Because you owe me," I replied.

"Nah, I don't. Owing someone comes from asking for help. I never asked for your help."

"And yet I graciously extended my hand to you when Ugo didn't."

"You're no different from him, are you? Wanting to collect your favor twelve years later."

"Say what you want about me. The fact remains I saved your family. I heard about your situation and I took care of things for you. Meanwhile, the man you gave everything up for refused ... even when you begged."

The very real possibility of losing Zola or having her hurt was frightening to me.

"What do you need from me exactly?" Tommy asked.

I briefly shut my eyes. "I've told you. Keep her safe for me."

"That's too vague a request. No, I can't do that."

"Do you know where she is?"

"I could find out."

"Please do. That's all I need."

Another long moment of silence ensued before he responded. "You know that he's going to find out it was me, right?"

"Don't worry, he won't be alive long enough to confront you about it."

"That better be the case," he said and abruptly ended the call.

Chapter 60
Zola

I was taken to a high-end townhouse in Greenwich Village. I had expected them to take me out of state and to a place I would probably never be found, instead, they had returned me to the city.

The door was pulled open by an unsmiling woman. I was led in, wet and shivering and filthy as hell.

The woman glanced at me with a disgusted look. I didn't need a mirror to know I looked very akin to something from a horror show. I could feel it with every fiber of my being. She communicated with the three men in rapid-fire Italian and they responded rudely and angrily. Shaking her head she walked away without a backwards glance.

The men followed her and I was left standing there alone, a bloodied, broken mess. My heart was beating fast in my chest. I turned to look at the front door. It was unlocked. It could be the only opportunity I got to escape.

"I wouldn't bother," a man's voice said sarcastically.

I whirled around and saw two men walking towards me. I instantly recognized one of them as my father's killer, Ugo.

God, how I hated him. He looked older than the photos the media were using and more sinister. His eyes were black and dead and his cold gaze settled on me as he approached. The other man stayed back and watched me expressionlessly.

"Please follow me," Ugo instructed and began walking further into the house.

I took one look at the nasty face and the folded arms of the other man and followed Ugo. The door shut behind us as the other man exited and left me alone with my enemy. He smiled suddenly, and to my astonishment began to behave in the way a well-to-do uncle welcoming his niece whom he'd not seen for some time would, rather than a mobster handling someone he had kidnapped.

"What a pleasure. It has been too long, Zola, my dear," he murmured affectionately.

I felt as if I was dreaming. Was this the feared man who killed my father? I nudged my tied arms toward him. "Can someone take these off, please? I'm in pain."

He studied my appearance and something like compassion showed in his face. "Yes, I imagine you must be, but I'm afraid, for now, I think it's best that we keep them on. So there are no surprises, you do understand, don't you?" He paused and smiled again, but it never reached his dead eyes.

"I promise, I won't cause any trouble," I said.

"Are you and Dante lovers?"

His question shocked me, but I tried not to show it. "Are you really expecting me to answer questions when I'm in this state?"

"Hmm," he said. "You're right. How inhospitable of me." He pressed a button on his intercom. "Francesca, could you please take care of Zola here, she's had a very hard day. Ensure she has a bath and some food. And get Doctor Falconi to give her a quick check."

Almost immediately the woman who had scolded the men earlier came in.

"Come with me," she said coldly and left the room. As soon as we were out of the room, she grabbed my arm and pulled me roughly through a corridor and down a set of stairs.

If I had harbored any thoughts that I was going to be treated well from now on, her surprisingly strong and rough hands showed me how mistaken I was. I was sure Ugo heard my struggling and fighting against being mistreated, but it was probably exactly what he wanted her to do.

I was unceremoniously thrown into a tiny bedroom and the door locked behind me. It was a plain room with a narrow wooden bed with a thin mattress on it, a metal toilet and a small sink. And that was it. I was too exhausted to make it to the bed so I just lay where I had fallen.

A little while later the door was pushed open and a burly man with a massive chest and large biceps in his late forties or fifties appeared. When he stepped aside, I saw another man with a stethoscope hanging around his neck behind him. Obviously, the doctor Ugo had spoken of.

The burly man led the doctor forward, then pulled a gun out.

"He's gonna check you," he said, gesturing toward the doctor. "Any sudden movements and I'll blow your head off."

I watched as the doctor knelt down beside me and set his kit down before him. I couldn't understand why they would tend to my injuries, but they were ready to blow my head off if I made a 'wrong move.' It all seemed so ludicrous.

"You're all scared, aren't you?" I asked.

Neither man responded to my taunt.

"You don't really dare to hurt me because of Dante. Kidnapping me is just to force his hand ... to make him do whatever you want ..."

The doctor checked the injuries on the back of my head, which hurt like crazy, and then he got to his feet.

"She'll need her wound cleaned and several stitches."

"Well, get to work then," the man said.

The doctor looked me in the eye for the first time. I could see that he was frightened and would have preferred not to be there. "Can you make it to the bed?"

My entire body was killing me, especially my head, and I wasn't stupid enough to not want relief. I had to find a way to survive this. I stood and stumbled towards the bed.

The doctor inspected my head and cleaned the wound, which caused me to wince. He got up and turned to the burly man. "I need a razor. I need to shave a part of her hair off."

"If you go and ask Francesca, she'll give it to you," the burly man said.

The doctor nodded and walked out. Something about the burly guy was incredibly intimidating.

"Have you worked with Ugo long?" I asked, and just as I expected, he didn't answer. Instead, he seemed to be listening to the doctor's footsteps.

"Why do you do this job? Is it because of the money? Is the money irresistible?"

He turned to stare at the door. "You sure do talk a lot."

"That's because I'm nervous. Hey, what are you doing?" I asked in a panic because he was advancing on me.

I tried to sit up to face him, but the pain immediately stopped me. I cried out at the pain coming from everywhere, but he did not strike me. Instead, he did something that shocked me. He pulled out a phone from his pocket and handed it over to me. I looked at the black thing as though it was a trap and then stared back up at him.

"You have twenty seconds," he muttered.

"What?" I exclaimed. Was he allowing me to call Dante? The fact I would be able to talk to Dante in any shape or form seemed way too good to be true.

"Fifteen seconds," he said, and there was no more time to waste.

I grabbed the phone from him and began dialing Dante's number. I kept my gaze on the burly man who had turned to stare at the door. I could hardly believe this was actually happening. Then Dante's voice came into my ear.

"Hello?"

Tears rushed into my eyes and I opened my mouth to speak, but no words would come out.

"Are you alright?" Dante asked urgently.

A sobbing sound came out of my mouth.

"Please give the phone to Tommy, sweetheart."

I handed the phone over. The man looked at it, then at me with such disdain that I suspected he would have preferred to shoot me. He walked away toward the door without a word.

"Ten seconds," he said.

I returned the phone to my ear.

"Where are you?" Dante asked.

"We're in the city. It looks like Greenwich. There are townhouses all over ... cobblestone streets. Um ..."

"What else?"

"I don't ..." I tried to think but a headache surged like a demon, perhaps fueled by my panic, and I could no longer think."

"That's it. Toss me the phone," Tommy said.

"Dante ... I'm-"

"I'll find you," he said. "I promise. I swear."

"I'm sorry. I'm so sorry," I whispered.

"Don't be. Stay strong," he said quietly.

My heart swelled with emotion, but before I could say another word, I heard a growl from across the room.

"Pass the fucking phone or we're both dead."

I didn't need to be warned again. I tossed the phone to him, and he caught it. Then he paused for a second and put it to his ear.

"We're even now." Then he ended the call and I heard the doctor's footsteps in the corridor.

Chapter 61
Dante

When the phone went dead I hurried to the door, yanked it open, and yelled as I hurried through the hallway.

"Giotto! Giotto!"

He appeared at the end of the hallway.

"Inform Andrea and the others right now. I need backup. Get my car."

I tossed him the keys and went back into my office to grab my gun and phone, by the time I had opened my front door my Range Rover was waiting outside.

I went over to the driver's seat to pull the door open, and Giotto immediately jumped out. I heard the second vehicle behind us starting, and in no time we were zooming out of the compound.

I wasn't sure exactly where she was. I searched my memories back to my days with him. Ugo didn't own a townhouse in the city then, but this could be a recent purchase. He would take her to a place most of his men didn't know about. By the time we arrived in Manhattan, I still didn't have a clue and I was forced to call the one person that I would have preferred not to. What if he insisted on interfering?

Detective Hudgens picked up on the second ring. "Are you calling to return our witness to us?"

"Does Ugo have any homes in the city?" I asked.

He paused for a moment and then he replied. "Why do you need that information? And why would I give it to you?"

"Because he has Zola and I'm heading over there right now."

"Are you out of your fucking mind?"

"No, I'm trying to get to her because he'll fucking kill her." I was irritated by his questions. It made me want to smash the phone to pieces.

"Um, we'll search for this and get back to you. Thanks for the tip. In the meantime, I need you to wait till you hear from us and not do anything rash. We'll handle this."

I slammed my fist on the steering wheel. I knew he was going to do this to me. "Stop being stupid, Hudgens. If he kills her before you get to her, imagine the scandal. You could even lose your job. Let me do it. I know him. I know how he operates. This way we both get what we want."

He paused, then sighed. "I'll find where she is and-"

"I'll call you back in ten minutes," I said and ended the call.

I could feel Giotto's gaze turn to me. He'd probably never seen me so riled up. I went as far as Greenwich Village, and then I had to stop because I didn't have any clue where to go, and I didn't want any delays if I had to cross Brooklyn Bridge. Ten minutes was up so I called Hudgens once again.

"What's the address?" I asked.

"This is off the record," he said.

"Sure, whatever."

"He has a property in Greenwich Village and that puts us forty-five minutes away without traffic. Too far to get there quickly. How far away are you?"

"Ten," I replied. "Give me the full address?"

He gave it to me and I repeated it aloud so that Giotto could hear it and key it into the GPS system.

"Don't do anything rash. This is-," Hudgens started to say but I ended the call and threw the phone aside.

Chapter 62
Zola

The night was quiet, quieter than I ever thought London could be, which if I was not in my situation, I would have found incredibly fascinating. From time to time, I would hear an occasional yell from streets away or shared laughter, and the low buzz of vehicles in the distance. Everything seemed far away and muffled, and it was an eerie sort of peace.

With every minute that passed, I felt as though I was aging ten years. I didn't know what to expect beyond the fact that Dante was possibly coming for me, but apart from that, I knew absolutely nothing. I was filthy and exhausted, and even when I lay down on the hard bed, there was no rest.

I thought of Dante and of the fact he was on his way, I prayed with all of my heart that he would be safe. Then I shut my eyes and tried to just rest so that when the time came, I would be able to act quickly and with great strength.

I had not eaten for hours and I knew having some food

in my system would help, but with no one offering, I had absolutely no appetite anyway.

About ten minutes later, the door was unlocked and pushed open.

"The boss wants to see you," Francesca said. "Someone will be here in a little while to take you to him, so be ready." She shook her head disapprovingly. "Wash your face or something. You look terrible."

She went out and locked the door.

I wasn't in a beauty contest and had absolutely no interest in making myself more presentable so I did nothing. After a few minutes, the door was unlocked and opened by one of his stoic-faced men standing at the door. I sat up, my heart rate quickening. He swung his head to the side, and the message was clear. I was to step out of the room with him.

I stood and followed him up the stairs. By the time I arrived at the ground floor, I could hear faint voices in conversation coming from different parts of the house. It looked like the house had become a hub of activity. I was led back to Ugo's office.

Ugo was behind his huge mahogany desk. He smiled and leaned into his leather chair. I didn't return the smile.

"You're quite a serious little thing, aren't you?" he commented, getting to his feet.

He walked over to his bar and poured himself a tumbler of golden liquid. He didn't offer me one. Then he returned to his seat behind the desk. He took a long sip of his drink and apologized.

"I'm sorry I didn't offer you one, but given the meds you've probably taken, I don't think it would be in your best interest." He continued drinking with his attention on me.

"I'm thinking about what to do with you," he said conversationally. "I've known Dante since he was a boy. Back then, he was just about your size, maybe a little taller, but he was broad and strong. A handsome lad."

He cocked his head slightly.

"He was completely under my control and I had countless chances to do away with him. If I had known he would end up becoming such a huge problem, I would have. He was quietly ferocious, never letting anyone get away with anything. I admired that about him, so I kept him around, sure that if I could get him to be loyal to me, I'd have the perfect guard dog by my side."

He took another sip of his drink.

"Too bad he turned on me. He crossed the line."

He drained the glass and set it down with a small clunk on the polished surface of his desk. Even though his voice was relaxed I felt waves of fury coming from him. He was livid.

"There can be no more excuses, no more leniency," he murmured. "Today was the last straw. Do you know he kidnapped my son? Can you believe it?"

Suddenly, his mild urbane demeanor changed. And the change was extraordinary. It was as if he was a different person or he was possessed by a demonic spirit. His black eyes glittered with fury and hatred.

"The arrogant bastard kidnapped *my* son," he screamed, spittle spraying from his mouth. His whole body shook with venom and animosity.

My eyes widened with astonishment at the amazing

transformation, and also because I'd never known he had a son. I had done a lot of research on him while I was idling my time away in the witness program.

"He thinks I'm going to negotiate with him," he spat indignantly. "I'd rather kill my son with my own hands than negotiate with that creature. Everything ends today, and that's where you come in. You will walk into Twenty-Third Street. Not run, not scream, just simply walk in a straight line. You are not to turn right or left. No matter what, straight always."

"What do you mean walk on the street?" I whispered in fear.

"Exactly what I said. While cars are zooming by at full speed all around you, you are going to walk in the middle of the street. They'll try to veer around you and miss you, or maybe they'll hit you, and your body will be thrown into and perhaps crushed by a lorry or bus that couldn't stop."

I stared at him in astonishment. The man was a raving lunatic.

"Why would you do that? What have I ever done to you? You're the one who has ruined my life." I screamed. "You're the one who has taken everything away from me."

"You're right," he said. "This has little to do with you, but you're connected to Dante so you must pay. As did your father. He's going to see you walking and he's going to come to you and try to help you, or maybe he won't. Who knows? We'll see. Now, I should warn you that if you stop walking in a straight line for even a second and choose to run, or even call for help, my men will empty an entire row of bullets inside you. The same if you try to get any good Samaritan to help you. And if you dare try to warn Dante about what is happening you will incur the same punishment."

I thought of what he had said. "Since I'm going to die anyway, why should I wait for Dante to come to me?"

"Because it's going to be a long walk, and if Dante gets here before you reach the intersection, then I'll spare your life. But if he doesn't, well, the city will take your life. If he arrives on time and comes for you, you will be spared."

I was trembling with fear. "If the choice is down to either me or Dante's life, then how do I know that even after Dante is gunned down, you will spare me?"

"You don't know," he said softly. "You'll just have to trust me. You might not know anything about the mafia, but we adhere to our word. It is our greatest honor. I've heard from reliable sources that he will be on his way here soon, so it is time for you to take your walk, my dear ..."

I started to charge at him, but I was caught in midair, turned around, and slammed so hard into a wall that I froze with shock and pain. I didn't even bother trying to get up. It was impossible.

He walked out of the room. I was picked up and deposited in the middle of the street and told to walk.

There was almost no one around, just a few passersby with their families and dogs. I looked filthy, covered with dirt and blood. If I was honest, I looked like the worst kind of homeless drug addict. Nobody came to help me. A few who saw me simply didn't want to get involved. Only one woman stopped and asked me if I was okay.

"I'm fine," I told her. I had to keep my wits about me.

"Do you want me to call an ambulance?"

"Please don't," I cried and saw the shock in her eyes.

I could only imagine how batshit crazy I looked, walking with such iron-like determination toward my own death. I considered screaming and perhaps ducking behind a car, but I couldn't risk it. I knew Ugo was deadly serious. I would be instantly shot dead, and then Dante would walk right into the trap with no one to warn him. And he would be gone as well.

All I could do was keep walking as I tried to figure out what the best course of action would be. Every step I took carried so much weight that it seemed like each one was the hardest I'd ever done.

I started thinking about Dante and it helped me to walk more calmly. I then started thinking of what I could do to make him understand there was something wrong with me. He had to be the smartest and most vigilant man I knew, and I had to trust he would notice I wouldn't just be walking up the street for no reason and come up with an effective counteraction.

Chapter 63
Dante

"What the fuck? Isn't that ... is that Miss Leone?" Giotto exclaimed.

My heart jumped into my throat as I looked in the direction he was pointing and could indeed see her walking down the street. I looked even closer, unable to believe my eyes.

My hands instantly went to the door. I pushed the latch and opened it, but suddenly, I felt a solid hand drop on my arm.

"Hang on, Boss ..."

I stopped and looked at him.

He shook his head. "Something's not right. It's too fucking easy."

The moment he said these words, I came back to my senses. I took in the dazed, disheveled, bruised state of her. She was alive, but Jesus, what had they done to her? I closed the door and stared at her. She was putting one foot before the other, but she looked extremely wobbly and weak as if she could collapse any moment. I had to clench my fists to stop myself from running to her. I had to think fast and assess the situation, but I was so shaken by the sight of her that I couldn't even think straight.

"What do you think is happening?" I muttered.

"Bait," Giotto replied, his eyes scanning the area around her.

I could barely control my temper. "Why? Do you think he was aware I was coming?"

Giotto turned to me. "It's not unfathomable."

"Tommy," I said, then shook my head. "No, it can't be him. He wouldn't have double-crossed me. Not after what I've done for him, and he's not that way."

"People change, Boss," Giotto said with a shrug.

I had no choice but to acknowledge his words as the truth. I definitely wasn't about to stick to my faith in him if it meant jeopardizing Zola's life.

"Let's assume he did tell him I was coming. Let's also assume he knew I had the means to be able to find the house."

"Yeah," Giotto replied. "Using her as bait makes perfect sense."

"I run out to meet her, and he takes me out. Or quite possibly, both of us. But what about his son? Does this mean he is willing to sacrifice his son?"

"Looks like it."

My blood ran cold. Giotto was right. It looked and smelled like a trap. One I couldn't work my way out of because the area was so built up. It was surrounded by huge buildings with many windows and flat rooftops, which meant we could be shot from any one of those vantage points. It would take a split second for it all to come to an end.

"Food truck," Giotto said suddenly.

"Where?"

"I spotted one on our way down a few blocks away. We could get him to drive over and arrange some sort of accident to distract them. In the meantime, he could shield her."

I considered this suggestion and then looked up at the rooftops of the buildings. "He might not be on the rooftops."

"Yeah. He might just be in one of the cars."

"The shooters can't be far from her if they want to get a clean shot. Get the men out on foot. They can start searching the area when I give the signal, but they have to be very careful or they will stand out like fucking gorillas at a chimpanzee party."

Giotto quickly made the call while I kept my eyes on her. I watched her walking and wondered if she was ever going to stop. What was Ugo's plan, to have her walk until I went to her, then shoot us both?

I needed to come up with a plan, but my brain was like mush.

She came to the intersection, and although there weren't any traffic lights, there was a stop sign. Instead of checking to see if she was walking into traffic, she just kept going as though she was a remotely controlled toy. I scowled. It was bizarre. Was she on drugs?

All the alarms in my body went off when I saw a vehicle heading directly towards her. The driver wasn't speeding, but she was walking straight into his path and he had to screech to a halt. The car skidded to keep from hitting her. She staggered away in shock, but then just kept walking in a straight line while everyone else on the street seemed horrified. The driver jumped out and began to rain down curses on her and I had to hold myself back from running out and protecting her from him.

She looked scared, but she turned away and continued walking like a battery-operated broken doll. Soon she would be out of my sight. That was when I saw the air pods in her ear.

Ah, he was directly communicating with her. Something else was clear too. She had been told to walk in a straight path, no deviations no matter what.

Chapter 64
Dante

I turned to Giotto. "She's heading to West 4th and will be out of sight soon. Get an extra set of eyes on her quickly."

"Yes, sir," he said, and the men already in the vicinity were called.

"She's still walking?" I asked, and one of them confirmed it.

"Should we call the cops? Add to the confusion," Giotto asked.

"No. To get to me he is willing to give up his own son. That tells me he has snapped. If they come, he will kill her. I'm sure he has her under some kind of clock, I just don't know what it is. Any interference to his plan will mean death for her."

"One thing's for sure, though," Giotto said.

"What?"

"Anyone who's going to shoot her is not on the rooftop. She's a moving target and she's left that street."

I nodded. "Have the men search the people in the cars discreetly."

I opened the glove compartment. "Don't you have a hat or a cap in here?"

"Sorry, Boss."

"Fuck this." I stuck an earpiece in my ear and got out of the car and walked as inconspicuously as I could toward the street. It was a good thing I was dressed casually in a pair of dark jeans and a T-shirt.

In front of me, I saw a man walking with another. He was wearing a mustard baseball hat. I hurried up to him and pulled a hundred-dollar bill out of my pocket.

"Sell me your cap," I said urgently.

He looked at me as though he couldn't believe what was happening.

"Sir, she's almost at the intersection," I heard the update in my ear. Instantly, I stuffed the bill into the man's hand, snatched the hat off his head, and hurried away. I took the shortcuts I knew in between the buildings and through alleys until I could glimpse the intersection.

"Is she here yet?"

"Almost," came the response.

In no time, she arrived at the end of the street. To my relief, the traffic light turned yellow and the cars gradually came to a stop. Now she would be forced to stop, but what I could never have anticipated was that she wouldn't. She continued walking into the traffic.

I couldn't wait a second longer then. I began walking briskly toward her rather than running so that attention wouldn't be drawn to me. As she neared the intersection

The Guardian

and stepped out on the road, I heard a screech. Then a loud horn pierced the air. Some cursed.

Regardless, she didn't stop. She crouched down for a moment in fear, then she quickly got up and began to walk. This was a major street, and a truck without the capacity to stop was coming along now. The entire street was in chaos as she kept walking, and the cars kept trying to avoid her.

She stumbled and fell.

I began to run as fast as I could. I no longer cared what happened anymore, just as long as I got to her fast enough and put my body over hers. Would I be a suitable enough shield?

I wasn't certain, but I was damn well going to find out.

Chapter 65
Zola

"If you don't get up right now and cross the road, I'm going to shoot you through the head," came the threat in my ears through the Air Pods.

"One," the counting began, and I was forced to get up.

Tears poured from my eyes, but I blinked them away and kept a sharp lookout for Dante. I wasn't under any circumstances going to let Ugo use me to hurt Dante. Instead, I was going to save him even if it meant my death. As soon as I spotted Dante I was going to scream at him and warn him to stay away.

The only thing I was grateful for was that Dante had not yet shown up. Maybe he wouldn't and that would be the best-case scenario. There was still a distance to get to the other end of the street. Ignoring the curses flying all around me I kept going forward. I was surprised no one had tackled me to the ground yet.

Trembling with nerves and fear, I kept walking.

Suddenly, I heard a woman scream from across the street. Then, other shouts. It didn't take me long to figure out what the panic was about. I looked to my left and saw a truck coming my way. There was absolutely no way he was going to be able to stop despite the fact that I could hear the screech of his brakes.

"Get the fuck out of the way," I heard multiple people yelling.

Instinct took over. I turned to run, but suddenly everything started happening in slow motion. All the sounds were magnified, I felt the air brush my face, as I turned, the colors were brighter, and my thoughts seemed crystal clear. I love you, Dante. Always did and always will. There was no surviving this. Death seemed so close. I could see the horrified expression on the truck driver's face. A whiff of someone's perfume filled my nostrils. I could feel the stitches in my head pulling. My jeans rubbed against a wound in my leg.

It didn't seem as if I was moving at all. Then something big and heavy smashed into me and knocked me to the ground.

I lay flat on the asphalt. All the pain was gone. Was I dead?

"Get up! Get up!" I heard a familiar voice, and in a flash, my eyes shot open. I saw Dante in a baseball cap on top of me. The truck zoomed past, its tires screeching and burning rubber.

The entire scene was unfolding so quickly that I couldn't even comprehend what was happening. I heard the hail of bullets. The air was filled with screams and the sound of metal slamming as vehicles crashed into each other. A few seconds of disorientation passed, and then I was pulled up again.

"You have to run, Zola," Dante yelled. "You must run. I can't put you on my back because they will shoot you."

That was all I needed to hear. I took his hand and with every bit of strength I had left, I ran. I ran like the wind, until I was being thrown into a vehicle. I rolled and landed on the floor. The door closed, and the car swerved and sped away as gunshots rained down on us.

"Dante!" I croaked and tried to sit up.

"Keep her down! Keep her down!" someone yelled.

A rough hand forced me down. Someone threw himself over me, but it wasn't Dante. I began to panic because if it wasn't him, then maybe he hadn't made it into the car before we drove off.

"Dante. Where is Dante? Dante? Where is he?" I began to scream maniacally. I was beside myself with terror. Everything I had suffered would have been for nothing if Ugo had managed to kill him.

"Shhh ... Shhhh ... I'm here. Just relax," Dante said from somewhere to my right, and I felt all the strength flow out of me. I lay still and let the world turn around me. Evil had not won. At least for now. Ugo had not won.

It was a long time before anything akin to normalcy returned to the car. I could hear voices, low but urgent, and through them, I heard the word "hospital."

"No, home, came the counter instruction. Dr. Muzio will be there."

Eventually, the other body moved off mine and I was pulled up from the floor and settled down on the seat.

I felt dizzy and my vision was blurry, but when it cleared, I saw Dante. His face was white as a sheet. He was clearly in immense pain and he had his hand pressed to his chest. Or rather, he had a cloth pressed to his chest, and copious amounts of blood was flowing out.

My God! Dante had been shot and he was bleeding out.

"Hospital," I said over and over again in my head, but it took a while before the words would come out.

He met my gaze and shook his head. "They'll take care of me at home. It's safer."

I could feel the nervousness and urgency of the other passengers in the vehicle, but I never once took my eyes off Dante. I couldn't hold him, but what I could do was watch him and pray. After what seemed like forever, we were back at the estate. There was a medical team already waiting for him. I stood back and watched as he was put on a stretcher and taken straight up to his room. They tried to close me out of his room, but I began crying loudly.

"Let her in," I heard him say weakly.

And I was allowed in. The doors to his bedroom were shut with only the needed personnel in it. There was a doctor and two assistants on hand. Together they began to work on him. They checked his vitals.

"You were lucky the bullet didn't hit any major organs," the doctor said.

I slumped with relief. I could see just how close the bullet had been to his heart. One centimeter closer, and it would have been over for the both of us.

The doctor gave instructions to the two nurses present, one male and one female. Then he got up and looked at us. Then he turned to me. "Now you must go. We need to operate on him."

I couldn't stop myself from walking over to Dante. His breathing was shallow and he appeared to have lost consciousness. I bent down and placed a gentle kiss on his forehead.

"I love you, Dante. I love you," I whispered.

He didn't respond and I stepped back. I knew not to linger.

Chapter 66
Dante

My night was riddled with nightmares. I woke up once or twice, my mouth dry and my heart pounding. And then I remembered. I got her back, and the panic subsided and I fell back into another restless dream.

Once I dreamed of Marco. There was no crumbling castle or maze. He was standing in his study.

"Don't let her go, Dante. Hold tight," he instructed and began to walk down the steps that led into the hiding place he had built to keep Zola safe.

When I woke, the sun was already up. I felt as though I had been run down by a freight truck. My body was sore and bruised and the crowning glory of it all, the burning pain under the bandage, wrapped across my chest.

There was no one in the room with me.

The first thing I thought of was Zola and the condition she had been in. I needed to check in on her to be certain she was doing well, but the moment I tried to get up I instantly fell back. The pain was excruciating.

My body was completely fucked and probably would be for the next couple of days. I had come away with my life so there was nothing to complain about. I gritted my teeth and tried again, but this time more cautiously.

After various maneuvering, I was finally seated upright. I was hooked up by wires to an EKG monitor. There was no need for it so I disconnected it. I left my IV in mostly because the stand helped me keep my balance.

Slowly, painfully, I walked out of my room towards hers. I considered knocking but decided against it. I didn't want to wake her if she wasn't already awake. I simply opened the door quietly.

I saw her lying in bed, safe, and soundly asleep. The bloodstained dirty clothes were gone. She was clean and dressed in white silk pajamas. One foot had worked its way out of the duvet. It looked so small and fragile.

A rush of love filled my chest. I thought my chest would burst with joy. Yes, it was worth it. I would do it all again. Death was nothing compared to the pain of losing her.

I went over to her bed and stared down at her. There were bruises on her face and along her neck and the part of her chest I could see, but she looked peaceful in her sleep. The wound in my chest started throbbing and I turned around to leave. Probably need more painkillers. As I arrived at the door, I heard a slight gasp behind me.

She had woken up.

I turned around very slowly. When our eyes met, I found her sitting up, her eyes as large as saucers in her pale face.

"*Dante,*" she breathed.

With the rays of sunlight coming through the window

behind her head, her face was lit in such a magnificent way that my heart skipped several beats. She was going to be a complete menace in my life, but I had never felt warmer or filled with more excitement.

"How are you?" she whispered.

"Not bad. I just came to check up on you. How are you feeling?"

"Twinges. Nothing to worry about."

"Okay."

"You must be starving. Do you want some food?"

"Marie will take care of that," I said. "Just focus on recovering."

"Is there anything I can do for you?" she asked, biting her bottom lip.

An image of my cock buried deep in her mouth flashed into my mind, and I was amazed at my own degeneracy. My pain seemed to be increasing with every moment I remained standing.

I shook my head. "Go back to sleep." I started to turn away.

"Dante?"

"Yeah."

"You were right. I'm really sorry I didn't listen to you."

I felt the weight of my doomed love for her then. She had no idea how madly, deeply and completely in love I was with her. To her, I was just an ex-mobster who was offering her some protection. Protection that she deemed so tainted she was only willing to accept it with misgivings and grudgingly.

I turned away and left before she could look into my tormented soul.

Chapter 67
Zola

Oh my God, he completely hated me!

I saw it in his eyes before he turned away. He loathed me so much he couldn't even look at me. I could hardly blame him. Because of me, he nearly died yesterday. I had also risked the lives of his men.

I clasped my hands together and watched as he exited my room. I could tell he was in a lot of pain from the way he moved which was labored and stiff, a far cry from the man I knew who did everything so effortlessly.

There was nothing I could do, at least there was nothing he wanted me to do except to get out of his way. After he left, I found it impossible to remain in bed so I got up and went to the bathroom.

I passed the full-length mirror by the door and almost shrieked. There were scrapes and bruises everywhere. I found a brush and pulled it through my hair. I slung on a robe and feeling decent enough I exited the room and headed down the stairs to the kitchen. The house felt unusually empty and quiet after the ruckus of yesterday.

The Guardian

It needed the sound of little voices and the pitter-patter of little feet running around. The moment the thought entered my head I came to a halt. What the hell was going on? Never in my life had I ever entertained the possibility of having babies with anyone. How had that thought just casually crossed through my mind as a desire?

Not that it was ever going to become a reality given the way Dante felt about me. If he had ever harboured any affection for me at all, I had killed it stone cold with the last stunt I pulled. I stood for a moment forlorn at the bottom of the steps, then I lifted my chin. He was mad at me at the moment, but his temper was sure to subside ... eventually.

Armed with this hope, I headed into the kitchen.

The kitchen was deserted and I was about to turn around and walk out when the back door opened and Marie came in with a basket of fruits in her hand. For a second she seemed startled to see me, but quickly recovered and gave me a big, happy smile.

"Good morning. How wonderful it is to know that you are feeling better."

"Good morning," I replied and watched as she started to retrieve a bunch of strawberries from the basket.

She washed one and offered it to me. "I'm truly glad to see that you haven't been harmed."

I accepted it. "Thanks. Has Dante eaten?" I asked.

She shook her head. "No, not yet, but I made chicken soup, my grandmother's old recipe. I hope it will help nourish and bring some strength back to him and you too."

"He's awake," I said. "Maybe I can take it to him?"

She smiled. "Alright. Let me warm it up."

Less than ten minutes later, I was headed up to his room

with a tray of food. He was seated in bed, and working on his laptop.

He closed his laptop and watched me as I brought the tray over to the coffee table. I hated how emotionless and detached he seemed, but at least he didn't order me out.

"You brought me a meal?"

I smiled. "Yeah. It's humble pie, but shaped like chicken soup."

He didn't smile and I felt a little part of me die. My little joke had not gone down well. He had not forgiven me. An awkward silence fell between us. I knew I deserved the cold treatment and had no right to complain, but he had no idea how much it hurt to be treated as if I was now a stranger to him.

I was trying to tread carefully, I knew I was literally on eggshells, but it seemed as though every time I opened my mouth, I simply made things worse.

I wanted to explain myself, but then I realized it was not about me feeling bad it was about him. He needed to recover. He needed time. I had simply come here to deliver his food and the last thing I wanted to do was give him trouble. I gave him a smile and started to walk out of the room. Just as I turned the doorknob, he stopped me.

"Have you eaten?" he asked, and my heart fluttered.

"No, but Marie has made some soup for me too," I replied.

He nodded, and I exited the room.

The moment I shut the door, I felt tears fill my eyes because it seemed as if he truly just didn't want anything to do with me anymore. The best course of action was probably to step away but after a few minutes passed, I found that I couldn't. I turned around and knocked on the door.

"Come in," he called.

"I just wanted to say that if you need anything, anything at all, just let me know. You can always call out to me and I'll get it done for you."

"Until you decide to run away again," he said softly.

I shut my eyes in guilt. Then I mustered up the courage to face him once again. "I know I was wrong to take matters into my own hands. I didn't intend for anyone to get hurt. I was trying to protect you. I'll never do that again. Please don't hate me."

His expression didn't change. "You were trying to protect me?"

"Yes."

He frowned. "How?"

"I thought they may try to punish you for kidnapping me."

"So ... you thought that was a good idea to leave my protection and hand yourself on a silver platter to Ugo?"

"I still don't understand what happened yesterday. Things spiraled out of control. I thought Sarah was the dirty cop, I never imagined Detective Mellor would do that to me."

"Let's get something straight here," he said. "It is very kind of you and I thank you very much, but it is not your job to protect me. Please don't ever do it again. The authorities can pin whatever they want on me, but like I have explained to you before, this is my territory. I've been involved with the law and the mafia since I was a child. So when I make decisions, even when they don't seem right to you, I would appreciate it if you don't go out of your way to oppose them even if it was with the intention of trying to help me. Because you will just make things a hundred times worse."

I couldn't look him in the eyes. He was absolutely right, and all I could do was lower my head and watch as my tears fell onto the rug.

"Zola," he called.

"Yeah," I mumbled without looking up.

"I don't hate you. I'm mad at what you did for sure, but it's impossible for me to hate you. We'll get through this together, okay?"

I nodded slowly.

These words coming from him meant the entire world to me and I wanted him to know that, but I couldn't find a way.

"Thanks for the food and make sure you get something to eat as well."

"I will," I nodded, wishing he would call me over to hug me, but there was no such invitation forthcoming, so I returned with a heavy heart to my bedroom.

Chapter 68
Dante

I smiled when she left. Contrite Zola was starting to become one of my favorite versions of her.

Although, I was certain it wouldn't last long. She was sure to snap sooner and return to her stubborn minx version, which I had to admit I secretly loved.

In the meantime, it was time for me to get a report about how the world had collapsed around me in my absence. I called Giotto into the room and moved over to the coffee table to eat the soup Zola had brought. I couldn't help smiling as I began to eat. She went all the way downstairs with her sore body just to get me a meal in an attempt to make up for her mistake. I wondered what she would do next to try to show me how sorry she was.

Giotto took his seat opposite me. "Did we lose anyone?"

He shook his head.

I let out a deep sigh of relief.

"Andrea got hit in the thigh, but he'll be fine?"

The fact that we hadn't lost anyone was nothing short of

a miracle. Even me sitting here eating was nothing short of a miracle.

"Tell me everything that has happened since last night," I instructed.

"Surprisingly there was little to no mention of the accident and although a few videos did surface online, none of the major news channels carried it. It's just on social media and since no one is really talking about it, it'll die down in a few days without any explanation whatsoever."

I frowned slightly and wondered why a gang shootout in the middle of one of the major intersections in the city was not getting more coverage.

Giotto shrugged. "Ugo might have more of the press under his control than we suspected."

"It appears we have a rat in our midst," I said. "And until we bring him to light, he will always be one step ahead of us."

"Do you have any suspects, Boss? I thought it might be Tommy," Giotto said.

"To me, that didn't make much sense, but there is one other explanation."

We shared a gaze and he instantly understood who I was referring to.

"Detective Hudgens," he said.

That was the name I'd been thinking of too.

"He has the means and given the way this news is being suppressed I think that your guess is right. It all points to him."

"It should be surprising, but somehow, I'm not surprised at all. Hudgens has made a deal with both the angels and devils of this industry and as far as I know, he's the only one who would have had the reach to pull this off. Or maybe it's someone even higher and he's working for them, but whatever it is the trail will take too long to uncover. And along with it are many pitfalls."

Giotto nodded in agreement. There was nothing else to discuss so he turned around and left me to my thoughts.

They ran rampant in my mind. Whatever trail we wanted to follow would take time to uncover. And we didn't have time. Or rather, I didn't want to spend my precious time pursuing it, but we couldn't just look away. The soup and the painkiller had done their job, and I went in search of Zola.

"She's in the gazebo," Marie told me when I painfully made it down to the kitchen.

"I'm so happy to see you walking again. I was so worried last night." Tears were glistening in her eyes, and I could tell she had been incredibly worried about me.

"Thank you," I said and began to stroll slowly across the yard.

From a distance, I saw that she had left the gazebo and was sitting on the edge of the pier with her legs dangling in the water. It was a dangerous place to be seated.

I called out to her and she turned. Getting up, she walked over to me.

"That pier is dangerous," I said.

She turned to give it a glance. "Is it not stable?"

"I'm not sure," I replied, "but it's been in place for years and we haven't inspected it for safety in a long time so you need to be careful. I would prefer it if you didn't go that far out at all."

I expected her to argue with me, but she simply nodded

and then took a seat in one of the rattan chairs by my side. Well, that was a turn-up for the books. An obedient Zola I had not expected.

Chapter 69
Zola

I saw in his gaze that he'd expected me to be defiant and to argue with him, but I had already promised myself that as long as he was in this state, I would listen to what he had to say. After all, never once had he asked of me something unreasonable.

But this also made me realize I had come to the point in our relationship where I respected him. Enough to pay serious heed to what he had to say and enough to be convinced that his admonitions could be extremely beneficial to me at this point in time.

He stared at me intently, and the more he did it, the more I fell in love with him. I couldn't look away, but at the same time, I couldn't stand him looking at me in such an intense way. It was as though he was studying me and I wasn't confident that whatever he was seeing was in my favor.

I began to admit my flaws. "I'm too stubborn, right?"

He cocked his head. "Yes."

I felt my face flame. Yup, I asked for that one. I decided

to just shut up and turn away to stare at the water. Finally, he did.

"Did Tommy tell you anything that sounded strange?" he asked.

"Tommy?"

"Ugo's underboss. He was the one that allowed you to speak to me on the phone."

"Ah, the man who told me he would shoot me in the head if I made any sudden movements." I thought back to the moment, but I didn't find anything that stood out. "He was extremely reluctant about wanting me to talk to you. Other than that, nothing else stood out."

Dante was deep in thought.

"Would he have done it?" I asked. "Would he have shot me?"

Dante's response was immediate. "No. He wouldn't have hurt you."

I was a bit surprised at how confident he sounded about this. "Really? He was very intimidating."

"He uses violence sparingly and fairly," he said. "He especially doesn't hurt women and children regardless of the circumstances."

"You worked with him during your days with Ugo?" I asked.

Something akin to a smile appeared in the corners of his mouth. "I worked for him. He was Ugo's second in command. His presence was a breath of fresh air because, unlike Ugo, he was fair, and he wasn't paranoid. God only knows how many of our lives he saved by talking sense to Ugo when Ugo felt like one of us was plotting something or another against him."

"So why did he refuse to help us?"

"He did plenty," Dante replied. "I would never have been able to find you if he hadn't allowed that phone call."

"But he didn't give you the address, so how did you find me?"

"Detective Hudgens found the address?" he said quietly.

Something about his voice bothered me. "What's wrong?"

"Mmm," Dante said. "For a very incompetent man, the detective sure does have a lot of tricks up his sleeves. All kinds of high-profile cases that should have been taken off his hands and given to more competent teams, or even different bureaus, yet they remain with him. I should have known from the onset that in itself was suspicious."

"Do you suspect him?" I asked incredulously.

"Maybe. I'll give him a bit more rope to hang himself."

He had a simple dress shirt on, with a light blue collar with its sleeves rolled up on his arms. It was left open several buttons down which showed a bit of his chest as well as a peek at the bandage wrapped across his shoulder. His arm was still in a sling which kept it suspended against his chest, but even in this state he still looked immensely in control and regal.

After my visit to Dante's room, I'd been unable to stop myself from going online, and I had seen a fair share of videos. Seeing him run out onto the road and throw himself completely on top of me, without any care whatsoever for his own welfare or whether he got shot or not was etched into my mind forever. He'd been shot and yet he'd acted like the bullet didn't mean anything as long as it went through his body but didn't reach mine. Even after he'd been shot he had pulled me up and run with me, always keeping his body as a shield.

Watching those videos brought tears to my eyes.

Now, as I looked at him and noted the calmness he exuded it struck me how much strength and guts lay underneath it all. How much loyalty and perhaps even care he had for me. I was itching to ask him if that was why he had done it. If it was solely out of an obligation or loyalty to my father, but I was chicken to find out the answer. It would break my heart if the answer was the former. I decided to just believe what I wanted until someone or something contrary was proven.

For now, all I could do was smile in gratitude. His gaze suddenly softened in a way that I hadn't seen since we were in London. I was so overwhelmed I could only stare at him.

"Come here," he said in that controlled, low voice of his and I didn't need a second invitation. He leaned forward. I wasn't sure what was happening, but I was hungry with anticipation. I felt his hands softly brush the tendrils of escaped hair away from my cheeks.

He gazed deeply into my eyes as though he was trying to understand something about me. His beautiful, blue, honest eyes pierced through me and for the first time in so long, I felt warmth fill me like sunshine.

"Can I kiss you?" I blurted out.

I was afraid he was going to reject me outright. But he didn't. My heart began to race out of control as I leaned forward, still slightly unsure of my boldness, but he met me halfway.

He pressed his lips to mine and my whole body relaxed.

Tenderly, he sucked my lower lip into his mouth, and I began to melt. This kiss meant the whole world to me. I wondered what he felt. He lifted his good arm and curved his hand gently against the side of my neck as he deepened the kiss. I realized this was one of the best feelings in the entire world.

By the time he pulled away, I was almost convinced he must be in love with me. Our eyes opened and met but neither of us said a single word to each other. He turned his head and I followed his gaze and laughed at the sight of Marie scurrying away with a tray.

"Please tell her to come back," he said. "I don't have the energy to yell."

"I'll go get it," I said and got to my feet.

"Don't be long," he said softly.

"I won't."

Chapter 70
Dante

I shut my eyes as soon as she walked away, but the taste of her kiss still lingered in my mouth. She had drunk something sweet and the aftertaste remained and I couldn't get enough of it.

I loved her.

I loved her like I'd never loved before. I never even dreamed I could love like this. She had become necessary, like air, sunlight, and food. I was also sure of the fact that I couldn't wait for another second to see her eyes free of worry and fear. Even though I was now persona non grata with the law I couldn't wait for them to resolve this absolute mess of a situation with Ugo. Ugo had shown me clearly that there was no negotiating with him. I had to return to my violent roots and deal with him ... the way he should have been dealt with from the very beginning.

Nothing but his head on a platter would do anymore.

And I wasn't going to make it quick or easy for him. Not after what he did to Zola. The sun beat down on my eyelids. I must have looked so peaceful. It was the peace before the storm. I heard her return and opened my eyes. She set the slices of peach pie that Marie had given her and it looked wonderfully golden in the sunlight. Life seemed indescribably beautiful. Here was everything I ever wanted.

Zola smiled at me as she put a small fork on the side of the plate and handed it over to me. I stared at the plate in contemplation wondering if I would spoil the beauty of the moment if I ate the pie.

She misinterpreted my gaze and leaned forward. "Do you need help with holding the plate?"

She sat by my side, sliced a small piece of pie with the fork, and held it out to me.

The beauty became a shining magnificence. "You're acting out of character. Where's the fire-spitting little dragon?" I teased.

She blushed. "Maybe." She placed the fork against my lips. "And maybe I'm not. Maybe this is just how I feel."

The pie was sweet in my mouth. I chewed it slowly. Savoring it. Remembering how perfect it was. Once it had been a fruit on a tree. Then it had been a slice of warm goodness in Zola's hands. Soon it will be part of me. Then I looked deep into her eyes. I felt as if I was drowning. Nothing felt real. It was too wonderful to be real.

"And how do you feel?" I asked.

She lowered her eyes. I understood it was too direct a question, but I didn't expect her to back away either. It wasn't her personality, and true to form she delivered.

"I care about you... quite... um... deeply. It's um... okay if you don't feel the same. I mean, I've been such a bitch to you and after the last stunt I pulled I don't expec-"

"What are you talking about?" I cut her off. "I'm in love with you."

Her eyes widened with shock. Then, she set the fork down slowly. "Can you please repeat that? I don't think I heard you right."

I chuckled. "I'm in love with you. Isn't it obvious?"

She buried her face in her hands.

"How could it be? You've been so cold to me all day."

"Of course, I have. I was mad at you."

"Ooh," she said and lifted her gaze. "Was mad?"

"I can't stay mad at you. You're too cute."

She dropped her head. "Actually, I'm deeply in love with you too. I just said care because I was afraid of being rejected by you."

I reached for the glass of deep red pomegranate juice on the tray, took a sip, and set the glass down contemplating what to say next.

I looked out at the beautiful spread of property and knew we would have to leave it for a little while. But it would be necessary to leave the country for a little while to forget about us once I had taken care of Ugo.

"How do you feel about London?" I asked. "I know you were there under duress the last time we were there."

"No, I loved my time there with you. When I was lying battered and bruised inside the freezer, I dreamed of that night you washed my hair. It kept me alive."

My fist clenched. I had hated Ugo before, but now I hated him with a passion. I wanted to boil him alive and laugh while he screamed in pain.

I took a deep breath. I understood that everything was too raw right now and both Zola and I needed time to mend our hearts and bodies. Slowly. Slowly, I would mend my sweet love and return her to the carefree creature she was before this mess began.

"How do you feel about living there for a little while? Just till things calm down here. It's an option I'm looking into."

"I don't care where I am as long as I'm with you. When are we going?"

"Not immediately. Once I've taken care of things ... and Ugo. Then we'll leave."

"We're going to be free before leaving. Free from Ugo?"

"Yes."

She looked me straight in the eye, her expression intense. "You kidnapped his small son. Where is he now? What's going to happen to him?"

"I believe he's having a great time in Disneyland. Ugo made the mistake of hiring the woman I sent over as a spy years ago. When I gave the word, she convinced the little boy they were going on a secret trip together. It was all too easy to arrange."

She frowned. "Yeah, that's what I thought."

I looked at her in surprise. "You knew I'd sent the boy to Disneyland?"

"No, I didn't know where you had sent him, but I knew he would be safe. I knew you wouldn't hurt him." Her voice became urgent. "You can't take on Ugo, Dante. You're too kind and good. He would eat you alive. I saw the real him. And he's a dangerous lunatic. A mad, out-of-control psychopath. He has no boundaries. He will go where you can't."

"I know you're worried, my darling, but there is a side to

me you have never seen before. I don't hurt women and children, but I have gazed so long into the abyss that I have now I become the abyss. I can promise you, Ugo will regret the day he decided to take me on."

"I'm learning not to question you. As you said earlier, this is your world and you know best how it functions. I can also see that Ugo will never stop, never give up. There is nowhere we can run to that will be safe, that he will not eventually find. He is a man possessed with the idea of punishing you for the disrespect you showed in that nightclub all those years ago when you refused to drink his urine. And I also know we can't keep living in fear, but I'm terrified, Dante. I'm terrified yesterday will happen again ... and maybe this time it will not be a clean wound. Maybe this time I will lose you."

I understood her fears, but there was no other option. Ugo left me no option. "Or maybe this old vendetta will finally be over."

My gaze went to the picturesque lake, and in silence, we both watched the setting sun.

"Will you keep this property?" she asked.

"Until the day I die."

She nodded, but I didn't miss the glistening of tears in her eyes. I didn't mean to say things that made her teary-eyed.

"I'm sorry, Zola. I'm sorry things are not different. You will just have to trust me that there is no other way for us to get out of this situation."

She nodded and sighed. "I know. Is there anything I can do to help?"

"Your father's files and notes about my case are in your possession, right?"

She stared at me. "They're back at his house."

"I'm going to need to go through them again. It's possible he noted down something about the detective that has helped us out."

"Oh okay," she said, understanding dawning on her.

"I need something on Hudgens, anything at all that will get him off our backs. Then I can do whatever I want."

"Tell Giotto exactly where they are and he'll go get them."

"Okay."

And that was my cue to leave. There was a lot for me to get done. I trailed my finger down her smooth cheek. "Stay here, *bella*, and enjoy the afternoon. I must go because I have stuff to do."

I stood and she looked up at me, and her eyes were shining with love.

Chapter 71
Zola

I felt frightened.

There was no doubt we were now heading into extremely dangerous territory where anything at any time could go wrong. But I understood him. It was either this or we put our fate in the hands of people like Hudgens and sat like sitting ducks while Ugo decided our fate.

It was the only real option, but it held terrifying consequences. One wrong move and Dante could either be killed or put away for a very, very long time.

But I couldn't think of that. I refused to. All I could do was support him, and when Giotto face-timed me from my father's house, I gave him detailed directions and watched while he located the relevant boxes of my father's files.

I looked at the clock on the library wall. It was almost midnight. I hadn't seen Dante since we had talked by the lake. He had been holed up in his office with the files Giotto had brought. I couldn't help but be worried about him, especially because he needed the rest.

Eventually, when I couldn't take the silence in the library any longer, I sent him a text message.

Need any help with going through the files?

I turned off the computer and got to my feet. His response was simple.

Sure, come over.

I got up and hurried down the stairs. I arrived at the door and gave a light knock. It was opened a few seconds later by Giotto, who inclined his head slightly in acknowledgment.

I felt guilty every time I saw him or any of the men for that matter because after watching the videos of me walking down the street like an automaton, I was even more aware of the risks they had undertaken to save me. I knew it wasn't on my behalf, he did it for Dante, but I couldn't help but be incredibly grateful. I gave him a big shining smile.

"Goodnight, Miss Leone. I'm heading off to bed, but call me if you need me, Boss," Giotto said as he walked out the door and closed it behind him.

"Goodnight, Giotto."

I walked into the warm room. It wasn't as huge as I had expected, but the best part about it was their little Eden area with a huge TV and the whitest, fluffiest rug on the floor. Dante was at his desk, leaning against the chair, with a pile of papers in his hand. He looked uncomfortable, and between his brows was a line of strain. I ached to smooth it out.

"Am I intruding?" I asked and he set the papers down and straightened slowly.

"No," he replied flatly. "Are you falling for Giotto?"

I grinned. "No, but I'm extraordinarily grateful for what your men did for me yesterday."

"Hmm ... if you smile any brighter at him, I'm going to have to fire the guy and I really don't want to do that, because he's hands down the best employee I've ever had."

I hid a smile. "I'll dim it down," I promised.

"Good. I'll appreciate it."

He set the papers down and got to his feet. It was with a little difficulty, much more than he had earlier, and I immediately stepped forward to help him, but he held up his hand.

"It's okay, I can manage." He got out from behind the desk and began to head over to me. He came to a stop in front of me.

"It's a bit sore now, isn't it?" I asked. "It aches more than before?"

He nodded. "Might have strained myself too much."

"Did you take medicine for it?"

"I have. The doctor said he'll be here early in the morning to check me and you as well."

Feeling daring, I lifted to my tiptoes to kiss him. It was supposed to be quick and sweet, but his hand curved around the side of my neck and I was lost. I felt it down to the depths of my heart. When our lips parted I found him watching me, a smile slowly appearing at the corners of his lips.

"I know what you're thinking," I said.

His eyes twinkled. "What am I thinking?"

"You're thinking that maybe it's a good thing if I mess up from time to time. This way, I'll be less headstrong, more kissable."

He laughed. "Marco's daughter is one smart cookie."

Slowly, he started moving towards the couch. He sat down and lifted a glass goblet half filled with brandy from the coffee table. He raised it towards me.

"My pain meds."

He took a huge sip of it while I got carried away simply watching him. His hair had gotten much longer, and it reminded me of how he had looked that first night I saw him, when he confused and excited me. When I had to reluctantly admit just how handsome he was to me. Now, the more I looked, the more I felt things that were definitely not appropriate right now, but I couldn't help it.

"Come over here," he invited, patting the space next to him.

I did as he asked and settled down by his side, but I felt suddenly amazingly shy and thought I might need some Dutch courage.

"I'm in pain too," I said softly.

He passed his glass over to me and watched as I took a sip, and then he took one as well before setting it down.

"Find anything interesting yet?" I asked.

He sighed and shook his head. "Not really." He looked at the boxes all around. "It's going to take a while to go through them."

"Sure you don't need any help?"

He was silent for a little while, and then he replied. "You won't know what to look for."

I turned to him. "You have another option?"

"Detective Mellor," he said. "I think it's imperative that I pay her a little visit."

I gasped. "You think she's gonna talk?"

"Yeah, I think she will. It's not like I'm going to use whatever I obtain from her in court anyway. It wouldn't have been obtained legally."

"What do you mean by it wouldn't have been obtained legally?"

"To wrap things up as quickly as I want to, I'll briefly have to revert to my old ways."

"I wish I could be there. I have a few questions for her too, but I can't, can I? Or can I?" I looked at him hopefully.

He shook his head decisively. "You can't. Anything can go wrong, and anyway, I don't want you to be there."

"Fine, but you will get some retribution for me ..."

His eyes narrowed. "Don't worry, I'll make sure she bitterly regrets doing what she did."

"Thank you," I said and burrowed deeper into the couch.

"You're becoming quite ... mafia-minded," he commented with amusement.

"Maybe that's the way to be," I said. "Otherwise, the entire world goes incredibly slowly, and people treat your life as though it's worth nothing."

"That was the lure," he agreed.

I leaned against him and shut my eyes, completely relishing the silence and his beautiful scent. I needed more of that, so I turned and leaned my nose into his neck. It felt like forever since I'd been intimate with him, and I missed it immensely. It was all I wanted now, to be as close to him as physically possible, but I was well aware this couldn't be the case given his injuries, but I had a trick or two up my sleeves.

. . .

The Guardian

"You smell so good and I have a present for you," I said.

His curious eyes were mere inches from mine. I noticed they seemed slightly glazed. "A present?"

"Yes, I got it ages ago in London and never got the chance to give it to you."

I slipped down to my knees in front of him and began to put my hair up. I wondered if he would stop me, but he didn't. His eyes were burning with blue fire. I'd seen them burn like that before ... in London. I was spurred to keep going. I undid the button of his slacks, pulled down his zipper, and positioned myself between his widened knees. As I did, he didn't take his eyes off me, and neither could I from him.

"Will it hurt you?" I asked.

"You call it hurt, I call it two spoons of sugar?" His voice was thick with lust.

I wrinkled my nose at his cockiness and gently pulled his beautiful, completely erect cock out of his boxers.

"You don't have to be so gentle," he said. "It won't break."

I looked up. Amusement glinted in his eyes. I wrapped my hand around the impressive length of him and watched it grow even harder and longer in my hands.

Teasingly, I massaged the rod, stroking from bottom to top until a little precum appeared at the head. I leaned forward and dipped my tongue into his slit to get a taste.

I heard a sharp intake of his breath, and I loved it. But I loved it even more when I completely covered the thick head with my mouth. A soft groan escaped from him and he leaned against the couch, his head tilted back, and his eyes shut.

He was ready to enjoy every single moment of it, and I was ready to suck him off with every ounce of energy I had in me. I took my time with it, running my tongue along his length and sucking on every inch of his slickness.

"Zola," he called out when I took his balls into my mouth, and how I loved it when I released them with a pop. I continued pleasuring him until I felt him inching closer and closer toward the edge.

His breathing was harsh, and his fingers raked into my hair. The slight tinge of pain and the idea that he was losing control completely aroused me. I could feel the wetness between my legs. He came in a rush and hot cream filled my mouth and rushed down my throat. He leaned forward to kiss me, his tongue swirling inside my mouth.

In a daze, I stared at him as he leaned away, a mischievous smile on his face. "Your turn."

I got to my feet and slipped off my underwear.

"Lose the dress… and the bra too," he ordered.

As naked as the day I was born I positioned myself astride him.

"Don't worry I'm going to go easy on you," I whispered as I settled lightly on him.

He stroked the bare flesh of my thighs. "Why? My chest is the only thing that's injured."

I found the head of his stiff cock was already bouncing and stroking my sex. My breath caught. Carefully holding onto the couch behind him, I looked into his eyes.

"Are you ready to go again?"

"Always," he said and impaled me deeply. His face contorted with pleasure as he filled me up.

Silky smooth skin grazed my walls as I rose and sank down on him again and again. My eyes were tightly shut as I relished the sweet feel of him inside me. That tightness was what I craved most. It never failed to amaze me how perfectly he fit inside me.

I had missed being so intimate with him.

I took my time and savored every moment of it. I rode him slowly, grinding my pussy against his groin, enjoying the friction, but I could see him fighting with himself not to quicken the pace. Eventually, I accelerated my movements until I nearly forgot he was injured.

My head fell back, forcing me to hold onto his arm, and only his slight wince of pain brought me back to my senses. Horrified by my carelessness, I came to an abrupt stop, but he didn't let me. He continued to thrust his hips into me until I met him thrust for thrust.

I cried out as I came, my muscles gripping his cock, my legs trembling.

"I'm sorry I hurt you," I said and tried to move away, but he held me to him and placed sweet kisses on my cheek.

"Wait a while, little one," he whispered.

He continued to pick up the pace, and it wasn't long before he gained his release. I shut my eyes, milked his hot seed, and relished the intimacy of our connection. I could feel the slickness from where we were joined, sliding out of my sex onto his thighs.

My heart swelled with love for him. I slanted my head and kissed him. Our tongues danced along with each other, and I began to feel him grow hard beneath me again.

"No," I pulled away, amused.

He caught my arm before I could move away.

"Why not?" he asked as I tried to get off.

"It'll hurt you," I said, but my knees were so wobbly that I ended up falling onto him. He cupped my face and kissed me once again.

I could no longer resist him. I melted into his embrace.

Chapter 72
Dante

"What do you want to know first?" Larry asked as I settled down at my desk in the office.

"Detective Mellor," I replied.

He began to look through his file of documents. "But before that, you do know a warrant has been issued for Zola's arrest, right?"

I nodded. "I'm aware."

"She's also been declared as a missing person."

"Hmmm ..." I reached for the report he was holding out to me.

"You're not worried they're gonna find her in your home sooner or later?"

"We'll be long gone by then," I replied. Thankfully he didn't push for an explanation.

"Good, I see you've got two private investigators on her tail day and night."

"Yeah," he replied. "You mentioned you needed this done immediately so they're on full duty. So far, there's not much to report. There has been no sign of her at her apartment so she might not even be there. But we'll see. The investigator is on his way to Utah as we speak to search for her aunt."

"That's her only living relative?"

"Yup," he replied. "I'm not sure putting the aunt in danger so she'll comply will be effective at all. She doesn't seem to be close to this aunt and the woman's well-being might not be of concern to her. If she was close enough to do what she did to Zola then maybe she wouldn't care about her aunt being in danger."

I carefully considered his words.

"Maybe," I said. "And maybe not, but emotions have a way of shifting when it's your only living relative at stake. I'm also curious about the compensation she received for selling Zola out. She doesn't have to report directly to Hudgens so maybe Ugo got to her personally. There might be a reason why she needs dirty money. Follow this thread as well so we can see what it uncovers for us within the next twenty-four hours."

"Twenty-four hours?" he repeated doubtfully.

"That's all I've got," I replied. "Right now, Ugo is aware I have been injured which means I am currently at my weakest thus it will be the best time to strike. I've always liked to believe they don't know the location of my hideout, but that might not be the case at all."

"I can trail just about anyone, and I'm sure Ugo has probably already done the same to me. We need to get to him before he finds us unprepared and at a disadvantage."

"Understood. I'll work on this 24/7," he agreed before he left.

The Guardian

My phone rang. I looked down at the screen and saw it was Hudgens. I wasn't surprised he was still reaching out to me. He didn't know I had figured him out and he was playing the role of the ever-vigilant officer.

"I just wanted you to know we're preparing another warrant for your arrest. There are more than enough eyewitnesses to the stunt you pulled at the intersection so we have to bring you in. This time around we don't think the possibility of bail will be given to you since it is now clear you're more dangerous than any of us could have anticipated."

I smiled at his words.

"Who is this *we,* you keep referring to? Yourself and Ugo?"

He went quiet for a few seconds but then tried to make up for the guilty silence by being super offended. "What the fuck are you talking about?"

"You know exactly what I'm talking about, Hudgens. And to think we were actually somewhat partners for years. I guess that weasel paid you more, but I would have coughed up whatever you wanted, if you had just asked. Because you were too stupid to ask, I'm going to ruin you. I hope you're ready."

"Did you just threaten me?" he blustered.

"Take it however you want to. Just know that as of now I consider you a dead man walking."

He shot back. "I think you're forgetting I was the one who informed you about Ugo's house location."

"Of course, you did. To throw me off your stink. After which you told Ugo to expect me, which led to the ambush. If it wasn't you, then who could it have been?"

"So, you're just guessing and throwing groundless accusations around. Good luck getting the evidence you need to prove that," he raged.

I smiled to myself. "You know, Hudgens, what made the mafia strong was what ruined it. Our code of silence. It was the foundation stone of our strength, but as soon as the first little crack appeared, the Mafia lost all its power and magic. And that's why you're going to be ruined because you've assumed every single person around Ugo is loyal to him."

"Oh, and you better warn Detective Mellor as well that we're coming for her. None of you are going to go scot-free for how you've handled this case."

I ended the call and got to my feet. I had set things in motion and there was no going back.

I called Tommy.

"I've told you we don't owe each other anymore," he harangued as soon as the call connected. "Why the fuck do you keep calling me?"

"Don't go with your guys," I told him. "Go with mine."

"What?" he asked.

"Ugo might have found out you were the one who ratted his location out to me."

"What the fuck does that mean? I just gave the girl a few seconds to talk to you."

"Ugo's dirty cop would have told him I had a description of the address. Someone gave that to me. He wouldn't hesitate to kill every person who came into contact with her. When you gave her the phone you were aware of the risk you were taking."

"Of course, I was."

"This is the last leg of this fight," I told him. "So, you

need to pick your side now. If you look just a few cars to the left of you, you'll see my men waiting. Head over and get in. They'll bring you somewhere safe."

"Thanks, but I'll take my chances with the devil I know," he scoffed.

"This is your last chance, Tommy. Decide wisely."

"You're telling me to throw away the last thirty-five years because of a single call from you?"

"You should have done it sooner and you know it. Take the fucking leap, man."

"What exactly do you want from me, Dante?" He sounded suddenly tired. In his head he knew Ugo couldn't be trusted. In the end, Ugo would kill him.

"You are gold," I said. "There's no one alive who knows more about Ugo's dealings than you do."

"Walk away and cut a deal with the cops so you don't end up holding the baby. You've already served your time."

"I'm not a rat," he muttered.

"You won't have to rat on Ugo. He's gonna be dead soon. I'm just extending my hand to be sure you don't end up the same way."

"And you gain nothing from this?'

"Nothing." And it was true. Tommy had done me a good turn and I wanted to make sure he didn't suffer for it.

Chapter 73
Zola

I spent the rest of the day working, or at least trying my best to, but I kept glancing at my phone. I hadn't sent him a message because I didn't want to distract him, but I was hoping he'd send a little note. It was already dinnertime and there was still no call or note.

When it was time for dinner, I headed to the kitchen with the intention of helping set the table or something, but I was told in no uncertain terms to either go back to the dining room to wait until I was served, or I could go pick a bottle of wine from his huge selection of great wines in the cellar. I opened the cellar and was amazed by how vast it was. Everything was clearly labeled and I found a vintage bottle of red wine that looked like it must cost the earth and took it upstairs. Marie said she would pop it open and decant it to let it breathe.

A message arrived on my phone.

On my way home. Shall we dine together?

I was surprised and so excited about the prospect I felt butterflies flooding into my stomach. He was coming home to eat with me. I'd never really had this before. Even when my father was alive, I'd always eat on my own, and it was one of the bones of contention between us. But here I was with Dante, creating something akin to a little family. With someone I felt so absolutely loved and cherished by. I didn't know how it happened or how it came together, but I was incredibly happy it had.

I texted him back.

Me: **How close are you? I'll wait for you.**
Dante: **About six minutes**.

I was impatient to see him. I wanted to go to the door and wait for him, but would that make me too clingy or house-wifey? I went to the kitchen instead, and despite Marie's protests, I was able to charm my way into letting me carry some plates and silverware to the table. At that moment we heard voices coming from the foyer, and before I could say a word she had taken the plates I was holding and pushed me off.

"He's here. Go," she urged, her eyes bright and encouraging.

I tried to control mine but found it incredibly hard to. I stood by the door but kept myself just out of sight till he dismissed the two men who were with him. He spotted me as soon as he turned, and he looked tired, I didn't miss the slight tilt of his lips in a smile.

Then the men left, the door was shut, and I was left alone with him. I ran toward him. I couldn't take my eyes off him, wishing his shoulder would heal quicker so he could be well and strong.

I threw my arms around him and laid my face against his chest.

"God, I missed you," I whispered, listening to the steady beat of his heart and breathing in the scent of him.

I could feel the fatigue and tiredness seep out of his body as ours connected, and it made me happy I could at least do that much for him. It also made me immensely worried that the state he was in brought even more danger into the mix. He was now a much slower and easier target, and this fear I couldn't hide from my eyes when I pulled away.

"What is it?" he asked, his voice noticeably softer. "I think we should wait till you're better before you take Ugo on."

He smiled crookedly. "Don't worry. I know I'm physically not in the best condition, but it's not brute force that will bring him down. In fact, it could actually be my hidden advantage. Thinking that I am weak will make him careless and overconfident."

"Okay," I nodded.

We started to head to the dining room, our fingers entwined. He took his seat at the head of the table and I sat beside him. I noticed that Marie had come in and already poured the wine into glasses.

He picked up his glass and held it up. "To a world without Ugo."

He set the glass down. "Do you like it?"

"I do."

Two of Marie's girls came in carrying plates of food and bowls of lemon water.

The first dish was a langoustine barbecued on open charcoal. The presentation was spectacular. Every bit of the meat had been meticulously removed from the shell and laid out. The blackened shell was filled with hot herb butter and bergamot mussel broth. We had to pour the fragrant liquid onto the charred meat, then clean our fingers in the bowls of warm lemon water.

I had to confess, my father had taken me to some of the top restaurants in the country, and I had never eaten anything so delicious. Indeed, Marie had magic fingers.

Someone had put on an Italian opera and the muted sound was piped into the dining room. We ate in silence because the outside world, meaningless conversations, and the mundane couldn't come into this sacred space. This was our universe where there was no need for words. We looked into each other's eyes and we smiled wordlessly because neither of us could believe how perfect everything was.

The main course was a freshwater fish, burbot. It had been specially flown in that morning. The tender meat had been skillfully wrapped in seaweed, skewered onto bamboo sticks and lightly grilled. It was served with a creamy coconut and cherry leaf sauce. As soon as my lips closed over the fish, it melted in my mouth. Heavenly.

Marie was not messing around. Dessert was ice cream made with hazelnut and caviar. I would never have imagined such a combination. The smile on Dante's face was all I needed to slip the spoon into my mouth.

It was divine!

Chapter 74
Dante

She was reaching for a chocolate when my phone began to ring and the sound was so jarring she froze midway, her head swinging around in my direction.

"It's okay," I whispered. "It's okay."

But the enchantment was gone.

I pulled out my phone, and I almost couldn't believe the name flashing on my screen.

"Tommy," I said.

"Can we meet and talk?"

I was instantly suspicious. "It can't be done over the phone?"

"Sure, it can, but I'm not exactly sure how to hand over all the evidence I have against Ugo over the phone. If you have a way, then let me know."

I wanted to believe he had turned on Ugo, but I wondered what had made him turn when he was so against it only a few hours ago. I had to make sure this wasn't some sort of trap.

"You know where all of my family is located. You can go hold them as hostages if that's the proof you want."

"No, no need for that. Even if you betray me, Ugo will never trust you again and kill you. Whether you take me out or not you're dead if Ugo lives," I said. "Where do you want to meet?"

"That place Joey took us to for his thirtieth birthday party."

"Yup, I remember."

"Just be on time," he said. "50 minutes."

"I'm an hour and a half away," I said, and he ended the call.

Zola had her full attention on me.

"Tommy seems ready to turn evidence in. I have to meet up with him to find out what kind of evidence he has."

She nodded, but nothing could take away the terrible fear I saw in her eyes.

"I'll be careful," I lifted my hand to gently stroke her cheek.

"What if it's a trap?" she whispered.

"It might be, but Tommy's no fool. He knows he's burned his bridges with Ugo. This is his only option. So it's a risk I'm willing to take. Please don't worry, all will be fine."

She stared at me anxiously, and I knew no matter how much I tried to reassure her, she would be afraid. Not wanting to waste any more time I turned to leave, but before I could, she held onto my hand and reached up slightly to place a kiss on my cheek.

I relished it for a second.

Then I grabbed my jacket and hurried out of the house.

I made for the restaurant's back room and I didn't have

to wait long for him. The moment he walked in and saw my men, he gave me a dirty look. He began to head to the table I was sitting at but was stopped and searched before he neared me.

"This is a private meeting, kid," he said.

"It is. They'll be leaving in a minute," I said with a smile. I was leaning casually against the chair, but there was nothing casual about the gun I had underneath the table and aimed directly at his crotch.

"You've nothing to worry about. I've made my decision. I've chosen a side."

I saw the deep frustration and devastation on his face, and suddenly, I understood.

"He set you up to take the fall, didn't he?"

"Yeah," he muttered quietly.

"Again."

Tommy smiled bitterly. "Yeah. He wants to make a deal with you. In exchange for his son, he will drop all charges against you. He wants me to confess to the murder. To admit that I set up the whole thing, staged the crime to implicate you, and everything afterward. It's actually very impressive how thoroughly he has covered all his tracks. He's thought of everything. My name was used in everything, signed on every transaction made. In exchange, he will not murder my family."

"Unbelievable," I marveled. The way Ugo treated his men never ceased to amaze me. It was almost as if he was running a cult of gullible, brainwashed followers.

"For a man so astute and with so much experience, it's pretty astonishing that he is unable to understand the very basis of human nature. What man in his right mind dies twice for the man who betrayed him?"

I lifted my hand from underneath the table, uncocked the gun, emptied the bullets in it, and placed it on the table.

"He does understand human nature," I said. "Which is why he chose you."

Tommy's ears perked up. "What do you mean by that?"

"You came back to work for him, didn't you?"

"Of course, I did. What else was I supposed to do?"

"You haven't shown any rebellion. You've been as calm as the sea on a hot day. So he's kept you cooling your heels, knowing that you can be used again."

"But this time he got it wrong ... so fucking wrong." He smiled. "Over the years, I've cleaned up everything for him, even his shit when he was sick. As a result, I've earned many friends along the way, many who have now become his enemies, though he doesn't know it. He will never truly understand how much I've shielded him from, but he's about to."

We needed a drink. I pulled the cord by the table, and almost immediately, a waiter opened the door and came into the room. I ordered a bottle of whiskey. When one was set on the table, I poured a large measure into two glasses.

Tommy lifted his glass. "Here's to Ugo! Let's see how he does without a moron to act as his buffer."

We drank and I refilled our glasses.

He looked at me with rage in his eyes. "I can't believe him. The audacity to sign my life away over and over again and give nothing in return. You were right to leave as early as you did. I wished I'd had half the guts."

"Don't beat yourself up. I had nothing to lose. You had a family to take care of."

"A family that I've lost. My sons are strangers to me and my daughter is ashamed of me. That's what this life does. It lures you in with all the promises of honor and brotherhood and while you're not looking it takes away everything that means anything to you and rips it apart." He wiped his mouth with disgust. "Anyway, this meeting has gone on long enough. What steps do we need to take now?"

"Let me talk to my lawyer and we'll take it from there. I won't let you down. You have my word."

He shook his head. "I can't believe it. In the end, I had to turn to a fucking kid for help."

Then he rose to his feet and walked away quickly. Giotto came in as soon as he left.

"He wasn't followed, was he?" I asked.

"No, Boss."

Chapter 75
Dante

"They've taken Giotto, Boss."

"What?" I shouted.

"They got him on his way here."

My heart sank. For a few seconds, I couldn't think. Giotto! Not Giotto. Then I knew exactly what I had to do. I owed him. I picked up my phone and called Ugo.

"I'm aboard my yacht and my Captain has just opened a splendid bottle of Petrus, Pomerol. Come over. We can drink and talk," he cordially invited and ended the call.

A wise man would say walking without any protection or weapons into Ugo's den as I was, was a death sentence. But I had a secret weapon in my bag of tricks. I had a psychopath's burning desire, not to save his son, but not to lose to me. To lose his only son to me would rankle like a cancer forever.

I made peace with my chances and went aboard.

I was thoroughly frisked and led to the top deck. Immediately, I saw the man who had been the bane of my existence since I was a kid. He was wearing a blue shirt and white trousers and standing by the railing, staring out at the ocean. The wind teased his hair and there was nothing to suggest that evil lived inside him.

He sensed my presence and turned.

"Ah, there you are," he said.

He nodded at his men and they disappeared from sight.

"Come, come. It's been years. Let us drink."

He led the way to a pure white, curved sofa. On the white table was an open bottle of wine and two glasses. He sat down and gestured for me to join him. I could smell the fragrance of the wine as he poured it out.

He held the glass up and studied the color of the wine. "This is my favorite wine, you know. I only drink it on special occasions."

"What's the occasion?" I asked.

He smiled softly and turned to look at me. "You are the occasion. I'm celebrating having you here. You'll probably laugh, but I've hated and loved you in equal measure. For a while, you were the son I never had."

"You have a son now."

His grip on the stem of the wine glass tightened. "Yes." He took a deep breath. "How is he?"

"This was taken yesterday." I brought a photo out of my pocket. A photo of him lying on a carpet and laughing uncontrollably while his nanny tickled his belly.

He took the photo and stared at it for a long time, then he carefully put it down on the table. His eyes were downcast. "I supposed I should thank you for not hurting him."

I shrugged. "As you said, I'm too squeamish for this job."

"Mmmm ... you're not drinking. The wine is not poisoned, you know."

"I know that. It's not your style to ruin good wine." I took the glass and swallowed a mouthful. I swirled it on my tongue and nodded approvingly. "Brilliant. You always did have excellent taste."

He looked deep into the red liquid in his glass. "Yes, and you were the only one who could appreciate it."

At that moment, one of his men appeared and nodded at him. He nodded back and looked at me and suddenly everything changed. He was no longer the urbane host. He was looking at me with undisguised glee.

The boat was being unmoored and we were about to sail away to the ocean. His intentions were becoming clearer. He was going to torture me, get the information he wanted, and then he was going to dump my body in the middle of the ocean. In a place where nobody would be able to find it.

However, I was wearing a tracker and my men were ready with speed boats that were waiting just out of sight. All they needed was a signal from me.

"I've spoken to Tommy. He's agreed to take the rap for you."

I leaned back and stared at him. "So why did you take Giotto?"

"To get you here. Why else?" he said simply.

It was clear I had walked into a trap, but what kind I didn't know yet. "Why did you want me here?"

"Bait. I used her to get to you and I used you to get to her."

I frowned. "What the fuck are you talking about?"

"Marco's daughter is on board."

I jumped to my feet. "You're lying," I yelled, but I knew he wasn't.

"You forget you've been making plans to destroy me for a few months, I've been doing it for years, more than a decade. I know everything about you. Even your secret hideaway. When you pulled out most of your men to follow you, my men sent a photograph of you boarding my boat to Marco's daughter."

He laughed. "It was easier than taking candy from a baby. They told her the only way to save you was to come away with them and she willingly came out of the fortress you'd built. Like a little lamb to slaughter."

I felt as if I was losing my mind. I was so livid I wanted to rush at him and strangle his thick ugly neck. I could deal with anything as long as it didn't involve Zola being in danger. Now that she was in the equation I couldn't even think straight.

"Would you like to go to her?" he asked glibly.

"Yes," I hissed.

As if we had been monitored the whole time, a few of his men came up and gathered around me. My hands were twisted to my back. Pain shot from my chest, but all I cared about was getting as quickly as possible to Zola.

Once I was handcuffed with zip ties, they dragged me down a short flight of stairs. A door was opened and someone shoved me hard from behind into a cabin empty but for a chair with my Zola on it. Her hands were secured behind her back and her ankles were tied to the front legs of the chair, but they had not harmed her ... yet. There were no new bruises, only the old ones that were slowly turning from blue and purple to dirty-yellow.

Her wide terrified eyes looked at me anxiously as if checking to see if I was alright. "Dante," she cried.

"Shut up," one of the men growled and roughly kicked the chair she was tied to.

She screamed with fear and I saw red.

"You bastard," I snarled and instinctively, like a maddened bull, I rushed forward and swung my knee into his groin. With a roar of pain, he went crashing to the floor.

The rest of the men were on me in seconds. They began to kick the shit out of me. I could hear Zola's screaming and begging for them to leave me alone. I regretted that I hadn't been able to control myself. Now she had to watch me get beaten to a pulp.

"That's enough," Ugo ordered from the doorway, and instantly, they moved back.

Zola was crying uncontrollably and I couldn't even reach up to wipe the blood dripping into my eyes. We were in a bad situation. A very bad situation.

Chapter 76
Zola

"Calm down, everybody. Stop crying my dear Zola," Ugo advised calmly.

I took a deep breath and looked at him.

He smiled in a friendly fashion and turned to Dante. "Here's the deal. You are both going to die. There is no getting away from that, but how Zola dies will be decided by you, Dante. Will she have a quick death? Or would you prefer to watch her suffer the slow agonizing death of being hacked piece by piece? I see you didn't like her chair being kicked so I should warn you now the cutting process could go on for hours."

I gasped with fear. Dante's head was bent so I couldn't see his expression, but I could imagine it being contorted with impotent fury.

"The way to spare her excruciating pain is to simply tell me where my son is being held. Or ... I start hacking her to death."

I felt my soul crumble further into pieces as an odd

silence fell upon the room. It was so quiet I could hear my heart racing and my blood pounding in my ears.

One of the men came forward and I was able to see what was in his hands and I felt dizzy with fear. It was a machete, but I had never seen any blade look dirtier or more rusted than what he held in his hand.

Ugo took the weapon and admired it with the glee of a child, and for the first time, I could see just how wicked of a person he truly was.

"It's blunt," he said, "as blunt as it can be, so I can only imagine just how long it's going to take to hack even one of your delicate limbs off, and we have so many body parts to go. This could be a long night and an interesting one too."

I knew he meant every word he said. I knew then we were both going to die. Let him have his son. Perhaps he would let us die in each other's arms. I told Dante once that I would go anywhere with him, and really meant it. We would hold hands and go together ...

Then I heard a familiar voice. A voice I would never forget as long as I lived. Tommy. He was not looking at me but at Ugo. He looked subservient and respectful. I couldn't stop myself from turning toward Dante in shock, but he was staring at Tommy, his face white and blank with pain, shock, and betrayal.

Ugo lifted his gaze to settle it upon me, and then he handed the blade over to Tommy. "Why don't you start the show? Nothing too drastic. Maybe a finger. He needs to know we mean business."

Tommy looked at me. I frowned at him in disbelief. I couldn't believe what he was about to do.

"Hold onto her chair," he told a man who was standing in the corner.

"Wait," Dante screamed.

But the machete had already swung and hacked into the side of the neck of the man behind my chair. I couldn't even scream as the blood gushed out and splattered all over me and Tommy. Calmly he reached up and wiped the blood off of his face in irritation. The other men in the room were frozen with astonishment.

"Fuck, this blade's blunt."

Ugo shot up to his feet. "What the fuck do you think you're doing?" he bellowed.

Wordlessly, Tommy swung the blade. It struck Ugo's shocked face with an awful clang. His face split into two. Bleeding profusely, he fell to the floor.

"The feds are never to be trusted," Tommy said with annoyance as he kept his foot pressed down on Ugo's neck. Underneath Tommy's shoe Ugo struggled, writhed, and slipped around in his own blood ... like a dying fish. He made strange gurgling noises in his throat, and then he became still.

"I gave them information about all of this on a fucking platter," Tommy continued, "and they still couldn't get their damn act together." He took his foot off and looked at Ugo's still body. "Should have done this years ago. Fucking asshole."

"Quick, free me," Dante urged.

Chaos was breaking outside as men began to shout and

hurry toward the room. Tommy moved swiftly to lock the door, and they began to bang on it.

"Tommy," a man yelled from the other side. "What the hell is going on? Open this fucking door now."

Tommy sliced through Dante's zip ties then he quickly cut through my binds too. "We don't have much time. They'll shoot the door down soon."

Dante came to me and held me close. "Where's Giotto?"

"I've got him," Tommy said. "He's safe."

Something akin to the sliver of a smile curved the corners of his mouth. "I thought you'd betrayed me."

"I gave you my word, and my word is always good. If I didn't appear to betray you, there would have been no way in hell to get you out of this mess."

Just then, gunshots rang out, and then more pounding on the door and voices. I recognized one of them and glanced at Dante, but he must have also recognized the voice because he began to smile. "Put the blade down, Tommy. My guys are here."

Tommy frowned. "How?"

"When I was being kicked around, I stamped hard on the tracker in my heel and smashed it. I knew the moment it stopped bleeping my guys would come to the spot it last flashed at.

"Alright then, here we go," Tommy said, and just a mere few seconds later, the door was busted in, and Dante's men rushed in.

"Took you long enough," I heard Tommy grumble loudly, but he was laughing with happiness.

"Are you alright, Boss?" someone asked.

"Yeah. Good job. Thanks!" Dante said.

My eyes landed on Ugo. His blood had turned the floor of the room a bloody red, and even as I shut my eyes, I knew it was an image that would haunt me for many years to come.

There was another image that would also linger in my heart for many, many more years to come. Of Dante's eyes staring straight at mine. There was a lightness to them that I couldn't recall ever seeing. Or perhaps it was a reflection of what I felt, which was the massive and almost crippling weight coming off my shoulders. We had faced death and come out on the other side.

"It's over," I whispered.

"It's over," he echoed.

Epilogue

Zola

I could hear the thunderous sounds of bullets the closer I got to the shooting range. Finding Dante here was a very easy indication to me that he was worried or unhappy about something, and this time around, I was very aware of what it was.

I felt the same unease too as it was the very first time we were accepting people into our home. However, it was a time for celebration, and I didn't want my paranoia to get the better of us.

I watched him in the cage for a little while, not wanting to bother him.

A few minutes later, after emptying his clip on the target, he took the headset and gloves off. As he turned around, I waved and he saw me. Immediately, the corners of his mouth tilted into a smile, and he came out toward me. I felt his arms encircle me and was grateful and happy to be held inside his safe warm embrace.

He hugged me tightly before pulling away and crouching down to place a kiss on my growing belly.

"You're so tense. Relax, my beauty. This party's for you."

I rubbed his hair. "You're such a liar."

"You are beautiful. More beautiful than any woman, living or dead."

I shook my head. It amused me whenever I heard him refer to me in this way. I was not one of those blessed with a glowing pregnancy. My hair was always greasy and because I was always hungry, I had put on a ton of weight in the last couple of months.

He looked around him quickly, his eyes alert and suspicious. He wasn't much different from how he had been when he hadn't completely cut off all ties with the mafia. His vigilance remained in all ways, but it was such a joy to see him happier and more relaxed than I'd ever thought possible. It had taken a while for us to get over everything that happened after the move from New York, but now we were both ready to open up our lives and welcome new people in again.

I took a peek at the gun range. "I can't believe I still don't know how to shoot."

He held my hand and began to lead me up the main stairs. "You'll learn after the baby comes."

I gave him a look. "That's what you said before our wedding, and then during the honeymoon. Then the first year went by, and the second ..."

"You had some lessons."

"Well, I'm still not as proficient as you are."

"You don't need to be." He paused to stare into my eyes.

"But I do," I said, as my hand went to my belly. "Especially now."

He completely understood my fears and proceeded to comfort me. "We're fine and we'll always be so. It's been three years, Ugo is where he belongs."

"At the bottom of the sea?"

"No, burning in hell with all the other psychopaths."

"Mmmm ..."

"And most of his men have been given sentences that will keep them in prison for many years to come. And we have all the security at hand that we could ever need. For the first time in my life, I'm truly living, and sometimes when I first wake up, it seems too good to be true and I think that I was dreaming. Then I turn over and I see you sleeping next to me and I remember I'm the luckiest guy on earth."

"You're right. I should stop being such a killjoy. I came out here to assure you the baby shower will go well, and I end up being the anxious one."

He walked back to the house and he rubbed the small of my back as we arrived at the kitchen.

"I'll just go check that everything is fine," I said.

"Okay. See you later."

I went into the kitchen and instantly Marie came up to me and began to shoo me away.

"Go upstairs and make yourself beautiful. Your guests will be arriving soon," she said, and gently pushed me out of the door.

I leaned against the door. Clearly, there was nothing for

me to do and still plenty of time left, so I should head upstairs and change or go and bother Dante. So I did just that and found Dante in the shower. Immediately, I stripped down and joined him.

He wasn't surprised at all to see me, but somewhat amused.

"Is everything ready?" he asked.

I nodded and turning around, leaned against him. His arms wrapped around my belly, and then he began to stroke me. I left all my anxiety about the party and slowly became aware of the man behind me. I turned around and stood slightly on the tips of my toes and gently brushed his hair out of his face.

"I know that look," he said.

I couldn't help the laugh that bubbled out of me.

"I don't know what you're talking about," I replied. My knees felt decidedly weak, but as always, he was there to support me.

I shut my eyes and melted into his warmth and strength.

"Has Tommy gotten back to you on the audio account you asked him for?" he asked as he positioned his cock between the folds of my sex. I shut my eyes to savor the feel as he slid in, and then I sank completely down onto him.

"No," I whispered hoarsely.

"Want me to send someone to pay him a visit in New York?" he asked.

I stopped moving. "That sounds like a threat."

"That's exactly what it is."

I turned to meet his eyes with an 'oh yeah' expression on my face.

"Fine. I'll let him keep making things difficult for you."

"Tommy doesn't respond well to threats of any kind," I told him. "You know this. Last month, I told him any further delays in cooperating with me in putting his book together would cause the publishing house to lose faith in him, but he pretended as though he didn't even hear me speak. When I mentioned it again, he told me to tell them to fuck off. Who does that?"

He laughed softly as he buried his face in my neck and began to press soft, passionate kisses along my wet skin.

"I still can't believe he agreed to a tell-all book with you," he said. "But then again, I don't know how anybody ever says 'no' to you."

His arms circled around my waist to hold me even more securely in place because his thrusts were slow, but each one of them was delivered with a force that I felt to my very core.

"I'm sorry," I breathed when I realized that my nails were digging into his arms.

"I told you before, when you hurt me, it's like two spoons of sugar."

Slowly, he fucked all the stress and anxiety out of me. By the time we were done and showered I lay on the bed too weak to get up.

"Hey, sleepy head. Aren't your guests arriving soon," he reminded me, as he sat down by my side.

I laughed, knowing full well I was going to use my pregnancy card to not show up on time.

"They'll have to wait."

He kissed me on the top of my head. "Rest a bit then, I'll get this underway."

With my heart filled with joy and peace, I shut my eyes

so my baby and I could steal a few more minutes for a very much-needed nap.

That's All Folks!

Coming Soon...

CHAPTER ONE

FRANCESCA

This is a sham.

A freaking deception.

We are desecrating the house of God.

These are the wild thoughts running through my mind as my grandfather, Nonno Franco Barbieri, walks me down the aisle. The ancient cathedral is bathed in a soft golden glow from the sun rays streaming through the stained glass windows. The lofty pillars are decorated with thousands upon thousands of fresh flowers flown in from around the world. Of special note is the magnificent Madagascan purple orchid arrangement behind the priest.

The wooden pews are packed with dignified people dressed in shades of pastel. Their hushed whispers of anticipation rise into the air and mix with the soft strains of music from the choir standing at the back of the altar.

Nonno and I approach the altar with small, demure steps. Nonno's back is proud and erect as he calmly walks me up the aisle, while I feel as if my whole life is falling apart and my stomach is churning so violently, I'm sure I'm going to be sick right there in front of everybody.

I lift my eyes and surreptitiously glance on either side of me.

I recognize almost none of the faces I see on my left, but on the right are the happy smiling faces from my side of the family. There's mamma, sitting in the front row, clutching her Dior bag. Through my lacy veil, I see the strain on her face. She's the only one whose smile isn't wide enough to break her face in half. She's the only one, other than me, who is truthful enough to admit that this marriage is a shameless sham.

As a little girl, I dreamed of the perfect wedding. Because my great-grandmother's Romanian gypsy blood runs in my veins, I saw myself in a big, white, meringue style wedding gown. My veil was so long it trailed for yards behind me as I walked up the aisle sprinkled with wild flowers to wed a dreamily handsome prince who would cherish me forever.

My wedding is a caricature of my innocent dream.

And I will never forgive all the people who made today a reality.

Especially the tall dark man waiting for me at the altar.

You see, everything is exactly the way I dreamed it: the breathtaking beauty of the church, the decorations, the gorgeous reception that I know is going to steal my breath away, and my pearl encrusted dress and antique lace veil are the price of a three-bedroom house in a good neighborhood. Yes, I deliberately chose one that is so exorbitantly expensive my bridegroom will understand that I'm either rebelling against him, or he has made a terrible mistake and agreed to marry the worst kind of spoiled brat that ever walked the earth. But all that trouble I went to was for nothing. The bastard is so wealthy he did not even notice.

I think you get the picture by now.

Everything is perfect except for the man.

Valentino Barone.

Instead of standing with his back to me like every other freaking bridegroom, he breaks tradition and stands facing me. Over six feet tall, his hands clasped in front of him, he watches me with a laser-like focus. But his stare is dead, like the man himself. At first, the desolation and lack of life in his eyes scared me. Now, it infuriates me that I will be shackled to him without reparations for the rest of my life.

No, this cannot be.

I find myself totally unable to accept that we will be husband and wife even as I am led towards the altar.

Incredible, right? Foolish? Asinine?

Maybe, but I have to hold on to the hope that there has to be a way out. I have accepted the fact that unless there is an act of God, a sudden tornado, or a terrible earthquake, I will lose the battle today... but one battle doesn't make a war. An unconsummated marriage can be annulled. I refuse to stay married to Valentino.

Not when I am in love with Thomas!

We reach the end of the aisle, and Nonno gives me over to Valentino. He takes my hand, and I expect worms to

Coming Soon...

automatically begin crawling under my skin. But no! Through my silk gloves, his touch burns, searing my skin until it feels as if the fabric will melt underneath his fire. When he releases my hand and I drag in a breath and rub the spot where he had held me.

It's okay, I console myself. Of course, his touch will burn. He might look like an ice-cold, heartless sculpture, but he is the devil himself. What bothers me though is the strange and undeniable pull between my thighs when he touches me. I tell myself it is simply nerves and fury. But I've been nervous and furious many times in my life and never felt such a thing. Must be a bride thing. All brides must experience this.

I push the bothersome thought away just as the music stops and turn my attention to the priest who descends to the dais.

"You may lift the veil, Don Barone, and look at your bride."

The hall quietens. For a moment, Valentino remains frozen and I stare at him in surprise. Then he steps forward, grasps the hem of my veil and raises it over my head. I see the involuntary widening of his eyes. As the priest officiates the ceremony, Valentino pins me with his gaze, and I'm astonished by how expressive those dead gunmetal eyes can be when they want.

He is not hiding the mockery in his eyes as his gaze boldly roams over my face and body. We met only once before, on the day Nonno decided I was to marry Valentino to save our family's fortune and secure the protection of the Barbieri clan. When Nonno called me to his office to meet Valentino, I had put on quite a show. It was my one and only chance, an act of desperate defiance. It was all I could do at the time and I had done my very best. Too bad it had not worked. The mad man that Valentino is, he didn't have the good sense to reject me as his bride.

I still cannot believe it because I had truly gone all out to appear as undesirable and unattractive as possible. If I could make myself look like a society outcast with a serious drug problem, no man in his right mind would want to marry such a woman.

I wore a gothic bat costume. I repeat, a gothic bat costume! My fingernails were painted black and I had managed to source the ugliest pair of black boots online to complete my outfit.

With the clever use of mascara and eyeliner I had made my eyebrows look thick and heavy. Purple eyeshadow, blue lipstick (couldn't find green), a clip-on silver septum ring, and an impressively large fake scorpion neck tattoo. The coup de grace, a SLUT tattoo on the apple of my left cheek. I had more or less gone all *barney with a serious drug problem* on him.

Nonno's face was a laughable mixture of horrified and disgusted when I clumsily entered in my clunky boots, but this cold monster had lazily shrugged, smiled, and agreed to the contract. *Smiled!*

I was, and am still heartbroken, but I'm trying with all of my heart to fight away the despair.

"Don Barone, please repeat these vows after me..."

As Valentino recites his vows, the mockery in his eyes intensifies. "...to love and to cherish, till death do us part. And thereto, I pledge to you... my faithfulness."

Fucking liar!

"Miss Barbieri," the priest says. "Repeat these vows after me."

I say my vows slowly, silently asking God for forgiveness because I'm being forced to lie through my teeth. This is wrong. Valentino has no desire to be faithful to me, and I definitely will not be to him because my heart belongs to someone else.

I think of Thomas and my heart aches. I wonder if he is here right now… watching as I am given to someone else. It amazes me how he can stay quiet. I would have shot Valentino dead on the spot if our roles had been reversed. I am considering doing it for him. Push comes to shove, I'll have to take my destiny into my own hands.

"I now pronounce you man and wife," the priest says with a beatific smile. "You may kiss your bride."

Absolutely motherfucking not.

Instantly, I try to look away, but Valentino, this mad man! Locks his gaze with mine again, and steps towards me. I freeze. His fingers touch my neck lightly, and his face moves closer to mine. My heart stops. I'm not surprised that he has no qualms about kissing me and once again this frustrates and annoys me.

Why? Why? Why?

When he knows just how much I loathe him. He knows just how much I am against this whole ridiculous charade. We should have just performed a simple ceremony at the registry office.

But in the next second I understand that perhaps we are all just slaves to life and our bodies because at his touch my blood betrays me. It ignites and runs like liquid fire beneath my skin. As I gasp with shock of my reaction, he swallows it into his mouth. I am supposed to be repulsed, however as his warm lips close over mine, for a brief yet never ending second, a hot flush of desire rolls from the top of my head to the soles of my feet.

I might have been able to ignore the brief sweet ache of desire earlier, but this one cannot go unnoticed. I wish with all my heart, I could, but I can't.

Valentino steps away, aloof and coldly unaffected. And I hate him even more for it. Damn him! How dare he make me feel these unwanted carnal desires while he feels nothing?

But even as I hate him, I understand why.

I may be young and naive, but I'm not blind. Valentino Barone is not just attractive, he's lethally magnificent. His face is perfectly chiseled like a piece of marble crafted by an old master sculptor. It's a look that makes you want to throw caution to the winds and do dangerous things. Punching him or riding him are two options.

Surprisingly, I don't think it is just the allure of his face that pulls me to him like a moth flying to its fiery death. Sure, it will lure me in, but the danger and ultimate appeal is in the man himself. There's an aura of darkness and mystery around him that is like nicotine—one drag. It pleads with me to take just one hit once. A little try. What can it hurt? But like I said, I'm not stupid. But I can very clearly identify it for what it is: a trap. And this is why I must never let myself get any closer.

This fake kiss on the altar is the only show of affection this man will ever get from me. From now on until he lets me go, I plan to make his life a living hell.

"*Congratulazioni!*" people shout and throw confetti at

us as we walk toward the exit. I don't bother smiling. They should all know without the shadow of a doubt that this is against my will. They don't seem to notice or care though because outside the church, I'm quickly swept away by laughing friends and family. They are all excited that I've married into the powerful Barone family, to their mafia head, Valentino.

I feel very betrayed by their pleasure and excitement.

"*Bravo!*" My cousin Louisa is suddenly in front of me with a cheeky smile. She's a few years older and would take me drinking sometimes. "Your husband is very handsome," she says. "I wish I had a man like him."

"I wish you had him," I responded, meaning every word.

The smile clears off her astounded face. She's about to say something when Mamma appears beside us.

She stares intently at me, but addresses my cousin. "Louisa, your mother requests your attention."

As Louisa hurries off, Mamma sighs heavily. "Bite your tongue, Francesca. Do you really want your cousin to have your husband?"

"I don't care who has him. I don't want him." The full extent of my vitriol comes out now that I'm talking to someone with whom I can be my true self. "I hate him."

"Francesca." My mom touches my face affectionately. "Most marriages in our world start this way. But you will see. You will fall in love with your husband."

"Never!" I declare. "He's just like Papa. I don't know how you were able to tolerate pure evil, but I cannot! I just cannot."

"Francesca, please trust that no matter how dire our

situation was, I would never have agreed to let you marry a man who is like your father. I did my due diligence on Valentino when your Nonno first mentioned him. He's not as bad as you think he is. He is hardworking, loyal, fair, and a good provider. All the things that make for a good husband and father."

Mamma lowers her head and I instantly feel guilty. I don't want her to worry about me when I'm away, and the more I voice my unhappiness the more she will. She's had to worry too much in her life, and I don't want to be an additional burden. I'm about to tell her not to worry about me when I see a lone figure standing outside the bubbling crowd. Unlike everyone else who is dressed in luxury and splendor, he is dressed in simple clothing.

My heart soars.

Thomas.

"Excuse me, mamma." I kiss her cheek and push through the crowd to where Thomas stands.

He sees me coming and forces a smile onto his face. "I'm sorry for crashing your wedding, Francesca. I just had... had... to... to come and see you." His nervous gaze flits around the garden, and my heart bleeds for him.

"Thomas-"

"Francesca," he says, and his voice breaks. "This hurts so much."

"Thomas, I'm so sorry." I shake my head. "I'm in hell as well."

"I know," Thomas says. "But I saw him kiss you, and I couldn't help but feel like a complete loser. He's handsome, wealthy, and has everything a woman would want."

His sandy hair falls onto his forehead. If I am brutally

honest, compared to Valentino Thomas looks like a squeaky clean, wet behind the ears, frat boy. But after witnessing the devilish life men like Valentino lead and the evil the wreck, a kind and compassionate activist like Thomas is the man my heart will always choose. I met Thomas in college, and even though my father had warned me before his death that I could never marry an ordinary man, I continued to keep Thomas in my life.

Because Thomas is the direct opposite of evil.

He chooses to remain poor because he refuses to work with corrupt organizations, and I couldn't admire him more for being so noble and upright. He stood for what I believed in, truth and goodness. It is also what I have believed in all of my life, given the very violent circumstances of my upbringing. What use is money when it is ill-gotten?

"Francesca," Thomas says passionately. "I wish everything was different, but I have to accept…"

I stare at him in shock. He is giving up? So easily? Why? I know having to see me marry someone else is horrible, but he knows I have no choice, it is a marriage in name only, and I have every intention of getting out of it as soon as humanly possible.

I expect him to say more, to change his words, but whatever he is looking at behind us seems to completely choke him up. He has also become white as a sheet and appears frozen with terror. I swing my head around to see the object of his fear.

Valentino is standing behind me, hell in his eyes.

He glances from me to Thomas before saying just one word, "Leave."

"Oh, okay." Without even a glance at me, Thomas scurries off like a frightened rabbit.

"Thomas!"

"Thom-"

"Say his name one more time, and he'll be dead by morning."

The half-spoken name freezes in my throat. I turn fully to face my new husband. Our gazes clash. Angry blue versus deadly gray. My automatic response to him has always been flight not fight, but this time the pain that rips through my heart makes me stand my ground and say exactly what I want to. "One of these days, while you're busy killing other people, I hope you kill yourself!"

He doesn't retreat. There is a strange madness in his eyes as he closes the distance between us. His fingers are cool as they stroke my neck softly. I swallow hard. I can't blatantly push his hand away. All eyes are on us and if he's anything like my father, he will not take kindly to being embarrassed in front of his whole clan. It would be stupid to test him while the killer in him roams his eyes. For the sake of the welfare of my family, I decide to exercise caution. I will fight him in private.

I inhale sharply as he tightens his fingers, not enough to hurt but enough to send a message. I get it. Loud and clear. He leans his mouth so close to my ear, I feel the warmth of his skin. My breath quickens.

"The car is here. We're leaving," he says quietly.

"What about the reception?"

"Sorry. Don't feel like one." He was clearly not sorry at all.

I gulp. "But... the cake..."

"I'm not a fan of red velvet cake with lemon icing," he says flatly.

My jaw drops. The fact that he knew a little detail like that shocks me. He had not been consulted about anything to do with the planning of the wedding because he had instructed my grandfather to hire the best wedding planner in town and expressed his desire not to be involved in the process.

With his hand on the small of my back he leads me towards a sleek black car. The engine was running and a uniformed chauffeur nodded and opened the passenger door closest to us. I look back to see Mamma standing next to Nonno. She is surprised to see us leave. The people who don't know the itinerary as intimately as she does are cheering and clapping. Tears spring to my eyes. I stop abruptly before the open car door. Our gazes meet. Fire and Ice.

"Where are we going?" I ask mutinously.

"You'll find out when we get there."

"What about my dress? I have to change out of it."

He looks down dismissively at my gown. "Why? A dress worth a quarter of a million dollars should be appreciated by as many people as possible."

Well, well, he does know how much my dress costs. I stand my ground. "I'd like to say goodbye to my mother."

"You spent your goodbyes on that freckled maggot," he says. "Get in the fucking car."

My heart drops to my stomach at his nasty tone. How dare he call Thomas a freckled maggot? One fingernail on Thomas is worth more than all of Valentino. I want to spit at him, but people are watching, and I don't want to make a scene and embarrass my family, so I pick up the big skirt of my dress and throw myself into the car, hating him even more for preventing me from saying goodbye to my mother one last time. A call would have to suffice. Valentino climbs in from the other side, and suddenly, it feels like the large interior of the vehicle has becomes too small. I feel suffocated in my beautiful dress.

I shift to the end of the seat and press myself against the door, but it's not far enough from him. As the vehicle moves away from the church, Valentino removes his jacket and loosens a few buttons of his dress shirt. As more of his chest is exposed, I turn my head away so fast I almost twist my neck.

We do not speak until we reach the airport. Everyone is looking at me in my bridal dress. If he thought he could embarrass me in this way, he was wrong. I hold my head up high and sweep across the floor. In half-an-hour, I'm seated in his private jet. Apparently we're on our way to Paris for our honeymoon, another notch in the number of scams we have done today. Honeymoons are for real couples, not people like Valentino and I.

The air hostess's eyes show surprise to see my attire. I smile blandly at her as if it is the most normal thing to board a plane in a big bridal dress. Once we are airborne, he opens his laptop and immediately becomes immersed in it. Infuriated by his attitude, I rip my silk gloves off and toss them on the little table in front of me.

"I'm going to the toilet," I announce.

He doesn't look up.

Bastard! I stomp huffily towards the toilet and stare at my reflection in the mirror. I'm in such a rage I feel like breaking something, but by the time I get back to my seat I have made the decision to act as cool as he is acting.

I spend the rest of the flight unable to relax in my pearl encrusted bodice and pretending to be totally engrossed in the pages of random magazines.

Food and drinks are served and still the bastard ignores me.

"Your dress is beautiful," the air stewardess serving me says.

"Thank you," I reply quietly, my eyes sliding towards Valentino.

Even though he is looking down I can see his lips curl upwards with mocking amusement.

Bastard!

Many painful hours later of me staring with unseeing eyes at the pages of magazines I have no interest in, the journey is over.

We are met at the airport and driven to a beautiful old hotel in the middle of the city. By now, my dress is a crushed mess and I'm sure I look terrible, but Europeans must be of a different temperament, because everyone we meet pretends everything is normal.

A bellboy dressed in a blue and gold uniform ushers us into one of the most gorgeous suites I've ever seen. While Valentino speaks on the phone, I head into the bedroom, admiring the exquisiteness of it all. I touch the rich curtain and sigh with pleasure. I don't know the exact extent of Valentino's wealth, but it's rumored that his riches multiply so quickly he himself cannot know what he is worth.

The door closes behind me and I jump. I whirl around to see Valentino walking into the room, his shirt is unbuttoned halfway down his chest. It's incredibly obvious what he wants... what this is, but every cell in my body screams, NO. The inevitability of sex with him has haunted me from the very moment I was 'persuaded' to wed him, but now that the moment is here, I am convinced I would rather die than sleep with this monster.

"I will not share a bed with you."

The room rings with my words. His dangerous eyes move towards me, and I begin to tremble, but I hold my head high.

"Why not?" His voice is calm and his posture is relaxed. I hate how unaffected he seems, how in control. How so damn unflustered.

"Because I will not ..." I glance haughtily at the king-sized bed. "I won't..."

"You won't what?" Valentino saunters toward me, like a predator toward its prey.

He stops in front of me, and to my shame, once again, my body reacts lustfully to his presence. It completely and utterly betrays me.

"I won't have sex with you, Valentino," I spit, staring into his expressionless gunmetal eyes. "I... I find you... repulsive."

"Repulsive?" A corner of his lips tugs upwards. "That's a rather strong word, my little pearl." He takes another step towards me, caging me against the wall. I can hear my heart going wild in my chest, and I fear he can hear it too. Suddenly, he touches me. One hand sliding into my hair to angle my head while his other hand roams my dress, eliciting responses I never knew my body to be capable of.

Coming Soon…

"Especially when I can see the way your body reacts when I touch you," he murmurs.

I press myself against the wall. "You are a bastard!"

To my shock, he drops his head and captures my mouth with his. I gasp, and he slips his tongue into my mouth and tastes me. His tongue hooks mine, pulls it into his mouth and sucks it. Pleasure spreads like wildfire through my body, but the moment a moan drops from my lips, he pulls away, putting several feet between us. I am astounded. This was nothing, nothing like the chaste kiss back in the cathedral!

Ashamed and breathing heavily, I catch his gaze, expecting to see mockery. Instead, his eyes are full of rage, which I quite frankly do not understand, I am the one who has been assaulted here.

"Keep your virginal bed. I'm sure I'll find a willing body elsewhere in this city. *Bonne nuit, Madame Barone.*"

I am struck dumb as I watch him walk out of the room. For a full minute I am too astonished to do anything, then I fall on the big lonely bed. Good God! My heart is beating so freaking fast I must surely be at risk of a massive coronary attack alone in Paris.

Curious to know what happens next?
:)
Pre-order here:
Fight Me, Little Pearl

About the Author

If you wish to leave a review for this book
please do so here:
The Guardian

Please click on this link to receive news of my latest releases
and great giveaways.
Georgia's Newsletter

and remember
I **LOVE** hearing from readers so by all means come and say
hello here:

Also by Georgia Le Carre

Owned

42 Days

Besotted

Seduce Me

Love's Sacrifice

Masquerade

Pretty Wicked (novella)

Disfigured Love

Hypnotized

Crystal Jake 1,2&3

Sexy Beast

Wounded Beast

Beautiful Beast

Dirty Aristocrat

You Don't Own Me 1 & 2

You Don't Know Me

Blind Reader Wanted

Redemption

The Heir

Blackmailed By The Beast

Submitting To The Billionaire

The Bad Boy Wants Me

Nanny & The Beast

His Frozen Heart

The Man In The Mirror

A Kiss Stolen

Can't Let Her Go

Highest Bidder

Saving Della Ray

Nice Day For A White Wedding

With This Ring

With This Secret

Saint & Sinner

Bodyguard Beast

Beauty & The Beast

The Other Side of Midnight

The Russian Billionaire

CEO's Revenge

Mine To Possess

Heat Of The Moment

Boss From Hell

Sweet Poison

Printed in Great Britain
by Amazon